Praise for George Pelecanos's Nick Stefanos novels

A FIRING OFFENSE

"A contemporary classic.... Pelecanos is a fresh, new, utterly hardboiled voice. *A Firing Offense* is full of virtuoso scenes of imaginative sex and substance abuse, suspenseful action, and brooding meditation on a newly lost generation."

—Pat Dowell, *Washington Post Book World*

NICK'S TRIP

"This particular entry in the series is as tough as they get: an urban nightmare of greed, betrayal, and kick-ass revenge."

—Bill Ott, *American Libraries*

DOWN BY THE RIVER WHERE THE DEAD MEN GO

"Nick and his incomparably seamy milieu, in their third outing, get an A."

—*Kirkus Reviews*

SHAME THE DEVIL

"Tough and skillful.... There are action scenes as fierce as any you will read and street talk that hits the ear as smart and accurate."

—Paul Skenazy, *San Francisco Chronicle*

DOWN BY THE RIVER WHERE THE DEAD MEN GO

By George Pelecanos

The Cut

The Way Home

The Turnaround

The Night Gardener

Drama City

Hard Revolution

Soul Circus

Hell to Pay

Right As Rain

Shame the Devil

The Sweet Forever

King Suckerman

The Big Blowdown

Down by the River Where the Dead Men Go

Shoedog

Nick's Trip

A Firing Offense

GEORGE PELECANOS

DOWN BY THE RIVER WHERE THE DEAD MEN GO

BACK BAY BOOKS
Little, Brown and Company
New York Boston London

Back Bay Books / Little, Brown and Company
Hachette Book Group
1290 Avenue of the Americas, New York, NY 10104
littlebrown.com

Originally published in hardcover by St. Martin's Press, June 1995
First Back Bay paperback edition, July 2011

Back Bay Books is an imprint of Little, Brown and Company. The Back Bay Books name and logo are trademarks of Hachette Book Group, Inc.

Library of Congress Cataloging-in-Publication Data

Pelecanos, George P.
Down by the river where the dead men go / George Pelecanos.—1st Back Bay paperback ed.
p. cm.
ISBN 978-0-316-07964-8
1. Stefanos, Nick (Fictitious character)—Fiction. 2. Private investigators—Washington (D.C.)—Fiction. 3. Washington (D.C.)—Fiction. 4. Bartenders—Fiction. I. Title.
PS3566.E354D69 2011
813'.54—dc22 2011016601

10 9 8 7 6 5 4 3

RRD-H

Printed in the United States of America

FOR PETER

DOWN BY THE RIVER WHERE THE DEAD MEN GO

ONE

LIKE MOST OF the trouble that's happened in my life or that I've caused to happen, the trouble that happened that night started with a drink. Nobody forced my hand; I poured it myself, two fingers of bourbon into a heavy, beveled shot glass. There were many more after that, more bourbons and more bottles of beer, too many more to count. But it was that first one that led me down to the river that night, where they killed a boy named Calvin Jeter.

This one started at the Spot, on 8th and G in Southeast, where I tended bar three or four shifts a week. It had been a hot day, hazy and soup-hot, like most midsummer days in D.C. The compressor on our ancient air conditioner had gone down after the lunch rush, and though most of our regulars had tried to drink their way through it, the heat had won out. So by ten o'clock it was just me behind the stick, lording over a row of empty bar stools, with Ramon in the cellar and Darnell in the kitchen, cleaning up. I phoned Phil Saylor, the owner of the establishment, and with his okay shut the place down.

Ramon came up the wooden stairs carrying three cases of beer, his head just clearing the top carton. He was smiling stupidly—he had just smoked a joint in the cellar—but the smile was stretched tight, and it looked as if he were about to bust a nut. Ramon in his cowboy boots stood five two and weighed in at 129, so seventy-two beers was pushing it. He dropped the cases at my feet and stood before me, wiping the sweat off his forehead with a red bandanna. I thanked him and tipped him out.

For the next fifteen minutes, I rotated the beer into the cooler, making sure to leave some cold ones on the top, while I listened to Ramon and Darnell cut on each other back in the kitchen. Through the reach-through, I could see Ramon gut-punching the tall and razorish Darnell, Darnell taking it and loving it and laughing the whole time. Then there were loud air kisses from Ramon, and Darnell saying, "Later, amigo," and Ramon motoring out of the kitchen, through the bar area, toward the door.

I finished with the beer and wiped down the bar and rinsed out the green netting and put the ashtrays in the soak sink, leaving one out, and then I washed up and changed into shorts and a T-shirt and high-top sneakers. Darnell shut off the light in the kitchen and came out as I tightened the laces on my Chucks.

"Whas'up, Nick?"

"'Bout done."

"Any business today?"

"Yeah. The catfish went pretty good."

"Used a little Old Bay. Think anybody noticed?"

"Uh-uh."

Darnell pushed his leather kufi back off his sweat-beaded forehead. "You headin' uptown? Thought maybe I'd catch a ride."

"Not yet. I'm gonna call Lyla, see what she's doing."

"All right, then. Let me get on out of here."

On the nights we closed together, this was our routine. Darnell knew I would stick around, usually alone, and have a drink; he'd always try and get me out of there before I did. A stretch in Lorton had straightened him all the way out, though no one mistook his clean lifestyle for the lifestyle of a pushover, least of all me; I had seen what he could do with a knife. Darnell went out the door. I locked it behind him.

Back in the main room, I counterclockwised the rheostat. The lamps dimmed, leaving the room washed in blue neon light from the Schlitz logo centered over the bar. I found WDCU on the house stereo and notched up the volume on the hard bop. I lit a cigarette, hit it, and fitted it in the V of the last remaining ashtray. Then I pulled a nearly full bottle of Old Grand-Dad off the call shelf, poured a shot, and had a taste. I opened a cold bottle of Bud, drank off an inch or two of that, and placed the bottle next to the shot. My shoulders unstiffened, and everything began to soften and flow down.

I looked around the room: a long, railed mahogany bar, mottled and pocked; several conical lamps spaced above, my own smoke swirling in the low-watt light; a rack behind the lamps, where pilsner and rocks and up glasses hung suspended, dripping water on the bar; some bar stools, a few high-backed, the rest not; a couple of vinyl-cushioned booths; a pair of well-used speakers mounted on either side of the wall, minus the grills; and some "artwork," a Redskins poster furnished by the local beer distributor (1989's schedule—we had never bothered to take it down) and a framed print of the Declaration of Independence, the signatures of our forefathers joined in various places by the drunken signatures of several of our regulars. My own signature was scrawled somewhere on there, too.

I finished my bourbon and poured another as I dialed Lyla's number. Next to the phone was a photograph, taped to the yellowed wall, of a uniformed Phil Saylor, circa his brief stint as a cop on the Metropolitan Police force. I looked at his round face while listening to Lyla's answering machine. I hung the receiver in its cradle without leaving a message.

The next round went down smoothly and more quickly than the first. During that one, I tried phoning my old buddy Johnny McGinnes, who had gone from electronics sales to mattresses and now to major appliances, but the chipper guy who answered the call—"Goode's White Goods. My name is Donny. How may I help you?"—told me that McGinnes had left for the evening. I told him to tell McGinnes that his friend Nick had called, and he said, "Sure will," adding, "and if you're ever in need of a major appliance, the name is Donny." I hung up before he could pry his name in again, then dialed Lyla's number. Still no answer.

So I had another round, slopping bourbon off the side of the glass as I poured. Cracking a beer I had buried earlier in the ice bin, I went to the stereo and cranked up the volume: a honking session from some quintet, really wild shit, the Dexedrined drummer all over the map. By the time the set was over, I had finished my shot. Then I decided to leave; the Spot had grown hellishly hot, and I had sweat right into my clothes. Besides, my buzz was too good now, way too good to waste alone. I killed the lights and set the alarm, locked the front door, and stepped out onto 8th with a beer in my hand.

I walked by an athletic-shoe store, closed and protected by a riot gate. I passed an alley fringely lit at the head by a nearby streetlamp. I heard voices in its depths, where an ember flared, then faded. Just past the alley sat Athena's, the last women's club in my part of town. Behind its windowless brick walls came the steady throb of bass. I pushed open the door and stepped inside.

I heard my name called out over a Donna Summer tune and the general noise of the place. I edged myself around a couple of women on the dance floor and stepped up to the bar. Stella, the stocky, black-haired tender, had poured me a shot when she saw me come through the front door. I thanked her and put my hand around the glass and knocked it back all at once. Someone kissed me on the back of my neck and laughed.

I found Mattie, my transplanted Brooklyn friend, by the pool table in a smoky corner of the room. We shot our usual game of eight ball, and I lost a five. Then I bought us a round of beers and played another game, with the same result. Mattie had the whole table mapped out before her first stroke, while I was a power shooter who never played for shape. Some nights I won, anyway—but not that night.

I went back to the bar and settled my tab and left too much for Stella. In the bar mirror, I saw my reflection, bright-eyed and ugly and streaked with sweat. Near the register hung a framed photograph of Jackie Kahn, former Athena's bartender and the mother of my child, a boy named Kent, now nine months old. I said something loudly to Stella then, my voice sounding garbled and harsh. She began to smile but then abruptly stopped, looking in my eyes. I pushed away from the bar and made it out the front door, to the fresh air and the street.

I unlocked the Spot's front door, deactivated the alarm by punching in a four-digit number on a grid, and went back behind the bar. I cracked a cold beer and drank deeply. Then I poured Old Grand-Dad to the lip of a shot glass and bent over, putting my lips directly to the whiskey, drinking off an inch of it without touching the glass. I shook a Camel filter out of my pack and lit it. The phone began to ring. I let it ring, and walked down toward the stereo, stumbling on a rubber mat along the way. I found a tape by Lungfish, a raging guitar-based band out of Baltimore, and slid that in the deck. I hit the play button and gave it some bass.

Black.

I sat on a stool at the bar, tried to strike a match. A cigarette had burned down, dead-cold in the ashtray. I lit a fresh one, tossed the match toward the ashtray, missed. I reached for my shot glass and saw the half-filled bottle of Grand-Dad in the middle of a cluster of empty beer bottles. I tasted whiskey. The tape had ended. There was not a sound in the bar.

Black.

I stepped off the curb outside the Spot. A whooping alarm screamed in the night. Stella walked by me, said, "Nicky, Nicky," went through the open front door of the Spot, reset the alarm. She asked for and took my keys, then locked the front door. A few women had spilled out of Athena's onto the sidewalk. Stella returned, held my keys out, then drew them back as I reached for them.

"Come on, Nicky. Come on and sleep it off in the back."

"I'm all right. Gimme my keys."

"Forget it."

"Gimme my keys. I can sleep in my car. What the fuck, Stella, it's ninety degrees out here. You think I'm gonna freeze? Gimme my fuckin' keys."

Stella tossed me the keys. I tried to catch them, but there was an open beer in one of my hands and the bottle of Grand-Dad in the other. I went to one knee to pick my keys up off the street. I looked up, tried to thank Stella. She had already walked away.

Black.

Driving down Independence Avenue, a Minor Threat tune at maximum volume, blowing through the speakers of my Dodge. I stopped my car in the middle of the street, let the motor run, got out of the car, urinated on the asphalt. To my left, the Mall, the Washington Monument lit up and looming, leaning a little toward the sky. Tourists walked hurriedly by on the sidewalk, fathers watching me from the corner of their eyes, pushing their children along, the singer screaming from the open windows of my car: "What the fuck have *you* done?" Me, laughing.

Black.

I drove down M Street in Southeast, the Navy Yard on my right. My first car, a '64 Plymouth Valiant, bought there at a government auction, accompanied by my grandfather. Must have tried to get back to the Spot, made a wrong turn. Lights everywhere, streetlights and taillights, crossing. I hit my beer, chased it with bourbon. The bourbon spilled off my chin. A blaring horn, an angry voice yelling from the car at my side. The beer bottle tipped over between my legs, foam undulating from the neck. My shorts, soaked; pulled my wallet from my back pocket and tossed it on the bucket seat to my right. Music, loud and distorted in the car.

Black.

The car went slowly down a single-lane asphalt road. Trees on both sides of the road. To the right, through the trees, colored lights reflected off water. No music now in the car. The surge of laughter far away, and trebly slide guitar from a radio. Blurry yellow lights ahead, suspended above the water, shooting straight out into the sky. Had to pee, had to stop the car, had to stop the lights from moving. Heard gravel spit beneath the wheels, felt the car come to rest. Killed the ignition. Opened my door, stumbled out onto the gravel, heard the sound of a bottle hit the ground behind me. Started to fall, then gained my footing, stumbling, running now to the support of a tree. Needed to lie down, but not there. Pushed off the tree, bounced off another, felt something lash across my cheek. Shut my eyes, opened them, began to float into a fall. Nothing beneath me, no legs, a rush of lights and water and trees, spinning. The jolt of contact as I hit the ground, no pain. On my back, looking up at the branches, through the branches the stars, moving, all of it moving. Sick. The night coming up, no energy to turn over, just enough to tilt my head. A surge of warm liquid spilling out of my mouth and running down my neck, the stench of my own flowing puke, the steam of it passing before my eyes.

Black.

A sting on my cheek. Something crawling on my face, my hands dead at my sides. Let it crawl. The branches, the stars, still moving. My stomach convulsed. I turn my head and vomit.

Black.

The slam of a car door. The sound of something dragged through gravel and dirt. A steady, frantic moan.

The voice of a black man: "All right now. You already been a punk, and shit. Least you can do is go out a man."

The moan now a muffled scream. Can't move, can't even raise my head. A dull plopping sound, then a quiet splash.

The black man's voice: "Just leave him?"

Another voice, different inflection: "Kill a coon in this town and it barely makes the papers—no offense, *you* know what I mean. C'mon, let's get outta here. Let's go home."

Black.

I OPENED MY EYES to a gray sky. I ran my hand through dirt and paper and grass, and something plastic and wet. I stayed there for a while, looking at the leafy branches and the sky. My back ached and I felt stiff behind the neck. I could smell the odor of garbage, my own bile and sweat.

I sighed slowly, got up on one elbow. I looked across the water at the sun, large and dirty orange, coming up in the east. I sat up all the way, rubbed a fleck of crust off my chin, ran my fingers through my hair.

I was down by the Anacostia River—in the marina district, where M Street continues unmarked. I recognized it straight away. My grandfather and I had fished here when I was a kid. He had always thrown back the perch and occasional catfish he had reeled in. The river had been virtually dead, even then.

I was sitting in a wooded area, the grass worn down to weeds and dirt, littered with plastic bags and fast-food wrappers, empty beer cans, malt liquor bottles, peach brandy pints, used rubbers, the odd shoe. I turned to the right and saw my car, nearly hidden in the start of the woods, parked neatly and without a scratch between two trees, all dumb luck. Beyond that, I could see the moored runabouts and powerboats of a marina, and past the marina the 11th Street Bridge, leading to Anacostia. Behind me was the road, cracked and potholed, and behind the road a denser block of trees, then railroad tracks, and then more trees. To my left, the woods gave to a clearing, where a rusted houseboat sat half-sunk in the water. After that, another hundred yards down the shoreline, the Sousa Bridge spanned the river, the lights of which I had noticed but not recognized the night before.

The night before. My memory flashed on something very wrong.

I got up on my feet and walked unsteadily through the trees to the clearing, continued on to the waterline. Wooden pilings came up out of the brown river, spaced erratically around the sunken houseboat. Something appeared to be draped around one of the pilings. The sun nearly blinded me, sent a pounding into my head. I shaded my eyes, went to where the scum of the river lapped at the concrete bulkhead, stood there on the edge.

A young black man lay in the water, his head and shoulders submerged, the shirtsleeve of one bound arm caught on a cleat in the piling. Duct tape had been wound around his gray face, covering his mouth. I could see an entry wound, small and purple, rimmed and burned black, below his chin. The bullet had traveled up and blown out the back of his head; brain stew, pink and chunked, had splashed out onto the piling. The gas jolt had bugged his eyes.

I fell to my knees and retched. The dry heave came up empty. I stayed there, caught air, stared at the garbage and debris floating stagnant in the river. I pushed off with my hands, stood and turned, stumbled a few steps, then went into a quick walk toward the trees. I didn't look back.

I picked up the empty bottle of bourbon at the side of my Dodge and opened the door. I dropped the bottle inside and fell into the driver's seat. My keys still hung in the ignition. I looked in the rearview at my eyes, unrecognizable. I checked my watch, rubbed dirt off its face: 6:30 A.M., Wednesday.

My wallet lay flat and open on the shotgun bucket. I picked it up, looked at my own face staring out at me from my District of Columbia license: "Nicholas J. Stefanos, Private Investigator."

So *that's* what I was.

I turned the key in the ignition.

TWO

MY GIRLFRIEND, LYLA McCubbin, stopped by my apartment early that evening. She found me sitting naked on the edge of the bed, just up from a nap, the blinds drawn in the room. I had thrown away my clothes from the night before and taken two showers during the course of the day. But I had begun to sweat again, and the room smelled of booze. Lyla had a seat next to me and rubbed my back, then pulled my face out of my hands.

"I talked to Mai at the Spot. She told me she picked up your shift tonight. You had a rough one, huh?"

"Yeah, pretty rough."

"What's all over your face?"

"Bites. Some kind of roaches, I guess. I woke up—I was layin' in garbage."

"Shit, Nicky."

"Yeah."

"I called you last night," she said.

"I called *you.*"

She looked in my eyes. "You been crying or something, Nick?"

"I don't know," I said, looking away.

"You got the depression," she said quietly. "You went and got yourself real good and drunk. You did some stupid things, and then you fell out. The only thing you can do now is apologize to the people you dealt with, maybe try and be more sensible next time. But you shouldn't beat yourself up about it. I mean, it happens, right?"

I didn't answer. Lyla's fingers brushed my hair back off my face. After awhile, she got up off the bed.

"I'm going to make you something to eat," she said.

"Sit back down a minute," I said, taking her hand. She did, and everything poured out.

Later, I sat on my stoop as Lyla grilled burgers on a hibachi she had set up on the brick patio outside my apartment. Lyla's long red hair switched across her back as she drank from a goblet of Chablis and prodded the burgers with a short-handled spatula. My black cat circled her feet, then dashed across the patio and batted at an errant moth. I watched Lyla move against a starry backdrop of fireflies that blinked beyond the light of the patio, and I smelled the deep-summer hibiscus that bloomed in the yard.

After dinner, Lyla drove up to Morris Miller's, the liquor store in my Shepherd Park neighborhood, for more wine. My landlord, who owned the house and lived in its two top floors, came out and sat with me on the stoop. I had my first cigarette of the day while he drank from a can of beer and told me a story of a woman he had met in the choir, who he said sang like an angel in church but had "the devil in her hips outside those walls." He laughed while I dragged on my cigarette, and pointed to my cat, still running in circles, chasing that moth.

"Maybe if that old cat had two eyes, she'd catch that thing."

"She might catch it yet," I said. "Nailed a sparrow and dropped it on my doorstep the other day."

"Whyn't you get you a *real* animal, man? I know this boy, lives down around 14th and Webster? Got some alley cats would fuck up a dog."

"I don't know. I bring a cat around here like your boy's got, might scare away some of your lady friends."

"Wouldn't want that." My landlord hissed a laugh. " 'Cause that woman I got now, that church woman? She's a keeper."

Lyla returned, uncorked her wine, and poured another glass. My landlord gave her a kiss and went back in the house to his easy chair and TV. Lyla sat next to me and dropped her hand on the inside of my thigh, rubbing it there.

"How you feeling?"

"Better."

"You'll be better still tomorrow."

"I guess."

She bent toward me, and I turned my head away. Lyla took my chin in her hand and forced me to meet her gaze. I looked into her pale green eyes. She kissed me then and held the kiss, her breath warm and sour from the wine.

After awhile, we went inside. I dropped a Curtis Mayfield tape into the deck while Lyla lit some votive candles in my room. I undressed her from behind, kissing the pulsing blue vein of her neck. We fell onto my bed, where we made out slowly in the flickering light. Lyla rolled on top of me and put my hands to her breasts. The candlelight reflected off her damp hair, the sweat on her chest like glass.

I shut my eyes and let her work it, let myself go with the sensations, the sounds of her open-mouthed gasps, the rising promise of my own release, the sweet voice of Curtis singing "Do Be Down" in the room. She knew what she was doing, and it worked; for a few minutes, I forgot all about the man I had become. Or maybe I had gone to another place, where I could let myself believe that I was someone else.

* * *

LYLA HAD PLACED MY coffee next to the *Post* on the living room table the following morning. I picked up my mug and sipped from it while I stood over the newspaper and stared blankly at its front page. Lyla walked into the room, tucking a cream-colored blouse into an apple green skirt.

"It made the final edition," she said. "Deep in Metro. The Roundup."

The *Post* grouped the violent deaths of D.C.'s underclass into a subhead called "Around the Region"; local journalists sarcastically dubbed this daily feature "the Roundup." As the managing editor of the city's hard-news alternative weekly, *D.C. This Week*, Lyla was not immune to criticism of local media herself. But her competitive spirit couldn't stop her from taking the occasional shot at the *Washington Post.*

"What'd it say?"

"You know," she said. " 'Unidentified man found in the Anacostia River. Fatal gunshot wounds. Police are withholding the name until notification of relatives, no suspects at this time'—the usual. When you read it, you automatically think, Another drug execution. Retribution kill, whatever. I mean, that's what it was, right?"

I had a seat on the couch and ran my finger along the edge of the table. Lyla kept her eyes on me as she pulled her hair back and tied it off with a black band.

I looked up. "You still got that friend over at the city desk at Metro?"

Lyla moved my way and stood over me. She rested her hands on her hips, spoke tiredly. "Sure, and I've got my own sources in the department. Why?"

"Just, you know. I thought you could see what else they got on this so far."

"So, what, you could get involved?"

"Just curious, that's all. Anyway, it's been awhile. I wouldn't know where to start." I thought of my last case, a year and a half earlier: William Henry and April Goodrich, the house on Gallatin Street—a bloodbath, and way too much loss.

Lyla leaned over and kissed me on the lips. "Get some rest today, Nick. Okay?"

"I'm workin' a shift," I said.

"Good," she said. "That's good."

She gave me one more knowing look and walked from the room. I listened to the slam of the screen door and slowly drank the rest of my coffee. Then I showered and dressed and left the apartment. The newspaper remained on my living room table, untouched, unread.

THE SPOT COOKED DURING the lunch rush that day. Darnell's special, a thick slice of meat loaf with mashed potatoes and gravy, moved quickly, and he was sliding them onto the reach-through with fluid grace. Ramon bused the tables and kept just enough dishes and silverware washed to handle the turns. Our new lunch waitress, Anna Wang, a tough little Chinese-American college student, worked the small dining room adjacent to the bar.

Anna stepped up to the service bar, called, "Ordering!" She pulled a check from her apron, blew a strand of straight black hair out of her eyes while she made some hash marks on the check. I free-poured vodka into a rocks glass and cranberry-juiced it for color. Then I poured a draft and carried the mug and the glass down to Anna, a lit Camel in my mouth. I placed the drinks on her cocktail tray just as she speared a swizzle stick into the vodka.

Anna said, "How about some of that, Nick?"

I took the cigarette out of my mouth and put it between her lips. She drew on it once, let smoke pour from her nostrils, and hit it again as I plucked it out. She nodded and carried off the tray. I watched Ramon go out of his way to brush her leg with his as he passed with a bus tray of dirty dishes. Anna ignored him and kept moving.

"Another martini for me, Nick," said Melvin, the house crooner, whose stool was by the service bar. I poured some rail gin into an up glass and let a drop or two of dry vermouth fall into the glass. I served it neatly on a bev nap, watching Melvin's lips move to the Shirley Horn vocals coming from the Spot's deck, and then I heard Darnell's voice boom from the kitchen over the rattle of china and the gospel music of his own radio: "Food up!"

I snatched it off the reach-through and walked down the bar toward Happy, our resident angry alki, seated alone, always alone. On my trip, I stopped to empty the ashtray of a gray beard named Dave, who was quietly reading a pulp novel and drinking coffee at the bar, his spectacles low-riding his nose, doing his solitary, on-the-wagon thing. Some ashes floated down into Happy's plate, and I blew them off before I placed the plate down in front of him. Happy looked down mournfully at the slab of meat garnished with the anemic sprig of wilted parsley and the gravy pooled in the gluey mashed potatoes. His hand almost but not quite fell away from the glass in his grip.

"This looks like *dog* shit," he muttered.

"You want another drink, Happy?"

"Yeah," he said with a one o'clock slur. "And this time, put a little liquor in it."

I prepared his manhattan (an ounce of rail bourbon with a cherry dropped in it, no vermouth) and placed it on a moldy coaster advertising some sort of black Sambuca we did not stock. Then I heard Anna's tired voice from down the bar: "Ordering!" I moved to the rail and fixed her drinks.

That's the way it went for the rest of the afternoon. Buddy and Bubba, two GS-9 rednecks, came in at the downslope of the rush and split a couple of pitchers. They argued over sports trivia the entire time with a pompadoured dude named Richard, though none of them had picked up a ball of any kind since high school. Before they left, they poked their heads in the kitchen and congratulated Darnell on the "presentation" of the meat loaf. Darnell went about his work, and Buddy sneered in my direction as he and Bubba headed out the door.

After lunch, I put some PJ Harvey in the deck for Anna while she cleaned and reset her station. Phil Saylor had instructed me to keep blues and jazz playing on the stereo during the rush, but Happy, dashing in his dandruff-specked, plum-colored sport jacket, was now the only customer in the bar. Sitting there in a stagnant cloud of his own cigarette smoke, he didn't ever seem to respond to the musical selection either way.

Anna split for the day after bumming a smoke, and Ramon retreated to the kitchen, where he practiced some bullshit karate moves on an amused Darnell while I began to cut limes for Mai's evening shift. I had just finished filling the fruit tray when Dan Boyle walked through the front door.

Boyle parked his wide ass on the stool directly in front of me and ran fingers like pale cigars through his wiry, dirty blond hair.

"Nick."

"Boyle."

His lazy, bleached-out eyes traveled up to the call rack, then settled back down on the bar. I turned and pulled the black-labeled bottle of Jack Daniel's off the call shelf. I poured some sour mash into a shot glass and slid it in front of him.

"A beer with that?"

"Not just yet."

He put the glass to his lips and tilted his head back for a slow taste. The action opened his jacket a bit, the grip of his Python edging out.

On any given night, the Spot could be heavy with guns, as the place had become a favorite watering hole for D.C.'s plain-clothes cops and detectives, the connection going back to Saylor. Guns or no, Boyle had earned a different kind of rep, topped by his much-publicized role in the Gallatin Street shoot-out. I had been there with him, right next to him, in fact, but my participation had remained anonymous. I was reminded of it, though, every time I passed a mirror: a two-inch-long scar, running down my cheek.

"Goddamn it, that's good," Boyle said, wiping his mouth with the back of his hand. "I'll take that beer now."

I tapped him one and set the mug next to the shot. Boyle pulled a Marlboro hard pack from his jacket, drew a cigarette, and tamped it on the pack. He put it to his lips and I gave him a light.

"Thanks." Boyle spit smoke and reached for the mug. I bent over the soak sink and ran a glass over the brush.

"Good day out there?" I said, looking into the dirty gray suds.

"Not bad today, if you really want to know. Picked up the shooter that fired off that Glock on school grounds over at Duval two weeks ago."

"The one where the bullet hit the wrong kid?"

"The wrong kid? If you say so. The kid that got shot, he had a roll of twenties in his pocket, and a gold chain around his neck thicker than my wrist. So maybe he didn't hit the kid he was going for, but he damn sure hit a kid that was in the life. Shit, Nick, you throw a fuckin' rock in the hall of that high school, you're gonna hit someone guilty of something."

"You're a real optimist, Boyle. You know it?"

"Like now I need a lecture. Anyway, you want to talk about sociology and shit from behind that bar, go ahead. In the meantime, I'm out there—"

"In that concrete jungle?"

"What?"

"'Concrete Jungle,'" I said. "The Specials."

"Gimme another drink," Boyle mumbled, and finished off what was in his glass. He chased it with a swig of beer and wiped his chin dry with the back of his hand.

Happy said something, either to himself or to me, from the

other end of the bar. I ignored him, poured Boyle another shot. I leaned one elbow on the mahogany and put my foot up on the ice chest.

"So, Boyle. How about that kid, the one that got it two nights ago—"

"The one they found in the river?"

"Yeah. I guess that was a drug thing, too."

"Bet it," Boyle said. "But it's not my district. So that's one I don't have to worry about."

"Let me ask you something. You know what the weapons of choice are on the street this month, right? I mean, it changes all the time, but you're pretty much on top of it. Right?"

"So?"

"These enforcers. They in the habit of using silencers these days?"

Boyle thought for a moment, then shook his head. He watched me out the corner of his eye as he butted his cigarette. Happy called again and I went down his way and fixed him a drink. When I came back, Boyle was firing down the remainder of his Jack and draining off the rest of his beer. He left some money on the bar, stashed his cigarettes in his jacket, and slid clumsily off his stool.

"Take it easy, Nick."

"You, too."

I took his bills and rang on the register, dropping what was left into my tip jar. In the bar mirror, I saw Dan Boyle moving toward the front door. He turned once and stared at my back, his mouth open, his eyes blank. Then he turned again and walked heavily from the bar.

I WORKED ANOTHER SHIFT on Friday, and in the evening Lyla and I caught a movie at the Dupont and had some appetizers after the show at Aleko's, the best Greek food in town for my money, on Connecticut, above the Circle. Lyla had a few glasses of retsina at the restaurant and a couple more glasses of white before we went to bed. I didn't drink that night—three days now without a drop, the longest downtime in a long, long while. I had some trouble going to sleep, though, and when I did, my dreams were crowded, filled with confusing detail, unfamiliar places, blue-black starlings rising in the corners of the frame.

On Saturday, Lyla went into the office to put the finishing touches on a cover story, and I rode my ten-speed down to the Mall to catch a free Fugazi show at the Sylvan Theater. A go-go act opened to a polite crowd, and then the band came out and tore it up. I saw Joe Martinson, a friend and contemporary of mine from the old postpunk days, and we hung together in the late-teen crowd that was getting off—clean off—on the music.

That night, Lyla and I stayed at my place and listened to a few records. Lyla drank a gin and tonic and switched over to wine, and around midnight she called me outside, where I found her sitting on a blanket she had spread in the yard. She smirked as I approached her, and as she opened her legs, her skirt rode up her thighs, and I saw what that smile was all about. It was a good night, and another day gone by without a drink. But my dreams were no better than those of the night before.

On Sunday, we drove down to Sandy Point and buried our toes in the hot orange sand, then cooled off in the bay, dodging the few nettles, which were late that year due to the heavy spring rains. In the evening, I drove over to Alice Deal Junior High and worked out with my physician, Rodney White, who ran a karate school in the gym. Though I had resisted "learning" tae kwon do—I had boxed coming up in the Boys Club and was convinced that hand technique was all I needed to know—I had been doing this with Rodney for years now, and he had managed to teach me some street moves as well as the first four forms of his art. I finished the last of those forms, and Rodney and I got into some one-step sparring.

"All right, man," Rodney said.

We bowed in, and then I threw a punch. Rodney moved

simultaneously to the side and down into a horse stance, where he sprang up and whipped a straight, open hand to within an inch of my throat. I heard the snap of his black gi and the yell from deep in his chest.

"What the hell was that?"

"Ridge hand," Rodney said. "Keep the first joints of your fingers bent. You'll be striking with the whole side of your hand. And the kicker's in the snap of the wrist, right before the strike. Step aside, and use the momentum coming up to drive it right into the Adam's apple. You do it right, man, you'll ruin somebody's day."

I tried it, then tried it again. "Like that?"

Rodney gave a quick nod. "Something like that. More snap, though, at the end. Like everything else, it'll come."

"What now?"

"Get your gloves, man," Rodney said. "Let's go a few."

After we sparred, I drove back to my place and grabbed a beer out of the refrigerator and took it with me into the shower. I didn't think about it one way or the other, as this was something I did every time I returned from Rodney White's dojo. No bells went off and I felt no guilt. The beer was cold and good.

I stood in the spray of the shower, leaned against the tiles, and drank. I thought about what had happened at the river, and what I had heard: the inflection of the voices, the words themselves, the animal fear of the boy. The memory had resonance, like a cold finger on my shoulder. Everyone else had this wrapped up and tied off as a drug kill, another black kid born in a bad place, gone down a bad road. But I had been there that night. And the more I went back to it, the more I suspected that they were wrong.

I got out of the shower and wrapped a towel around my middle, then got myself another beer. I cracked the beer and went to the living room, where I phoned Dan Boyle.

"Yeah," he said, over the screams and laughter of several children.

"Boyle, it's Nick Stefanos. What's goin' on?"

"These fuckin' kids," he said, letting out a long, tired breath into the phone. "What can I do for you?"

I told him, and then we went back and forth on it for the next half hour. In the end, against his better judgment, he agreed to do what I asked, maybe because he knew that we both wanted the same thing. I set a time and thanked him, then hung the receiver in its cradle. Then I tilted my head back and killed the rest of my beer.

I could have called Boyle back and ended it right then. If I had just called him back, things might not have gone the way they did between Lyla and me, and I never would have met Jack LaDuke. But the thirst for knowledge is like a piece of ass you know you shouldn't chase; in the end, you chase it just the same.

THREE

AFTER MY MONDAY shift, I walked out of the Spot and headed for my car, with Anna Wang at my side, a colorful day pack strung across her back. She wore black bike shorts and a white T-shirt that fell off one muscled shoulder, leaving exposed the lacy black strap of a bra. I let her into the passenger side and then went around and got myself behind the wheel.

"Boss car," Anna said as she had a seat in the shotgun bucket of my latest ride.

"I like it," I said with deliberate understatement. Actually, I thought it was one of the coolest cars in D.C.: a '66 Dodge Coronet 500, white, with a red interior, full chrome center console, and a 318 under the hood. After my Dart blew a head gasket a year earlier, I had gone into the Shenandoah Valley and paid cash—two grand, roughly—to the car's owner in Winchester, and I hadn't regretted it one day since.

Anna snagged a cigarette from the pack wedged in my visor

and pushed in the dash lighter. I hit the ignition, and the dual exhaust rumbled in the air. Anna glanced over as she lit her smoke.

"What are you, some kind of gearhead, Nick?"

"Not really. I just like these old Chrysler products. My first car was a Valiant with a push-button trans on the dash. After that, I had a '67 Polara, white on red, the extralong model, a motel on wheels. My buddy Johnny McGinnes called it my 'Puerto Rican Cadillac.' It had the cat-eye taillights, too. A real beauty. Then I had a '67 Belvedere, clean lines, man, and the best-handling car I ever owned. I guess because of the posi rear. Then my old Dart, and now this. I'll tell you something, these Mopar engines were the strongest this country ever produced. As long as there's no body cancer, I'll keep buying them."

Anna took a drag off her cigarette and smirked. "'Posi rear'? Nick, you *are* a gearhead, man."

"Yeah, well, I guess you got me nailed." I looked her over and caught her eye. "Speaking of which, there's this tractor pull, next Saturday night? I was wonderin'... if you're not doing anything, I'd be right proud if you'd care to accompany me—"

"Very funny. Anyway, you can just take your girlfriend to that tractor pull, buster."

At the top of 8th, we passed an old haunt of mine, a club where you used to be able to catch a good local band and where you could always cop something from the bartender, something to smoke or snort or swallow in the bathroom or on the patio out back. I had met my ex-wife Karen there for the first time one night. The original club had closed years ago, shut down at about the same time as my marriage.

Anna looked out the window. "You ever go in that place?"

"Not anymore."

"I thought 'cause, you know, they cater to that thirty-plus crowd."

"Thanks a lot." I could have backhanded her one, but she was so damn cute. "Where you headed, anyway?"

"Drop me at the Eastern Market Metro, okay?"

I did it and then got on my way.

I DROVE DOWN M Street, past the Navy Yard and the projects and the gay nightclubs and the warehouses, and kept straight on past the 11th Street Bridge ramp as M continued unmarked, past Steuart Petroleum, down through the trees toward the water, past a couple of marinas and the Water Street turnoff, to the wooded area where the rusted houseboat sat submerged in the river amid the wooden pilings. I pulled off in the clearing and parked my car next to Boyle's.

An old man with closely cropped salt-and-pepper hair sat in a metal folding chair, holding a cheap Zebco rod, a red plastic bucket and green tackle box by his side, a sixteen-ounce can of beer between his feet. Two young men leaned against a brilliantly waxed late-model Legend parked beneath the trees and looked out toward the carpet green of Anacostia Park across the river. Boyle stood on the edge of the concrete bulkhead, his shirtsleeves rolled above his elbows, his beefy hands at his side, a manila envelope wedged under one arm, a hot cigarette drooping lazily from his mouth. I walked across the gravel and joined him.

"You're a little late," Boyle said, glancing at his watch.

"Had to wait for Anna to clean her station. Gave her a lift to the subway."

"What're you, sniffin' after that Chinee heinie now?"

"Just gave her a ride, Boyle."

"Like to have me some of that. Never did have a Chinese broad when I was single. Any suggestions on how to get one?"

"You might start by not calling them 'broads.' Women don't seem to like that very much these days. They haven't for, like, forty years."

"Thanks for the tip. I'll work it into my next sensitivity discussion. The department's very big on that now, since those uniforms handcuffed that drunk broad—I mean, *inebriated woman*—to that mailbox last winter. Maybe I could get you to come down and lecture."

I looked at the envelope under Boyle's arm. "So what you got?"

"Not yet," Boyle said. He transferred the envelope to his hand and dragged deeply on his cigarette. A large drop of sweat ran down his neck and disappeared below his collar. "Where were you that night?"

I pointed to a dirt area of paper and cans and garbage just inside the tree line, behind the fisherman. "Right about in there." One of the young men leaning on the Legend gave a brief, tough glance my way, and the other stared straight ahead.

"If they were parked where we are—"

"I don't know where they were parked. I didn't see anything. I couldn't even lift my head."

"Well, the freshest tire prints we got were there. We were lucky to get those—someone called in an anonymous on the murder pretty soon after it happened. That was you, right?"

"Yeah."

Boyle moved his head in the direction of our cars. "So if that's where they were parked, and they took the kid straight down to the water and did him, then went right back to their vehicle, it's possible they didn't see you layin' back there in the trees."

"What, you don't believe me?"

"Sure, I believe you all right." Boyle took a last hit off his smoke and ground it under his shoe. "Just tryin' to figure things out. C'mon, let's take a walk, get away from those two entrepreneurs."

"Those guys dealers?"

Boyle shrugged. "That's a thirty-thousand-dollar car, and they ain't real estate developers. Anyway, I'm Homicide, not Narcotics, so I couldn't give a rat's ass. But it's a bet that they aren't holdin' right now. This road dead-ends up ahead, past the bridge at the last marina. The locals know not to do business down here—no place to run to. Those guys are probably just relaxing before going to work later tonight. But I don't need any witnesses to what I'm about to do. Come on."

We went back to the road and walked north toward the Sousa Bridge. A mosquito caught me on the neck. I stopped and slapped at it, looked at the smudge of blood on my fingers. Boyle kept walking. I quickened my step and caught up with him.

Boyle said, "That thing you pulled with the silencer. That was pretty cute. It didn't hit me until I got off my bar stool. 'Course I phoned the detective in charge of the case soon as I left the Spot. Ballistics report had come in earlier that day."

"And?"

"You were right. A silenced twenty-two. A Colt Woodsman, I'd guess, if it was some kind of hit."

"A twenty-two. That proves it wasn't a gang thing, right?"

"It doesn't prove anything. A kid on the street can get his hands on any piece he wants, same as a pro, and for all I know, a twenty-two is the latest prestige weapon. Don't get ahead of yourself, Nick."

We went beneath the bridge and moved to the last set of legs before the river. A gull glided by and veered off toward the water. The metallic rush of cars above us echoed in the air.

Boyle leaned against a block of concrete, one of many that sat piled near the legs. "Tell me why else you think this isn't a drug kill."

"Let me ask you something, Boyle. You ever know whites and blacks to crew together in this town?"

"'Course not. Not in this town or any other town I ever heard of."

"It was a white man and a black man killed that kid. I heard their voices. And I'll tell you something else. You might want to check up in Baltimore, see if some similar shit has gone down. The white guy, he talked about going 'home,' used that extra long *o* the way they do up in South Baltimore. The guy was definitely out of BA."

"You got it all figured out. A pro hit, out-of-town talent. Come on, Nick, you're puttin' an awful lot together with nothin'."

"I'm telling you what I heard."

Boyle looked down at the manila envelope in his hand, then back at me. "I give you what we got, what are you gonna do with it?"

"I know what's going to happen to this if the shooters aren't found in a few more days. Not that it's the fault of you guys. They got you working two, maybe three homicides at a time, and I know it doesn't stop." I shrugged. "I'm just going to get out there, ask around like I always do. I find anything you can use, I'll head it in the direction of the guy who's assigned to the case."

"Through me."

"Whatever. Who's on it?"

"Guy named Johnson's got it. He doesn't come in the Spot, so you don't know him. He's a competent cop, a little on the quiet side. But he is straight up."

"If I find out anything, it'll come to you." I pointed my chin at the envelope.

Boyle breathed out slowly. "Well, we got nothing, really. Nothing yet. The kid's name was Calvin Jeter. Seventeen years of age. Dropout at sixteen, high truancy rate before that, no record except for a couple of f.i.'s, not even misdemeanors. Johnson interviewed the mother, nothing there. Said he was a good boy, no drugs. It's like a broken fuckin' record. Jeter didn't run with a crowd, but he hung real tight, all his life, with a kid named Roland Lewis. Haven't been able to locate Lewis yet."

"Lewis is missing?"

"Not officially, no."

"What about forensics, the crime scene?"

"The slug was fired at close range. You saw the burn marks yourself. A twenty-two'll do the job when the barrel's pressed right up there against the chin." Boyle's eyes moved to the river.

"The tire tracks indicate the doers drove some kind of off-road vehicle. Similar tracks were found in a turnaround area at the end of the road, past the last marina. Which tells me that when they left, they headed right for the dead end, had to backtrack—so maybe they weren't local guys after all." Boyle looked at me briefly, then away. "Like you said."

"What else?"

"One important thing, maybe the only real lead we got. There's a potential witness, someone who actually might have seen something. A worker down at the boatyard says there's this guy, some crazy boothead, sits under this bridge"—Boyle patted the concrete—"sits right on these blocks, wearing a winter coat, every morning just before dawn, reading books, singing songs, shit like that. And the estimated time of death was just around dawn."

"That's about right," I said.

"And if your friends drove under the bridge, then turned around and drove back, and if this mental deficient was here, there's a very good chance he got a good look at the car. Maybe he noticed the license plates. Maybe he can ID the shooters themselves."

"So who's the guy?"

"The guys at the boatyard, they don't know him. They never introduced themselves, on account of the guy was stone-crazy."

"Anybody interview him since?"

Boyle flicked a speck of tobacco off his chin. "He hasn't been *back* since. We don't even know if he was here that particular morning. Johnson's checked it out a couple of times, and we've got a couple of uniforms sitting down here at dawn for as long as we can spare 'em. But so far, nothing."

"All this stuff in the reports?"

"Yeah." Boyle pushed the envelope my way but did not hand it over.

"What's the problem?"

"I know what's going with you, that's all. You think because you got polluted and happened to fall down near where a kid got shot, that makes you responsible in some way for his death. But you ought to be smart enough to know that you had nothin' to do with it—that kid woulda died whether you had been laying there or not. And consider your being drunk some kind of blessing, brother. If you coulda got up off your ass, most likely they woulda killed you, too."

"I know all that."

"But you're still gonna go out and ask around."

"Yes."

Boyle sighed. "You got no idea what kind of trouble I could get into." He pointed one thick finger at my face. "Anything you find, you come to me, hear?"

"I will."

Boyle tossed me the envelope. "Don't fuck me, Nick."

He walked away and left me standing under the bridge.

FOUR

THAT EVENING, I categorized and studied the Xeroxed police file on the Jeter case, and in the morning I sat at the desk of the small office area in my apartment and studied it all over again. I showered and dressed, grabbed some of the pertinent material, and took a few legitimate business cards and some phony ones and slid them in my wallet. Then I took a dish of dry cat food and a bowl of water, placed them out on the stoop, and got into my Dodge and headed downtown.

I stopped for some breakfast at Sherrill's, the Capitol Hill bakery and restaurant that is the last remnant of old Southeast D.C., and had a seat at the chrome-edged lunch counter. My regular waitress, Alva, poured me an unsolicited coffee as I settled on my stool, and though the day was already hot, I drank the coffee, because you have to drink coffee when you're sitting at the counter at Sherrill's. Alva took my order, watching me over the rims of her eyeglasses as she wrote, and five minutes later I was sweating over a plate of eggs easy with a side of hash browns and sausage and toast. After the food, I had a second cup of coffee and a cigarette while I listened to a nearby conversation—the uninitiated might have called it an argument—between the owner, Lola, and her daughter, Dorothy. I kept my eyes on the Abbott's ice cream sign hung behind the counter and grinned with fondness at the sound of their voices.

Out on the street, I fed the meter and walked the four blocks down to the Spot. Darnell was in the kitchen prepping lunch and Mai sat at the bar, drinking coffee and reading the *Post.* The sandaled feet at the end of Mai's stout wheels barely reached the rail of the stool, and her blond hair was twisted and bound onto her head in some sort of pretzelized configuration. Phil stood at the register, his back to me, his lips moving—I could see them in the bar mirror—as he counted out from the night before.

"What's going on, Mai?" I said, walking toward the phone.

"Jerome," she said happily. Jerome had to be her latest Marine from the nearby barracks, but I didn't ask.

I placed the list of numbers and addresses in front of me on the service bar and picked up the phone. I began to dial Calvin Jeter's mother, then lost my nerve. Instead, I dialed the number for the Roland Lewis residence. Ramon walked from the kitchen, smiled a foolish gold-toothed grin, and sucker punched me in the gut as he passed. I was coughing it out when a girl's voice came on the other end.

"Yeah."

"Is Roland there?"

"Uh-uh."

"How about Mrs. Lewis? Is she in?"

"Nope." Some giggling by two other females in the background over some recorded go-go. I listened to that and watched Mai send Ramon down to the basement for some liquor.

"You expect her in?"

"She's workin', fool." A loud explosion of laughter. "Bah."

I heard the click of the receiver on the other end. I hung up the phone and checked the list for Mrs. Lewis's work number, saw that I had it, and decided, Not yet. Phil walked by me without a glance or a word, took his keys off the bar, and split.

I went into the kitchen. Darnell stood over a butcher block, chopping white onions, a piece of bread wedged inside his cheek to staunch the tears.

"Goin' on, Nick?"

"Just stopped in to make a couple of calls."

"You see Phil?"

"Yeah. He's still punishing me over last Tuesday night."

"You got all liquored up, left his place wide open, and walked out into the street. You can't really blame the man, can you?"

"I know."

"Yeah," Darnell said. "You know. But do you *really* know?"

"Thanks, Father. Light a candle for me the next time you're in church."

"Go on, man, if you're gonna be actin' funny." Darnell cocked his head but did not look up. He said quietly, "I got work to do."

I left the kitchen and walked through the bar. Ramon came up from the cellar, both hands under a bus tray filled with liquor bottles and cans of juice. I slapped him sharply on the cheek as he passed. He called me a *maricón* and we both kept walking. He was cackling as I went out the door.

THE LEWIS RESIDENCE, A nondescript brick row house with a corrugated green aluminum awning extended out past its front porch, was on an H-lettered street off Division Avenue in the Lincoln Heights area of Northeast. I had taken East Capitol around the stadium, over the river, past countless liquor stores, fried-chicken houses, and burger pits, and into the residential district of a largely unheralded section of town, where mostly hardworking middle-class people lived day to day among some of the highest drug and crime activity of the city.

I parked my Dodge on Division, locked it, and walked west on the nearest cross street. I passed a huge, sad-eyed guy—a bondsman, from the looks of him—retrieving a crowbar and flashlight from the trunk of his car. Three more addresses down the block and I took the steps up the steeply pitched front lawn of the Lewis house to its concrete porch, where I knocked on the front door. No one responded and no sounds emanated from the house. The girl who had answered the phone earlier and her friends were obviously gone. I stood there, listening to a window-unit air conditioner work hard in the midday heat.

I waited a few minutes, looked over my shoulder. The bondsman had gone off somewhere, leaving an empty street. I went to the bay window, stepped around a rocker sofa mounted on rails and springs, and looked through an opening in the venetian blinds: an orderly living room, tastefully but not extravagantly furnished, with African-influenced art hung on white-washed walls.

I dropped my card through the mail slot in the door and walked back down to the street.

DIVISION LIQUORS STOOD ON a corner a couple of blocks south of the Lewis house, between an empty lot and the charred shell of something once called the Strand Supper Club. Two other businesses on the block had burned or been burned out as well, leaving only the liquor store and a Laundromat open on the commercial strip. I parked in front of the Laundromat and walked towards Division Liquors.

Several groups of oldish men stood in front of the store, gesturing broadly with their hands and arguing dispassionately, while a young man stood next to his idling Supra and talked into a pay phone mounted on the side of the building that faced the lot. The young man wore a beeper clipped to his shorts—some sort of statement, most likely meaning nothing—and swore repeatedly into the phone, punctuating each tirade with the words *my money*. I passed a double amputee sitting in a wheelchair outside the front door. His chair had been decorated with stickers from various veteran's groups and a small American flag had been taped to one of its arms. The man sitting in it had matted dreadlocks tucked under a knit cap, with sweat beaded on the ends of the dreads.

"Say, man," he said.

"I'll get you on the way out," I said, and entered the store.

I grabbed two cans of beer and a pack of Camels, paid a white man through an opening at the bottom of a Plexiglas shield, and left the store. Out on the sidewalk, I slipped a couple of ones and some coin into Knit Cap's cup, checked to see if the young man was still using the phone, saw that he was, and walked back to my car. Sometime later, as I finished off my first can of beer, the young man dropped into the bucket of his Supra and drove off. I got out of my car and walked to the pay phone, where I sunk a quarter in the slot and punched in a number that was written on the notepad in my hand.

"Mrs. Jeter, please."

A bored young female said, "Hold on." A television set blared in the background, competing against the sounds of young children yelling and playing in the room. A woman's voice screamed out, silencing the children. She breathed heavily into the phone.

"Yes?"

"Mrs. Jeter?"

"Y-y-yes?"

"My name is Nick Stefanos. I'm working with the Metropolitan Police on your son Calvin's murder," I said, breaking some kind of law with the lie.

"I've done talked to the p-p-police three times."

"I know. But I'd like to see you if possible. I'm in your neighborhood right now." I gave her the name of the liquor store.

"You're in the neighborhood all right. Fact, you're just

around the corner." I listened to the TV set and the kids, who had started up again, as she thought things over. She told me how to get to her place.

"Thanks very much. I'll be right there." After I shotgun another beer, I thought, hanging the phone in its cradle.

THE JETER APARTMENT WAS in a squat square structure housing five other units, oddly situated on a slight rise in the middle of a block of duplex homes. I parked in a six-car lot to the right of the building, beside a green Dumpster filled to overflowing with garbage. Bees swarmed around a tub-sized cup of cola abandoned on top of the Dumpster, and two boys stood nearby on brown grass and swung sticks at each other in the direct sun. I finished my beer, popped a stick of gum in my mouth, locked my car, and walked across the grass. One of the boys, no older than eight, lunged at me with his stick. I stepped away from it and smiled. He didn't smile back. I walked around to the front of the apartment.

A woman sat in a folding chair outside the entrance, her huge legs spread, the inside of each wrinkled thigh touching the other, fanning herself with a magazine. Some kids stood out on the street, grouped around an expensive black coupe, the name MERCEDES scripted along the driver's side rocker panel. Bass boosted and volumed to distortion thumped from the sound system, burying the rap. A kid looked my way and spread his fingers across his middle, and one of his friends smiled. I approached the woman and asked her the number of the Jeter apartment. A wave of the magazine directed me to a dark opening centered in the front of the building.

The Jeter apartment was one of two situated down the stairs. The stairwell smelled of urine and nicotine, but in the depth and insulation of the cinder block, things were cooler and there was less noise. I wiped sweat off my face and knocked on a door marked 01.

The door opened, and a woman who could have been forty or sixty-five stood in the frame. She wore turquoise stretch pants and a T-shirt commemorating the reunion of a family name I did not recognize. Her breasts hung to her belly and stretched out on the fabric of the T-shirt. Her face was round as a dinner plate and her hair was doing different things all at once on different parts of her head. By anyone's standard, she was an unattractive woman.

"Mrs. Jeter? Nick Stefanos." I put out my hand.

She took it and said, "C-c-come on in."

I walked into a living room crowded with a plastic-covered sectional sofa and two nonmatching reclining chairs. Over the sofa, on a pale yellow wall, hung a black blanket embroidered with a fluorescent wild pony. A rather ornate sideboard of cheap material stood against the next wall, with just about a foot of space between it and the sofa. Except for one dusty teacup, the shelves of the sideboard were empty. A big-screen television sat flush on a stand against the next wall, with wires extending from the Sega beneath it, the wires leading to the hands of a young man sitting on the sofa next to a young woman. Around them both, and on the table where the young man's feet rested, were scattered junk-food wrappers and plastic cups. The young man played the game with intensity, his features twitching with each explosion and laser simulation from the set. As I entered, he glanced up briefly in my direction with a look that managed to combine aloofness with contempt. The young woman, who I guessed had answered the phone when I called, did not acknowledge me at all.

I followed Mrs. Jeter toward the kitchen, looking once into a deep unlit hallway where a little boy and a toddler of indeterminate sex jostled over a rideable plastic fire engine. In the shadows, I saw another young man move from one room to the next.

The kitchen, lit with one circular fluorescent light and a bit of natural light from a small rectangular window, was through an open doorway to the right of the television. Mrs. Jeter leaned against an efficiency-size refrigerator and folded her arms.

"Can I get you somethin', Mr. Stefanos?"

The heat, oppressive in the living room, was stifling in the kitchen; I rolled my sleeves up over damp forearms to the elbow. "Water. A little water would be great, thanks."

"H-h-have a seat."

She gestured to one of four chairs set tightly around a small folding table with a marbleized red Formica top. I sat in one, under a clock whose face featured a Last Supper depiction of white disciples grouped around a white Jesus. Mrs. Jeter turned her back to me, withdrew a glass from a sinkful of dirty dishes, rinsed the glass out, and filled it from the spigot. She placed the glass in front of me and took a seat in a chair on the other side of the table.

Mrs. Jeter watched my face as I looked at the grayish water in the glass, the lip of which was caked yellow. I turned the glass inconspicuously in my hand and had a sip from the cleanest side. The water was piss-warm and tasted faintly of bleach. I put the glass down on the table.

"Mrs. Jeter—"

"Call me Vonda, if you don't mind. I ain't all t-t-that much older than you."

I nodded. "My sympathies on your son's death, Vonda."

"Your sympathies," she said quietly and without malice. "Your sympathies gon' bring my baby back?"

"No," I said. "It's just that... I'd like to help, if I can." I rotated the glass in the ring of water that had formed beneath it and listened to the sounds of the toddler crying in the hallway and the explosions coming from the game on the television set in the other room.

"You say you're with the p-p-police?" She closed her eyes tightly on the stutter, as if she could concentrate her way through it.

"Unofficially, yes. I'm working with them on this," I said,

repeating my lie. "I know what you've told them already. I need to know if there's anything else."

"Like?"

"Things the police may not have asked. Like where Calvin usually went when he went out. What he did for money. That sort of thing."

"You mean, was he druggin'? Ain't t-t-that what you mean to say?" Her eyes flared momentarily, then relaxed. "Calvin wasn't in the life. He was just a boy. Just a boy."

I looked away from her. The crying from the toddler in the hallway intensified. I wondered, Why doesn't someone pick that goddamned baby *up?*

"Those your children out there?" I said, hoping to loosen what had fallen between us.

"The girl is my oldest. The babies, m-m-my grandchildren, are hers. That boy out there, on the couch? That's Barry. He's the father to the youngest child. His little brother, the one back in the bedrooms, he's stayin' with us awhile. Got put out, up his way."

"Mind if I talk to your daughter?"

"She don't know nothin' more than what I told you. What I already told the police."

The television set clicked off and the sound from it died. The front door opened and shut, and soon after that the toddler stopped crying. The older child came into the kitchen then and stood by his grandmother's side, patting his hand against her thigh. She picked him up and sat him in her lap, rubbed her palm over his bald head.

"Have the police been back in touch with you?"

"'Posed to be," she said, brushing some crumbs off the child's lips.

"They're trying to find Calvin's friend Roland," I said. "Know if they had any luck?"

"Roland? If they did, n-n-nobody said nothin' to me."

I rubbed a finger down the scar on my cheek. "Mind if I have a look in Calvin's room?"

"You can look," she said, with a shrug and a grunt as she picked up her grandson and rose from the chair. "Come on, Mr. Stefanos."

We walked out and through the living room, where the girl sat on the sectional couch, giving the toddler a short bottle of juice. I followed Vonda Jeter into the hallway, past a bathroom and then four bedrooms, which were really two rooms divided by particle-board in one and a shower curtain hung on laundry cord in the other. Three of the rooms contained single beds and scuffed dressers and small television sets on nightstands or chairs. In one of the rooms, the younger brother of the toddler's father slept on his back, bare-chested in his shorts, with one forearm draped over his eyes. Vonda Jeter directed me into the last room, which she said was Calvin's. She pulled on a string that hung from the ceiling and switched on a light.

The room was windowless, paneled in mock birch, separated from its other half by a chair-supported board running floor to ceiling. An unfinished dresser stood flush against the paneling, and next to that an army-issue footlocker. Some change lay on the top of the dresser, along with a set of house keys on a rabbit's foot chain and a knit cap with the word TIMBERLAND stitched in gold across the front.

"The detective, that Mr. Johnson? He went through C-C-Calvin's stuff."

I looked back at Vonda Jeter. Her eyes, yellow and lifeless before, had moistened now and pinkened at the rims.

"Do you have a photograph of Calvin that I could borrow? In the meantime, I'd just like to have a quick look around. I won't disturb anything."

"Go on ahead," she said, and walked from the room without another word.

I went through the dresser drawers, found nothing to study or keep. As a teenager, I had always kept a shoe box in my dresser filled with those things most important to me, and in fact, I still had it; Calvin's drawers were filled with clothing, nothing more, almost obsessively arranged, as if he had no personal connection to his own life.

In the footlocker, a basketball sat in the corner on a folded, yellowed copy of *D.C. This Week.* Several shirts hung on wire, along with a couple of pairs of neatly pressed trousers. I ran the back of my hand along the print rayon shirts, my knuckle tapping something in one of the breast pockets. I reached into the pocket and withdrew a pack of matches: the Fire House, a bar on 22nd and P in Northwest. Across town, and in more ways than one a long distance from home. I slipped the matchbook into my shirt pocket, switched off the light, and left the room.

Vonda Jeter stood in the living room, by the door. I stepped around the couch and met her there. She handed me a photograph of a tough, unsmiling Calvin wearing a suit jacket and tie. He looked nothing like the boy I had seen lying in the river.

"Thank you," I said. "I'll be in touch."

"Whatever you can do," she said, looking away.

She opened the door. I stepped out, quickly took the concrete steps up the stairwell, and walked out into the white sunlight. I heard her door close behind me as I moved across the grass.

I went to my car, unlocked it, and rolled the windows down. The father of the toddler, the game player from the couch, stood looking under the hood of a burnt orange 240Z parked beside my Dodge. He wore shorts that fell below his knees and a black T-shirt showing Marley hitting a blunt. Like most of the young men I had seen that day, he was narrow-waisted, thin, and muscled, with hair shaved to the scalp, broken by a short part. I put him somewhere at the tail end of his teens.

"Is it burnin' a lot of oil?" I said, walking up beside him.

He pulled the dipstick, read it, wiped it off with a cranberry red rag, and pushed it back down into the crankcase.

"Nick Stefanos," I said, extending my hand. "It's Barry, isn't it?" He ignored the question and my gesture. "These old Zs, they're trouble. But they do have style. The two-forties have those headlights—"

"Somethin' I can do for you? 'Cause if not, whyn't you just go on about your business." He closed the hood, wiped his hands off on the rag.

I placed my card on top of the hood. He read it from where he stood without picking it up.

"I'm looking for Roland Lewis," I said. "Thought maybe he could tell me something about Calvin's death."

"That punk," he muttered heavily, staring at the asphalt. He went around to the driver's side and began to fold himself into the bucket. I could see some sort of garishly colored uniform thrown on the floor behind the seat.

"Let me ask you something, Barry," I said, stopping him. "What do *you* think happened to Calvin? At least you can tell me that."

He stopped, chuckled cynically, and looked me in the eyes for the first time. "What do *I* think happened? Whyn't you just take a look around you, chief, check out what we got goin' on down here." Barry made a sweeping gesture with his hand and lowered his voice. "Calvin *died*, man. He died."

He got into his car, started it, and backed out of the lot. My card blew off the hood, fluttered to the asphalt. It landed next to a fast-food wrapper dark with grease. I left it there, climbed into my Dodge, and steered it back onto the street.

I STOPPED FOR ANOTHER can of beer at Division Liquors and went back to my car, where I found some dope in the glove box and rolled a joint. I smoked half the number driving across town, slid an English Beat into the deck. By the time I hit my part of the world, upper 14th around Hamilton, "Monkey Murders" poured out of the rear-deck speakers of my Dodge, and I was tapping out the rhythms on my steering wheel, and singing, too, and many of the things I had seen that day seemed washed away.

I stopped at Slim's, near Colorado Avenue, for a beer, drank it while I listened to some recorded jazz, then hit the Good

Times Lunch on Georgia for an early dinner. Kim, my Korean friend who owned the place, put a can of beer on the counter when I walked in, then went off to fix me a platter of fried cod and greens and potatoes. I took the beer to a pay phone near the front register, stood beneath a malt-liquor poster featuring a washed-up black actor embracing a light-skinned woman with Caucasian features, and dialed the number once again to the Lewis residence.

This time, the mother of Roland Lewis answered the phone. She had just gotten in from work and had found my card in the pile of mail inside her door. Her tone was cool, even, and clear. I explained to her that I needed to speak with her son, adding for the third time that day that I was "with" the police on the Calvin Jeter case. I listened to my own voice, caught the slur in it from the alcohol and the pot, wished then that I had waited to straighten up before I called. But after a moment or two, she agreed to meet me, and I set something up for the next day at her place of business, on M Street in the West End.

I returned to my stool at the counter and ate my food. A man came into the restaurant and ordered a beer, talked to himself as he drank it. I pushed the empty plate of food away and smoked a cigarette while I watched rush hour dissipate through the plate-glass window of the Good Times Lunch. I butted the smoke and went to the register to get my check from Kim.

"Any trouble down this way lately?" I asked as he ripped a green sheet of paper off a pad. There had been two gun deaths, merchant robberies on the strip, in the last six months.

Kim produced a snub-nosed .38 from somewhere under the counter. He waved it briefly, then replaced it as quickly as he had drawn it. Kim blinked, wiped a forearm hard as pine across his brow.

"Take care," I said. I went back down to my spot, left ten on seven, and walked out under the damp veil of dusk.

When I got back to my apartment, I fed the cat and phoned Lyla. Her recorded message told me that she had gone out for happy hour with a friend and that she'd check the machine later that night. I left my own message, asking her to come by, adding, "I could use some company."

But Lyla did not call back or drop in on me. I ended the night sitting on a bench in the back of my yard, another beer in my hand, listening to the crickets sounding out against the flat whir of air conditioners from the windows of the neighboring houses. My cat slinked out from the darkness and brushed against my ankles. I scratched behind her ears. After awhile, I walked back inside and fell to alcohol sleep.

FIVE

THE POLICE REPORT had the only potential witness to the Jeter murder as a black male, mid-forties, average height and build, with no distinguishing characteristics, a typically blank cross-racial description. It wasn't much to go on, not anything at all, in fact, but the boatyard worker had mentioned that the man wore a brilliant blue winter coat year round. Everyone concerned had accepted the worker's opinion that the man who sat singing under the bridge every morning at dawn was crazy. Crazy, maybe, but not necessarily stupid. If he knew that he had witnessed a killing and understood the implications, then he had probably disposed of the coat by now, or, at the very least, quit wearing it. I was reminded of the time when, as kids, my friends and I had stood on a hill and thrown hard-packed snowballs at cars driving south on 16th Street. One of my buddies had winged a smoker that shattered the side window of a green Rambler Ambassador, bloodying the driver's lip. We all scattered and ran; the cops nailed me at the end of a nearby alley, identified me by my neon orange knit cap, which I had neglected to remove from my head. The hat had been the only thing the driver had remembered from his brief look at us on the hill. I figured that nobody, even a straitjacket candidate, is as mindless as a kid who is running from the cops for the first time. But I hoped that I was wrong.

So the next morning, I woke up in the dark and headed downtown and into Southeast, down M Street to the waterline, in search of the man in the brilliant blue coat. By the time I got there, the sky had lightened and a line of orange had broken the green plane of Anacostia Park across the river. A blue-and-white sat parked beneath the Sousa Bridge, with two uniforms in the front seat. They noted me without incident as I went by. I turned the car around at the end of the road and passed them again on my way back out. No man sat singing or reading on the concrete pilings beneath the bridge, blue coat or otherwise. I moved on.

I drove all the way across town, bought a go-cup of coffee at a market on Wisconsin and P in Georgetown, then went up to R and parked near Dumbarton Oaks. I walked through open grounds, down into the woods of Rock Creek Park, and found my seat on a large gray rock at the crest of a winding bridle trail overlooking the creek and Beach Drive. I watched the cars and their occupants, making their morning rush to wherever it is that people who wear ties and business suits go, and I listened to the serpentine creek running to the Georgetown Channel and the songbirds in the trees above. Everyone has their own spot in their hometown, and this was mine.

Afterward, I walked to the iron fence surrounding Oak Hill, wrapped my hands around the rungs, and admired the most beautiful cemetery grounds in D.C. Privileged people lead privileged lives, and even find privileged places to rest. I wondered idly about the final whereabouts of Calvin Jeter's body. Then for a while I thought of nothing earthbound at all. I noticed an old man in a physical-plant uniform sitting atop a small tractor in the cemetery, and for a moment our eyes met. Then he looked away, and we both went back to what we had been doing for the last half hour: trying to find a kernel of spirituality before returning to the cold reality of our day.

I spent that morning reading local history in the Washingtoniana room of the Martin Luther King Memorial Library, then walked into Chinatown and met Lyla for lunch at a nondescript restaurant packed with locals at the corner of 7th and H. I crossed the dining room with a bag in my hand and had a seat next to Lyla.

"Hey," I said, kissing her mouth.

"Hey, you." She looked me over. "Why so sporty?"

I wore an open-necked denim, sleeves up, and a pair of khakis, with monk-straps on my feet. "You think this is sporty?"

"Well, you ran an iron over the shirt."

"Just for you, baby. And, I'm meeting a woman this afternoon."

"What, I'm not a woman?"

"Sweetheart, you're all woman. But I'm talking about a business appointment. Over at Ardwick, Morris and Baker, in the West End."

"That's the firm that defended those S and L boys."

"I don't know anything about that. I'm meeting one of their secretaries."

"Uh-huh." She smiled maternally. "You're poking around on the Jeter murder, aren't you? I can see it on you, Nick. The only time you get wired during the daylight like this is when you're juiced on some kind of case. Am I right?"

"I'm asking around, that's all. Maybe I'll kick something up."

"Yeah," she said.

Our waitress, an angular woman with coal black hair and bad teeth, arrived at the table. I ordered steamed dumplings with a main of squid sautéed in garlic, and Lyla ordered the special, asking only if it contained chicken. We avoided anything in the way of chicken here, as several of them hung plucked in the midday heat of the window. Lyla asked for white wine, and I took ice water.

"What do you suppose is in the special?" Lyla said.

"I'm not sure," I said. "But it's probably better you didn't ask."

The waitress came back momentarily with our drinks.

Lyla lifted her wineglass. "Takes the edge off," she said, and had a sip. "Yeah, that'll do it."

"I thought you looked a little thick today," I said. And I had noticed her hand shaking as she picked up her glass.

She shrugged apologetically. "Happy hour stretched to last call. Sorry I didn't make it over last night."

"That's okay."

She flicked the brown paper on the table. "So, what's in the bag?"

"Some stuff I picked up at the Chinese store on H. Something for you."

I withdrew a small ceramic incense burner, hand-painted lilacs on a black background, and put it in front of her.

"Love it." She smiled, turned the burner in her hand. "What else?"

"Something for me." I took a videotape from the bag and waved it in front of her. "A Ringo Lam flick, for the collection."

"Okay. What else?"

"Something for us." I pulled out a tub of cream, labeled completely in Mandarin characters. "The lady at the counter said it was 'very special lotion for lovers.' "

"What's so special about it?"

"I don't know. But we've got a date, tomorrow night, right?"

"Yeah?"

"So I was thinkin'—"

"Oh boy," she said.

"That, at the end of the night, maybe you'd care to dip your fingers in this jar and give me a back rub. And maybe after that, I could return the favor and give you a front rub."

"Here it comes."

"And then we could rub it all over us and get some kind of friction going."

"You could get a burn like that."

"And maybe we'd get so much friction going, that, I don't know, the two of us could just explode."

"At the same time?"

"Well, we could try."

"Nick, why are you such a dog?"

"Speaking of dog," I said, "here comes your food."

Lyla and I spent a couple of hours in the restaurant, enjoying the food and talking and having a few more laughs. There was a sign over the kitchen door that read MANAGEMENT NOT RESPONSIBLE, and Lyla commented dryly on that. I stuck with water and she had another wine. Lyla paid the check and I left the tip, and we kissed outside on the street. I stood there and watched her walk in the direction of the subway stop, moving in that clipped, confident way of hers in her short peasant dress, her red hair brilliant in the sun and long on her back. You're a lucky bastard, I thought, and then I added, Nick, just try not to fuck this up.

THE OFFICES OF ARDWICK, Morris and Baker occupied the top floors of an Oliver Carr building on M Street at 24th. I have to laugh now when I hear any law firm's name; a guy by the name of Rick Bender comes in the Spot for a vodka gimlet once a week—I don't know what Bender does, but he's a profoundly silly guy, and I know he's not an attorney—and always leaves a business card on the bar with his tab: "Rick Bender, Esquire." Printed below his name is the name of his "firm": "Bender, Over, and Doer."

I passed through the marble-floored lobby and made an elevator where a couple of secretaries stood huddled in the back. I was of the tieless variety, and after a quick appraisal, the two of them went right on complaining about their respective attorneys. A few floors up, a paralegal joined us, a guy in his twenties who was struggling mightily in his attire and haircut to look fifteen years older. Then on the next floor, we picked up a real attorney, wearing a real charcoal suit with chalk stripes and a really powerful tie. I said hello to him and he looked both confused and scared to death. Finally, we made it to the top floor of the building, where I put my back to the door to let the ladies out first, which seemed to perplex everyone further. My grandfather taught me to do that, and it isn't done much in D.C. anymore. I'm almost never thanked for it, but that doesn't mean that I'm going to stop.

I announced myself to the receptionist, had a seat in a very comfortable chair, and leafed through a *Regardie's* magazine set on a round glass table. I wasn't far into it when Mrs. Lewis walked into the lobby on two nice cocoa-colored legs and stood over my chair. I got up and shook her hand.

She wore a tan business suit and a brown blouse with an apricot scarf tied loosely around her neck. Her face was long and faintly elastic, with large brown eyes and a large mouth lipsticked apricot like the scarf. She was younger than the voice on the phone, and I bet she had a good smile, but she wasn't using those muscles just yet. I looked at the fingernails on the spidery fingers that rested in my hand; the polish on the nails was apricot, too. Neat.

"Nick Stefanos. Thanks for seeing me."

"Shareen Lewis. We can use one of the conference rooms. Follow me."

I did it, walked behind her, passing open-doored offices where men stood reading briefs or sat talking on telephones. They wore British-cut suits with suspenders beneath the jackets and orderly geometric-patterned ties. I thought, Why the suspenders? Did these guys collectively buy their pants in the wrong size?

Shareen Lewis directed me into a conference room whose

center held a long, shiny table with gray high-backed swivel chairs grouped around it. The shades had been drawn, and when she closed the door the room became cool and quiet as a tomb. We sat next to each other by the windows. She turned her chair in my direction, folded her hands on the table in front of her, and faced me.

"Are we being recorded?" I said, kidding only by half, trying to break things down.

"Should we be? You look a little uncomfortable."

"Well, I'm playing an away game here. This isn't my usual arena."

"That much I can see." Her enunciation was careful, slightly forced.

"So I'll be brief. I've got to get to work myself."

"What do you do, Mr. Stefanos? Besides...this."

"I work in a bar, a place called the Spot. Over on 8th in Southeast."

"I don't know it."

"You wouldn't," I said, intending it as a compliment. But she didn't know what I meant by the remark, and the muscles of her jaw ratcheted up a notch.

"What can I do for you?" she said.

"Like I told you on the phone, I'd like to have the opportunity to speak with your son, Roland. Everything I've been able to uncover tells me that he was the closest friend that Calvin Jeter had. I'm assisting the police on the Jeter murder."

"I don't believe that I can help you."

"Maybe Roland might like to help."

"I don't think so."

"Could you tell me where to contact him?"

"No."

"Is that because you don't know where he is?"

"Roland is seventeen years old. Almost a man. He comes and goes as he pleases."

"So he's not missing."

"No."

"But he didn't attend Calvin's funeral, did he?"

"How do you know that?"

"The police haven't talked with Roland since the murder. Don't you think it's odd that Roland didn't attend Calvin's funeral, seeing that the two of them were best friends?"

She spoke quietly, but for the first time her voice registered emotion. "I would hardly say, Mr. Stefanos, that Roland and Calvin were best friends. Roland might have felt sorry for that boy, but nothing in the way of real friendship. After all, the Jeter boy lived in a welfare setup, down in those... apartments."

So she was about that. I didn't like it, and stupidly, I've never been one to hide it. I leaned forward. "I've been to your house, remember? And those apartments are just a few blocks away from you. The people who live in them are your neighbors. And I've got to tell you, Calvin's mother—that welfare mother you're talking about—treated me with more dignity and grace than you're showing me here." I relaxed in my chair, then tried to throw some water on the fire. "I'm only trying to help."

But it didn't move her. If anything, she sat up straighter, eyeing me coldly. She tapped her fingernail on the lacquered table—the only sound in the room.

"All right," she said. "Let me tell you why I agreed to see you today. It's not to talk about my son, I can assure you of that. You just told me that you were 'assisting' the police on the Jeter case. It's the second time you've told me that. And not only is what you're telling me a straight-up lie; it happens to be a criminal offense. I work in a law firm, Mr. Stefanos. I'm not an attorney, but I'm not just a message-taker, either, and I've had this checked out. I could turn your ass in to*day*, my friend, bust you right out of your license. I don't know what your business is with this, but I'm telling you, I don't want to know. I don't ever want to see you or hear from you or have you around my house or near my children again. Understood?"

"Yes."

"This conversation is over." She stood from her chair and left the room.

I waited a couple of minutes to let the heat dissipate. I found my way out.

I FIRST NOTICED THE white sedan as I drove east on Constitution toward the Spot. The driver had tried to catch up by running a red, and the horns from the cars starting through the cross street caught my attention. It wasn't until I got stuck in a bus lane and saw the white sedan deliberately pull into that same stalled lane that I knew I was being tailed. I made a couple of false turn signals after that, saw the tail make the amateur's mistake and do the same. I hit the gas at the next intersection and hooked a wild right into the 9th Street tunnel. I lost him in the Southwest traffic and went on my way.

The Spot was empty of customers when I arrived. Mai untied her change apron as I entered and tossed it behind the cooler. She wore her angry face, splotched pink, and she left without a word. An argument with Jeremy, most likely—or had she said Jerome? Anna Wang had hung out past her shift and now stood in the kitchen, talking with Darnell, showing him some crystals she had bought in Georgetown. The week my son was born, when I flew out to San Francisco to visit Jackie and her lover, Sherron, Anna had given me four crystals wrapped and tied in a square of yellow cloth, crystals specifically selected to protect me on my journey. The crystals hung now in their cloth sack from the rearview of my Dodge, along with a string of worry beads given to me by my uncle Costa, the two elements forming some hoodoo version, I suppose, of a St. Christopher's medal.

I changed into shorts and a T-shirt, poured myself a mug of coffee, put some music on the deck, and began to slice fruit for the tray. After that, I washed the dirty glasses from lunch, soaked the ashtrays, and wiped down the bar. Mai should have prepped all that, but I didn't mind. The dead time between lunch and happy hour, standing idly in front of the sexy, backlit pyramid of liquor with nothing much to do, was just plain dangerous for a guy like me.

Mel came through the door as I finished the prep. He found his stool, ordered a gin martini, and requested "a little Black Moses." I managed to find our sole Isaac Hayes tape buried in a pile of seventies disco and funk and slipped it into the stereo. Mel closed his eyes soulfully, began to sing off-key: "You're my joy; you're everything to me-ee-eee." Happy entered at about that time, sat at the other end of the bar, complained about the speed of my service as I placed his manhattan down in front of him, stopped complaining as he hurriedly tipped the up glass to his lips. Then it was Buddy and Bubba taking up the middle of the place, two pitchers deep, and later a gentleman I'd never seen before, who started off fine but degenerated spectacularly after his first drink, and an obnoxious judge named Len Dorfman, who spouted off to a dead-eared audience, and Dave, reading a paperback Harry Whittington, and a couple of plainclothes detectives talking bitterly about the criminal-justice system, cross-eyed drunk and armed to the teeth. Finally, after all of them had gone or been asked to leave, it was just Darnell and I, closing up.

"You about ready?" Darnell said, leaning one long arm on the service bar.

"Yeah, but—"

"I know. You're gonna have yourself a drink."

"Just one tonight. If you want to stick around, I'll give you a lift uptown."

"That's all right." Darnell tipped two fingers to his forehead. "Do me good to catch some air, anyhow. See you tomorrow, hear?"

"Right, Darnell. You take care."

He went through the door and I locked up behind him. I dimmed the lights and had a shot and a beer in the solitary coolness of the bar. I smoked a cigarette to the filter, butted it, and removed my shirt. I washed up in the basin in Darnell's kitchen, changing back to my clothes from the afternoon. Then I set the alarm and walked out onto 8th.

Parked out front beneath the streetlamp was a white sedan, a big old piece-of-shit Ford. I recognized the grille as belonging to the car that had tailed me earlier in the day. No one sat inside the car. I looked around and saw nothing and began to walk. A voice from the mouth of the nearby alley stopped me.

"Stevonus?"

"Yes?"

I turned around and faced him. He walked from the shadows and moved into the light of the streetlamp. He had a revolver in his hand and the revolver was pointed at my chest.

"Who are you?" I said.

"Jack LaDuke," he said. He jerked the gun in the direction of the Ford. "Get in."

SIX

I STOOD THERE staring at him. He had a boyishly handsome face, clean-shaven and straight-featured, almost delicate, with a long, lanky body beneath it. His light brown hair was full and wavy on top, shaved short in the back and on the sides, a *High Sierra* cut. His manner was tough, but his wide brown eyes were curiously flat; I couldn't tell what, if anything, lived behind them. He tightened his grip on the short-barreled .357.

"Why aren't you moving?" he said.

"I don't think I have to," I said. "You're not going to mug me, or you'd already have me in that alley. And you're not going to shoot me—not with your finger on the outside of that trigger guard. Anyway, you're not throwing off that kind of energy."

"That a fact."

"I think so, yeah."

He shifted his feet, tensed his jaw, and tilted his head toward his car. "I'm not going to ask you again, Stevonus."

"All right." I moved to the passenger side and put my hand to the door.

"Uh-uh," he said, and tossed me his keys. "You drive."

I walked around to the front of the car and got into the driver's seat. LaDuke settled into the shotgun side of the bench. I fitted his key in the ignition and turned the engine over.

"Where to?"

"It doesn't matter," he said, the gun still pointed at my middle. He wore a long-sleeved white shirt and a plain black tie tightly knotted to the neck. His slacks were no-nonsense, plain front, and he wore a pair of thick-soled oxfords on his feet. A line of sweat had snaked down his cheek and darkened the collar of the shirt. "Drive around."

I pulled the boat out of the space and swung a U in the middle of 8th. I headed toward Pennsylvania Avenue, and when I got there, I took a right and kept the car in traffic.

"You gonna tell me what this is about?"

"I'll tell you when I'm ready to tell you."

"That's a good line," I said. "But you're in the wrong movie. Let me help you out here. This is the part where you're supposed to say, 'I'm asking the questions here, Stevonus.'"

"Shut up."

"You're making a mistake," I said, speeding up next to a Mustang ahead of me and in the lane to my left. "You've been making mistakes all day. Your shadow job was a joke. Stevie Wonder could have made your tail."

"I said, shut up."

"Then you sit out front of where I work for I don't know how long. How many people you figure walked down 8th in that time happened to see you? Those are all people that could ID you later on."

"Just keep pushing it," he said.

"And now this. 'You drive'—that's some real stupid shit, pal. You let me drive, and who do you think's got the power? Yeah, you're holding the gun, but I've got both our lives in my hands. I can drive this shitwagon into a wall, or into a cop car, or I can drive it right into the fucking river if I want to. Or I can do this."

I stuck my head out the window and yelled something at the driver of the Mustang. The man turned his head, startled. I yelled again and flipped him the bird. The driver was alone, but he was a Southeast local, and he wasn't going to take it. He screamed something back at me and swerved into my lane.

"Now he'll remember us," I said, talking calmly over the man's angry shouts. "And he'll remember the car. In case you got any ideas of doing me and dumping me out somewhere. I guess I better make sure he's got our plate numbers, too."

I accelerated and cut in front of the Mustang, then jammed on the brakes. The Mustang missed us, but not by much. I floored it, leaving some rubber on the street.

LaDuke's fingers dug into the armrest on the door. "What the fuck are you doing, man!"

"Put that gun away," I said, and cut across two lanes of traffic. The oncoming headlights passed across LaDuke's stretched-back face. I jetted into a gas station without braking. The underside of the Ford scraped asphalt, and as the shocks gave it up, the top of LaDuke's head hit the roof. I continued straight out of the station lot, tires screaming as I hit the side street.

"Put it away!" I said.

"Fuck," he muttered, shaking his head. He opened the glove box in front of him, dropped the revolver inside, and shut it. I pulled the car over in front of some row houses and cut the engine.

LaDuke wiped his face dry with his shirtsleeve and looked across the seat. "Fuck," he said again, more pissed off at himself than at me.

"Just sit there and cool down."

"You know," he said, "she told me she had the feeling you were some kind of headcase."

"Who told you?"

He turned his head and stared out the window. "Shareen Lewis."

"What is she to you?"

He withdrew his wallet from the seat of his pants and slid out a business card. I took it and read it: "Jack LaDuke, Private Investigations." His logo—I'm not kidding—was one large eye. I stifled a grin and slipped the card into my shirt pocket.

"You know," I said, "you didn't need to pull that gun."

"Just wanted to see how you'd handle it."

"Am I auditioning for something?"

"You might be," he said, giving the mysterious routine one last try.

I shrugged and fished a smoke out of my pack and pushed in the dash lighter. "Cigarette?"

"I don't smoke."

"Okay." I lit the Camel and drew some tobacco into my lungs. I noticed that my hand was shaking, and I put it by my side. On the corner up ahead, a neighborhood market stood open for business, moths swarming in the spotlight mounted above the door. Young people walked in and out carrying small packages and forties in brown paper bags wrapped to the neck. An older man leaned against the store's plate glass and listlessly begged for change, barely raising his head. I sat there calmly and smoked my cigarette and waited for Jack LaDuke to regain his composure and enough of his pride to the point where he could talk. After awhile, he did.

"Shareen Lewis hired me to find her son," he said.

"So she *is* worried about him."

"Yes."

"Why'd she call you?"

"She didn't," he said, "at first. She called a bondsman she knew named William Blackmon."

"I've heard of him."

"Yeah, they tell me he's been around forever. But he farms out a lot of his work now. First thing I did when I came to town,

I went to all the skip tracers and bondsmen, went to see if I couldn't work something out."

"Blackmon recommended you to Shareen Lewis."

"They go to the same church. Blackmon took me for a flat referral fee."

"And when I dropped my card in the Lewis's door, she wanted to know what was going on." LaDuke nodded. "She agreed to meet with me just so you could set up the tail, check me out."

"That's right," LaDuke said. "Now I've been straight with you. What *is* going on, Stevonus?"

"I'm working on the Calvin Jeter murder," I said, "just like I told her. Roland Lewis seems to be the key."

"Working for who? And don't kid me with that 'police assistant' crap, okay?"

I considered how much I wanted him to know. "I was the first one to find Jeter's body. I came on it by accident. I called it in anonymously to the cops. The cops have gone as far as they're going to go on it. I'm doing some digging on my own."

"For who?" he repeated.

"Jeter's mother. And me."

LaDuke eyed me suspiciously. "There's more to it than what you're telling me. But I guess that's good enough for now, Stevonus."

"The name's *Stefanos*. What have you got, a speech impediment or something?"

"I've got trouble with names," he said with a touch of embarrassment. "That's all."

"Call me Nick, then. You can remember that, can't you?"

"Sure."

I flicked my cigarette out the window and watched its trail. LaDuke shifted nervously in his seat, tapped his fingers on the vent window.

"So what are we going to do now?" I said.

"Well," LaDuke said, "I could use a little help on my end."

"I bet you could." I looked him over. "How long you been in D.C.?"

"Does it show?"

"A little."

"I don't know. Six, maybe seven months."

"Six months. Shit, LaDuke, you don't even know your way around yet. You're never gonna find that kid."

"It's beginning to look like that." He rubbed the top of his head. "How much have you got on the Jeter case?"

"A few things," I said.

"I was thinking…maybe you and me, we ought to work together on this. You know, feed each other information. I mean, you're not getting paid right now, isn't that right? We could cut it straight down the middle."

"Cut what? After Blackmon's piece, that doesn't leave enough for two."

"I've got a couple of other cases I'm working on," he said. "I'm after a deadbeat husband, for one. Maybe you could help me out there, too."

"I don't think so," I said.

"Sleep on it," he said. "Because, the thing is, if you're set on talking to Roland Lewis about Jeter, you're going to have to go through me. Shareen Lewis isn't going to let you near her house, that's for sure. I don't think she cares too much for you."

"She must prefer them on the clean-cut side," I said, scanning his shirt-and-tie arrangement, damp and limp now in the evening heat.

"Yeah, well, this is a business. If you're going to make it, you've got to treat it like a business, act in a businesslike manner, and be presentable."

"And brush your teeth after every meal."

"What's that?"

"Forget it. We about done?"

"Yeah," he said, "let's go. But move over, will you? This time, I'm gonna drive."

* * *

HE PARKED THE FORD in front of the Spot and let it idle. I got out, went around to the driver's side, and leaned my arms on the lip of the open window.

"Think about my proposition," he said.

I nodded and said, "I will."

He looked at me curiously. "Something else?"

"There's one thing I wanted to tell you."

"What's that?"

"Don't ever pull a gun on a man unless you intend to use it. And even then, don't pull it. Do you understand?"

"I know all about guns," he said. "I grew up in the country. I've known how to shoot since I was a kid."

"Congratulations. But it's not the same thing. An animal's not a man."

"No shit," he said with a cocky grin.

I pushed off from the car and stood straight. "Well, I guess you already know everything there is to know. So you might as well get on home."

"Right. I'll call you tomorrow."

"Take care, hear?"

I walked across the street to my car. LaDuke drove away.

SEVEN

I WOKE UP early the next morning, fed my cat, went outside and picked my *Post* up off the stoop, then went back in and read it over a couple of cups of coffee. After a week, there had still been no follow-up on Calvin Jeter's murder. Nothing in the *Post* or in the *Washington Times*, and nothing on the TV news.

I phoned Boyle, and when he phoned me back he confirmed it: "This one's already cold, Nick."

He asked me what I had. I said, "I've got nothing." It wasn't exactly the truth, but it was close enough. Boyle told me to keep in touch before he cut the line.

I paced around some after that, did a few sets of sit-ups and push-ups in my room, showered, dressed for work, and paced around some more. I found Jack LaDuke's business card on my dresser and rubbed my finger across its face. I put it down and walked into another room. A little while later, I returned to my bedroom and picked the business card up off the dresser once again. I went to the phone and dialed LaDuke's answering service. He phoned me back right away.

"Glad you called," he said.

"Just wanted to make sure you were all right after last night."

"I've got a hell of a stiff neck. All that bouncing around and shit. Where'd you get your license, anyway? Sears?"

"You were holding a gun on me, remember?"

"Yeah, well..."

"Listen, last night's over, as far as I'm concerned. You say you can get me into the Lewis house."

"Sure I can."

"Well, let's do it. Today."

"It'll have to wait until after Shareen gets off work."

"That's fine. I've got a day shift at the Spot. I can swing by afterward, pick you up. Where's your crib?"

"Never mind that," he said. "I'll pick you up at the bar. You tellin' me we got a deal?"

"Not so fast. Let's take this a little bit at a time, okay?"

"Just don't want to give everything away and get nothing back."

"I don't blame you. But let's see if we can work together first. And LaDuke?"

"Yeah?"

"Don't forget your tie."

He didn't forget it. He was wearing it, a solid blue number on a white shirt, knotted tightly despite the heat, when he walked into the Spot at half past four that afternoon. LaDuke had a seat next to Mel, who had stretched a lunch hour into three and was working on his fifth martini of the day. Anna stood by the service bar, counting the sequence of her checks. She glanced at LaDuke when he entered, then gave him a second look as he settled onto his bar stool.

"Nice place," LaDuke said. "Really uptown." He wiped his hands off on a bev nap and left the crumpled napkin on the bar.

"Thanks," I said. "Get you something?"

"I'll just have a Coke, please."

"So you don't drink, either."

"Not really, no."

"Okay, Boy Scout. One Coke, coming up." I shot a glassful from the soda gun and placed it in front of him. "Want a cherry in it?"

"No. But do you have a place mat I can color on?"

I heard Anna laugh from the service end of the bar. Ramon walked behind her on his way to the kitchen and patted her ass. She slapped his hand away. Mel continued to croon along to the Staple Singers coming from the system, doing a Mavis thing with his pursed-out mouth. Happy sat in the shadows, his hand curled listlessly around a manhattan.

"I'll be ready to go," I said, "soon as my replacement shows up."

"I'll just sit here and soak up the atmosphere," said LaDuke.

"Cash in!" Anna yelled.

I went to her and took her tip change, all lined up in neat little rows, and turned it into bills. I handed it over to her and she put her hand into my breast pocket and withdrew a smoke. I lit it for her and she blew the exhale away from my face.

"Who's the guy?" she said.

"Name's Jack LaDuke."

"I like it," she said.

"The name?"

"The whole package."

"You go for the puppy-dog type?"

"Not usually," she said. "But he's cute as shit, man. What's he do?"

I winked broadly. "Private dick."

"Why's he keeping it private?"

"I don't know. Why don't you ask him?"

She did, but it didn't work out. She started by getting herself a beer and having a seat next to LaDuke and initiating some conversation. LaDuke was polite, but clearly uncomfortable. Anna took his manner for disinterest; she downed her beer quickly and drifted away. Darnell came out of the kitchen and introduced himself, and soon after that Mai arrived in a chipper mood and relieved me of my position behind the stick. I changed into something presentable and told LaDuke that it was time to go.

We headed into Northeast in LaDuke's Ford. He stared ahead as he drove, his hands tight on the wheel, ten and two o'clock, right out of driver's ed. I tried to get a station on his radio, but he reached across the bench and switched it off. I wondered, What does this guy do to get off?

"Anna thought you were interesting," I said.

"You know that little guy? The busboy, the guy with the gold tooth?"

"You mean Ramon?"

"Yeah," LaDuke said. "Him. Does he like her or something?"

I laughed. "Ramon likes anything that has to sit down to take a piss. But no, they got nothin' going on."

"Well, she's really cute."

"That's what she said about you. So why'd you blow her off?"

LaDuke blinked nervously. "I didn't mean to, exactly. I'm not very good with women, to tell you the truth."

"I'm not very good with them, either. But when I find one I like and I think she likes me back, I give it a better shot than you did. Anyhow, a pretty motherfucker like you shouldn't have any problems."

"I'm not pretty," he said, a touch of anger entering his voice.

"Relax, man, I'm only kidding around."

"Look," he said, "just forget it, okay?"

"Sure."

We drove for a couple of miles in silence. LaDuke looked out the window.

"Maybe I'll give her a call," he said.

* * *

SHAREEN LEWIS WAS SITTING on the rocker sofa on her porch when we reached the top of the steps leading to her house. She stood and took LaDuke's hand, then briefly shook mine without looking in my eyes. She wore linen shorts and a short-sleeved blouse, with a masklike brooch pinned beneath the collar. As on the day before, the makeup somehow managed to match the clothes. She was a handsome woman, nicely built; she might have been lovely had she simply smiled.

We followed Shareen through the front door and found seats in her comfortably appointed living room. For my benefit, LaDuke repeated to Shareen what they had obviously discussed earlier over the phone: that I would team up with him in trying to locate her son, and that the teaming could only double our chances of finding him. Her eyes told me that she doubted his reasoning, but she nodded shortly in agreement. I asked her for a recent photograph of Roland. Shareen Lewis nodded with the same degree of enthusiasm. I asked her if she had heard from her son either directly or by message and she said, "No." I asked her if she had any idea at all as to his whereabouts. To that one, she also said, "No." We sat around and listened to the clock tick away on her mantelpiece. After some of that, I asked to see Roland's room.

We took the carpeted stairs to the second floor—three small bedrooms and a bath. We passed the largest room, which I guessed to be Shareen's. Its absolute cleanliness and frilly decor told me that, under this roof at least, Shareen Lewis slept alone. The next room belonged to the teenaged daughter, Roland's sister, who had blown me off two days earlier on the phone. She was in there, sitting at a desk, listening to music through a set of headphones. She was already heavier than her mother, and she had chunkier features, or it could have been that she was at an awkward age. We made eye contact, and for some reason, I dumbed up my face. She laughed a little and closed her eyes and went back to her groove. Then we were in Roland's room at the end of the hall.

Shareen pulled the blinds open and let some light into the space. LaDuke leaned against a wall and folded his arms while I took it in: another clean room, too clean, I thought, for a boy his age. Maybe Shareen had tidied it up. But even so, there was something off about it, from the rather feminine color scheme to the schmaltzy souvenir trinkets on the dresser. A large dollar sign had been cut out and tacked to the wall. On an opposite wall, a poster of the group PM Dawn. No pictures of fat-bottomed women, no basketball stars, no hard rappers, no gun-culture or drug-culture symbolism, nothing representative of the mindless, raging testosterone of a seventeen-year-old city boy trying to push his manhood in the 1990s. Nothing like my own bedroom at seventeen, for that matter, or the bedrooms of any of my friends.

"Mind if I look in the closet?" I said.

"Go ahead," Shareen said.

I went to it, opened it. I scanned a neat row of clothing, shirts of various designs and several pairs of slacks, the slacks pressed and hung upside down from wooden clamps. I put my hand on the shelf above the closet rod, ran it along the dustless surface. I found a back issue of *D.C. This Week* and took it down. I looked at it with deliberate disinterest, folded it, and put it under my arm.

"Anything?" LaDuke said, nodding at the newspaper.

"No," I said, and forced a smile at Shareen. "You don't mind if I take this, do you?"

"I don't mind," she said, looking very small, hugging herself with her arms as if she was chilled.

"Thanks. By the way, did you clean this room recently?"

"I haven't touched a thing. Roland always kept it this way."

"Have you noticed anything missing? Did he take any clothes with him, pack anything before...the last time you saw him?"

"I don't think so," she said, a catch in her voice.

"You keep a nice house," I said, trying to keep things light.

"Thank you. It's not easy with these kids, believe me."

"I can imagine," I said, but it was too much.

"You can?"

"Well, no. Actually, not really."

"Then don't patronize me." The resentment crept back in her tone. "Let me tell you how it is. When I inherited this house from my mother, I also inherited the balance of the mortgage. That, and everything else it takes to be a single working mother—car, clothing, new stuff for the kids all the time. You come into this part of town, see what it is over here, and maybe you make a judgment about where I prioritize my family in the scheme of my life. What you don't know is, I'd like to get my children out of this neighborhood, too, understand? But the way it is out here, in this economy, me and everyone I know, we're all one paycheck away from the street. So, no, it's not easy. But I've done pretty good for them, I think. Anyway, I've tried."

I didn't ask for all that, but I allowed it. LaDuke cleared his throat and pushed off from the wall.

"I'll take that photograph of Roland now," I said, "if you don't mind. Then we'll be on our way."

She left the room. I walked out with LaDuke and told him to meet me at the front door. After some hesitation, he followed Shareen downstairs. I went to the daughter's room, knocked on her open door. She pulled one earphone away from her head and looked up.

"Yeah."

"I'm Nick Stefanos."

"So?"

"What's your name?"

"Danitra."

"So how's it going?"

"It's goin' all right."

"Listen, Danitra, I'm here because your mom hired me and my friend to find your brother, Roland."

"So?"

"Just wanted to introduce myself, that's all. What are you listening to?"

"Little bit of this and that. Nothin' you'd know."

"Yeah, you're probably right. But I recognized that Trouble Funk you and your friends had on the other day when I called."

"That was you?"

"Yep."

For a second, she looked like she might apologize for her attitude that day, but she didn't. Instead, she shrugged and began to replace the earphone over her ear.

"Hold on a second," I said.

"What?"

"You got any idea where your brother went off to?"

"Uh-uh."

"You think he's okay?"

"That fool's all right," she said.

"Why are you so sure?"

"'Cause if he wasn't, he would've called. Listen, most likely he's off on one of his money things. That boy just wants to be large, know what I'm sayin'? Always wantin' to be like some movie star, ride around in a limousine. When he finds out it ain't like that, he's gonna come home."

"You think so, huh?"

I stood there and waited for a reply. But she turned away from me then and went back into herself. I left her alone and headed back down the stairs.

"MRS. LEWIS REALLY DIGS you, man," LaDuke said with a laugh as he negotiated the Ford around RFK, then got it on to East Capitol. "Every time you open your mouth, she'd like to bite your head off."

"Yeah, thanks for all your support back there."

"Kinda liked watchin' you bury yourself."

I fired a smoke off the dash lighter. "Well, the funny thing is, in some ways I agree with what she's saying. She's out there working for a big firm, and she probably knows just about as much law now as the people she's working for. You know how that goes, Xeroxing and taking messages for people who really have no more intelligence than you. I mean, lawyers, they've got the degree, and they worked for it, but that doesn't necessarily make them geniuses, right? But I'm sure that doesn't stop them from condescending to her all day long. Then she's trying to raise those kids in a bad environment, with no way to get out.... I don't know... I guess I can see why she's so angry. 'Course, that doesn't explain why she's so angry at me."

"Maybe you remind her of the type of guy that left her with those kids," he said.

"Yeah, maybe." The thought of my failed marriage crossed my mind. The thought must have transferred to my face.

"Hey look, Nick, I didn't mean anything."

"Forget it."

LaDuke punched the gas and passed a Chevy that was crawling up ahead. He drove for a couple of miles, then said, "You get anything from the sister?"

"Uh-uh. Typical teenager with no time for me, and nothing good to say about her brother. She thinks he's just out there being an entrepreneur, trying to make some kind of score."

"You saw the dollar sign plastered on his bedroom wall. Maybe that *is* all he's into. Maybe he's running some kind of game."

"What else you see in that room?"

"I saw what you saw," he said.

"No, I mean the details."

LaDuke rubbed the top of his head, something I had seen him do over the last couple of days when he was trying to think. "Well, it's kind of a funny room for a seventeen-year-old boy. It looked like it could have been his sister's room."

"Right. How about that PM Dawn poster?"

"PM Dawn? What the hell is that?"

"It's a rap group—but soft, man, all the way soft. Not what anyone down here would call 'street authentic.' Like what U2 is to rock and roll."

"U2?"

"Yeah. The Eagles, in black leather."

"What?"

"Never mind. It's just not the kind of music a kid in that neighborhood would want to advertise that he was into. That and the room, you know, if it got around, it's something that could get your ass kicked for you."

LaDuke breathed out through his mouth. "You sayin' that maybe him and the Jeter kid were boyfriends?"

"No, not exactly."

But I thought of Barry calling Roland a "punk." And the killer had called Calvin one, too. And then there was the Fire House matchbook from Calvin's room. I dragged on my cigarette, blew the exhale out the open window.

"What, then?"

"It's just that this Lewis kid is different, that's all, at an age when being different from your peers is the last thing you want to be. It might not mean anything. I don't know if it does, not yet."

I picked up Roland Lewis's photograph: unsmiling, like Calvin's, but with a certain vulnerability. Unlike the sister, Roland looked very much like his mother. I slipped the photograph in the folded-up newspaper. LaDuke watched me do it.

"What's with the paper, anyway?" he said.

"Nothing."

"Bullshit. Don't hold out on me, Nick."

I hot-boxed my cigarette and pitched it out the window. "I'm not."

"Yes you are," he said. "But you won't keep holdin' out, not for long. 'Cause we're gonna do this thing, you and me. You hear me?" He was pumped, his face lit and animated. A horn blew out as he lost his attention and swerved into another lane.

"Okay," I said. "We'll find the kid, LaDuke. But do me a favor."

"What?"

"Keep your eyes on the road."

He dropped me in front of the Spot. I thanked him for the lift, picked up the newspaper, and started to get out.

"What are we, done already?"

"I am. I've got a date tonight." He looked a little deflated. "Listen, man, we'll get on this again, first thing tomorrow. Hear?"

"Sure, Nick. I'll see you later."

He pulled away from the curb and drove down 8th. I went to my Dodge and fumbled with my keys. When LaDuke was out of sight, I walked into the Spot, phoned Lyla, and told her I'd be a little late. Then I returned to my car, ignitioned it, and headed back into Northeast.

EIGHT

THE HEAVY WOMAN with the elephantine thighs sat out front of the Jeter apartment, her folding chair in the same position as it had been two days before. I turned into the lot and parked beside Barry's Z, walked across the worn brown grass, into the cool concrete stairwell, and down the steps to the Jeters' door. I knocked on it, listening to the noises behind it, television and laughter and the cry of a baby, until the peephole darkened and the door swung open. Calvin's sister stood in the frame, her baby resting on her hip.

"Yes?"

"Nick Stefanos. I was here the day before yesterday, talking to your mom."

"I remember."

"Is she in?"

The girl looked behind her. Barry's younger brother and another shirtless young man about his age sat on the couch, describing a movie they had both seen, talking loudly over the minstrel-like characters acting broadly on the television.

"Uh-uh," the girl said. "She's at the store."

"Can I talk to Barry for a minute?"

She thought about it while I listened to the shirtless young man talking about the movie: "Carlito" did this and "Carlito" did that, and "Carlito, he was badder than a motherfucker, boy." Then the young man was on his feet, his hand figured in the shape of a pistol, and he was jabbing the hand back and forth, going, "Carlito said, bap-bap-bap-bap-bap."

"Come on in," the girl said, her lips barely moving.

I followed her into the room and back through the hall. The young men stopped talking as I passed, and when my back was to them, they broke into raucous laughter. I supposed that they were laughing at me. Calvin's sister gestured me toward a bedroom. I stepped aside to let her pass back through the hall.

I went to the bedroom and knocked on the frame. Barry stood next to an unmade double bed in a room as unadorned as the rest. He read from a book, one long finger on the page. He looked up at my knock, gave me an eye sweep, and returned his gaze to the book.

"Wha'sup?"

"I need to get something out of Calvin's room. It's nothing personal of his. Would that be all right?"

Barry closed the book and sighed. "Come on."

He walked with me to Calvin's bedroom. Barry folded his arms, watched me go to the footlocker and get the folded copy of *D.C. This Week* that sat beneath the basketball. When I turned around, he was looking at the paper. I thought I saw some kind of light come into his eyes.

"What am I, getting warm or something?"

Barry said, "You're really into this shit, aren't you?"

"I'm going to find out who killed Calvin, if that's what you mean."

"And if you do? What's that, gon' bring Calvin up from the dead?"

"No. But maybe his mother might rest a little easier if she knew what happened to her son. You ever think about that?"

Barry breathed out heavily through his nose. "Moms ain't worried about no justice. She thinks Calvin's up there, sittin' by the right hand of Jesus and shit, right now. Anyhow, who *asked* you to get on this?"

"That doesn't matter. The point is, I'm being paid now, and that makes it work. And when someone pays you to do something, you do it. Once you accept that, you don't think about why, and you finish whatever it is you started."

"I wouldn't understand about all that."

"The thing is, I think you do understand. See, I noticed that uniform in the back of your car. You got that fast-food job of yours—what do you make, five and a quarter an hour, maybe five-fifty?"

Barry's eyes narrowed. "So?"

"So, you could be like all those other knuckleheads out there, making ten times that a week on the street. But instead, you're being a man, trying to be right for your family."

"Listen, man, I ain't got time for all this bullshit, understand? Matter of fact, I got to get into work, right now."

I withdrew my wallet, slipped out a card, and handed it to Barry.

"Here," I said. "You dropped this the first time around."

"I got to go to work," he said softly, slipping the card into his shorts. "Come on, I'll let you out."

We walked back into the living room. Barry stopped by the TV set and I headed for the front door.

The shirtless young man said, "Hey, Barry, who's your boy?"

"Man's a private detective," Barry said mockingly. "He *finds* things."

Barry's younger brother said, "Maybe he could find Roger

some onion, know what I'm sayin'? 'Cause Roger ain't *had* none in a long time."

"Go on, man," Roger said. "I forgot about more pussy than you ever had, boy." Barry's brother and Roger touched hands and began to laugh.

I looked at Barry. He wasn't laughing, and neither was I. I tucked the newspaper under my arm and left the room.

ON THE WAY TO my place, I stopped at Athena's and had a seat at the bar. I lit a cigarette, drew on it, and laid it in the ashtray. It was early yet for any kind of crowd, but I recognized a couple of regulars in quiet conversation, along with an Ultimate solo drinker who was as beautiful as a model and an intense woman I knew who was running the pool table on a youngish woman I had never met. Stella came over and wiped the area in front of me with a damp rag. She cocked her head and raised her eyebrows. I nodded my head one time. She reached into the cooler and pulled a bottle of beer. She popped the cap and set it down on a dry coaster. I thanked her and had a swig.

"So you're back to it," she said.

"Never had any intention of getting off it. I've never kidded myself about what I am. I've just got to try and not be so stupid about it, that's all. Like I was that night."

Stella adjusted her eyeglasses, put her fist on her hip. "That some kind of back-door apology?"

"Yeah, and a thank-you at the same time. I was probably rude about you stepping in—you know how I get. I know you were just trying to look out for me."

"Don't worry about it," she said. "You'd do the same for me, right?"

"You bet."

"Anyway, nobody got hurt."

I left that alone and reached across the bar and shook her hand.

"So what're you up to tonight, Nick?"

"Date with Lyla. But I wanted to ask you something."

"Go ahead."

"You still play in that gay and lesbian bartenders' softball league?"

"Every Monday night."

"You know anybody from over at the Fire House, on P?"

Stella rubbed a finger under her nose. "There was this guy, Paul Ritchie, played for a long time on our team. Knees went out on him a couple of years back. Good guy. Good ballplayer, too. Ritchie, he could really hit."

"You ever in touch with him anymore?"

"He still comes to the games. It's more a chance to see old friends now than it is a competition. So, yeah, he stays up with us."

"He still tends at the Fire House?"

"He's been there, like, a hundred years. Where's he gonna go?"

I drank off some of my beer. "I need to talk with him, if I can. I'm working on something that might involve that place."

"Something that could get him into trouble?"

"Not unless he's directly involved. The truth is, I don't know yet. But I'll do my best to keep him out of it. Could you hook me up?"

Stella took her hand off her hip, pointed a stubby finger at my face. "I thought you came in here to apologize, Nick."

"I did, Stella."

"Uh-huh. Well, I'll give Paul a call, see what he says."

"Tomorrow would be good for me," I said.

"Don't push it," Stella said sternly. "I'll call him."

I told her to leave a message about it on my machine. She nodded and went to fix a cocktail for a customer. I drank the rest of my beer and put my cigarette between my teeth. Stella winked and gave me a little wave. I left ten on three and went out the front door. I walked to my car in the gathering darkness.

* * *

THE TWO COPIES OF *D.C. This Week* were identical, the last ones printed before Calvin Jeter's murder. That the issues were the same couldn't have been a coincidence, but as I looked through them, sitting at the desk of my makeshift office in my apartment, I saw no connection to either Calvin's death or Roland's disappearance. I skimmed every article, weekly feature, arts review, and column and came up empty. So I showered, changed into slacks and a blue cotton shirt, and went to pick up Lyla.

"Wow," I said as she opened her door.

She wore a gauzy green-and-rust sundress cut high above her knees. Her hair was pulled back, with some of it left to fall around her lovely face, the light catching threads of silver in the red.

"You're late, Nick."

"I know. I'm sorry, I just got hung up in what I've been working on."

"That's okay." She held up her goblet of wine. "But I got started without you."

"I'll catch up," I said. "Let's go."

We drove across town in my Coronet 500, all four windows down, some Massive Attack pumping from the deck. Lyla was moving her head, digging on the music and the night, and I reached across the buckets and put my hand in her hair. At the next stoplight, we kissed and held it until the green. The air felt clean, with a crispness running through it, a rarity for that time of year; it was a fine summer night in D.C.

We ate at a Thai place on Massachusetts Avenue, in a row of restaurants east of Union Station. We talked about our respective days over satay and spring rolls and a barbecued beef salad; Lyla stayed with white wine while I worked on a couple of Singhas. By the time the waitress served our main course, a whole crispy fish with hot chili and garlic, the subject turned to Lyla's newspaper and what I had found that day.

"Any thoughts?" I said.

"If you think something criminal is going on in relation to the newspaper, a good bet would be the personals."

"What do you mean?"

"There's all sort of things happening in there—messages for meeting places that are really drop locations, model searches looking for porno candidates, stuff like that. Nick, you wouldn't believe how many of the entries are just ads for prostitution, or for some other scam that's even worse."

"And you guys know about it?"

"We don't knowingly take any ads or personals that are criminal. But we're running a business. The *Post* and *City Paper* are doing it and making good money at it, and we have to do it, too. With the personals—it's a nine hundred number—we get ninety-five cents a minute. There're a couple hundred of those in each issue. When you annualize the revenue—well, you figure it out."

"Yeah, I see what you're saying. I'll go back to it, check it out." I cut a piece of fish off and dished it onto Lyla's plate. "Here."

"Thanks." Lyla had a bite and signaled the waitress for another wine.

"You're hittin' it pretty good tonight," I said.

"It's all this hot stuff," she said. "This fish is making me thirsty."

"It's making me thirsty, too. Next time that waitress goes by, get me a beer, as well."

After dinner, we walked across Mass to a nice quiet bar in a fancy restaurant run by friends of Lyla's. We ordered a couple of drinks—a bourbon rocks for me and a vodka tonic for Lyla—and had them slowly, listening to the recorded jazz that was a particular trademark of the house. A local politician whom Lyla had once interviewed and buried in print stopped on his way to the men's room and talked with her for a while, leaning in close to her ear, a toothy smile on his blandly handsome face. I sat on my stool and drank quietly and allowed myself to grow jealous. On the way out of the place, Lyla tripped on the steps and fell and scraped her knee on the concrete. We got into my car and I leaned forward and kissed the scrape, tasting her blood with my tongue. From that fortuitous position, I tried to work my head up under her dress. She laughed generously and pushed me away.

"Patience," she said. I mumbled something and put the car in gear.

We stopped once more that night, to have a drink on the roof of the Hotel Washington at 15th and F, a corny thing to do, for sure, but lovely nonetheless, when the city is lit up at night and the view is as on time as anything ever gets. We managed to snag a deuce by the railing, and I ordered a five-dollar beer and a wine for Lyla. We caught a breeze there, and our table looked out over rooftops to the monuments and the Mall. A television personality—a smirky young man who played on a sitcom called *My Two Dads* (a show that Johnny McGinnes called *My Doo-Dads*)—and his entourage took a large table near ours, and on their way out, Lyla winged a peanut at the back of the actor's head. The missile missed its target, but we got a round of applause from some people at the other tables who had obviously been subjected to the show. I could have easily had a few more beers when I was done with the first, could have sat in that chair for the rest of the night, but Lyla's eyes began to look a little filmy and unfocused, and her ears had turned a brilliant shade of red. We decided to go.

We drove to Lyla's apartment off Calvert Street, near the park, and made out like teenagers in her elevator on the way up to her floor. At her place, I goosed her while she tried to fit her keys to the lock and then we did an intense tongue dance and dry-humped for a while against her door, until a neighbor came out into the hall to see what the noise was all about. Inside, she pulled a bottle of white from the refrigerator, and we went directly to the bedroom. Lyla turned on her bedside lamp and pulled her dress up over her head while I removed my shirt. The sight of her—her freckled breasts, the curve of her hips, her full red bush—shortened my breath; it never failed to. She draped the dress over the lamp shade, kicked her shoes off, and walked naked across the room, the bottle in her hand. She took a long pull from the neck.

"We don't need that," I said.

Lyla pushed me onto my back on the bed and spit a mouthful of wine onto my chest. She straddled me, bent over, and began to slowly lick the wine off my nipples.

"You sure about that?" she said.

I could only grunt, and close my eyes.

LYLA'S HEAVY BREATHING WOKE me in the darkness. I looked at the LED readout on her clock, laid there for a half hour with my eyes open, then got out of bed, ate a couple of aspirins, and took a shower. I dressed in my clothes from the night before, made coffee, and smoked a cigarette out on her balcony.

I came back into the apartment, checked on Lyla. In the first light of dawn, her face looked drawn and gray. Her mouth was frozen open, the way she always slept off a drunk, and there was a faint wheeze in her exhale. I kissed her on the cheek and then on her lips. Her breath was stale from the wine. I brushed some hair off her forehead and left the place, locking the door behind me.

I drove straight down to the river, passed under the Sousa Bridge, turned the car around, and parked it in the clearing. No sign of a crazy black man in a brilliant blue coat. No cops, either; I guessed that, by now, the uniforms had been pulled off that particular detail.

I got out of my car, sat on its hood, and lit a cigarette. A pleasure boat pulled out of its slip and ran toward the Potomac, leaving little wake. Some gulls crossed the sky, turned black against the rising sun. I took one last drag off my cigarette and pitched it into the river.

Back in Shepherd Park, my cat waited for me on my stoop. I sat next to her and rubbed the hard scar tissue of her one empty eye socket and scratched behind her ears.

"Miss me?" I said. She rolled onto her back.

I entered my apartment and saw the blinking red light of my answering machine. I hit the bar, listened to the message. I stripped naked, got into bed, and set the alarm for one o'clock. Stella had come through; I had an appointment with Paul Ritchie for 2:30 that afternoon at the Fire House on P.

NINE

THE FIRE HOUSE had changed hands several times in my lifetime, but as long as I could remember, it had been a bar that catered primarily to homosexuals, in a neighborhood that had always been off center in every interesting way. This particular corner unofficially marked the end of Dupont Circle, where the P Street Bridge spanned the park and led to the edge of Georgetown. There were many hangouts down here, restaurants and a smattering of bars—the Brickskeller for beerheads, Badlands for the discophiles—but the Fire House had become something of a landmark for residents and commuters alike. For many years, gas logs burned day and night behind a glass window that fronted P at 22nd, the logs being the establishment's only signage. The building's facade had been redone now in red brick, and the window and the logs had been removed. But the fire imagery remained in the bar's name, a small nod to tradition.

I had taken the Metro down to Dupont, then walked down P.

By afternoon, the day had become blazing-hot, with quartz reflecting off the sidewalk and an urban mirage of shimmering refraction steaming up off the asphalt of the street. My thrift-shop sport jacket was damp beneath the arms and on my back as I reached the entrance to the Fire House. I pushed on the door, removed my shades, and entered the cool darkness of the main room.

Several couples and a few solo drinkers sat in booths and at tables partitioned off from the empty bar. I went to the stick and slid onto a stool, dropping the manila folder I had been carrying on the seat to my right. The heat had sickened me a bit, that and my activities from the night before. I peeled a bev nap from a stack of them and wiped my face.

A thin young waiter stepped up to the service area and said in a whiny, very bored voice, "Ooordering." The bartender ignored him for the time being, walked down my way, and dropped a coaster in front of me on the bar.

"How's it going?" he said. He was large-boned, with some gut to go with it. His brown hair had streaks of red running through it, and there was a rogue patch of red splotched in the chin area of his beard.

"Hot."

"Not in here, it isn't. Thank God for work, when it's air-conditioned. What can I get you?"

"A cold beer."

"Any flavor?"

"A bottle of Bud. And a side of ice water, thanks. By the way, where's the head?"

"Top of the stairs. You'll see it."

I took the stairs, passed an unlit room where a piano sat in the middle of a group of tables. The men's room was at the end of the hall. I went in and took a leak at one of two urinals. A mirror had been hung and angled down, centered above the urinals. I understood its purpose but didn't understand the attraction. Years ago, I had a date with a woman who at the end of the night asked me to come into her bathroom and watch her while she took a piss. I did it out of curiosity but found it to be entirely uninteresting. I never phoned her again.

I zipped up my fly, bought a pack of smokes outside the bathroom door, and went back down to the bar. The bartender had served my beer and was placing the ice water next to it.

"Nick Stefanos," I said, extending my hand.

"Paul Ritchie." He shook my hand and said, "How do you know Stella?"

"I tend at the Spot. A couple times a week, I go into Athena's, shoot a little pool."

"You that guy that used to hang out with Jackie Kahn?"

"You knew Jackie?"

"Sure. I heard she had a kid."

"Yeah."

"Heard she had some straight guy impregnate her."

"I heard that, too."

"You know, I think I met you, in fact, one night when I was in Athena's with a friend." His eyes moved to the beer in my hand, then back to me. "I guess you don't remember."

"Must have been one of those nights," I said. "You probably know how that is."

"Not anymore," he said.

"Ooordering, Paul!" said the prematurely world-weary voice from down the bar.

Paul Ritchie said, "Give me a minute," and went to the rail to fix the waiter a drink. I gulped down the ice water and lit a cigarette. By the time Ritchie returned, I had finished half my beer; my stomach had neutralized, the quiver had gone out of my hand, and my head had become more clear.

"Thanks for seeing me."

"No problem. What can I do for you?"

I put the manila folder on the bar, opened it, and slipped out the photographs of Calvin Jeter and Roland Lewis. I turned them around so that Ritchie could have a look.

"You recognize either of these guys?"

Ritchie studied the photos. "Uh-uh. I don't think so."

I searched his face for the hint of a lie, saw nothing irregular. I tapped my finger on Calvin's photo. "This one here, I found a book of Fire House matches in one of his shirts."

"What'd he do?"

"He got himself murdered."

Ritchie breathed out slowly. "I don't work every shift, obviously, so I can't say he's never come in here. But I know he's not a regular. And these two look like minors on top of that, and we make a pretty good effort not to serve minors. They *are* minors, right?"

"Yeah. What else?"

"To tell you the truth, neither of these kids look like my type of clientele."

"You mean they don't look gay."

"Look schmook, Stefanos. I don't have much of an idea what a gay person 'looks' like anymore. Do you?"

"I guess not. But what *did* you mean? They're not your clientele—what, because they're black?"

"No," he said tiredly, "not because they're black. Turn your head and take a look around this place."

I did. I saw some men getting on into their thirties and forties, some wearing ties, most of them with expensive haircuts and fine watches. The racial mix seemed to be about 80 percent white to 20 black; on the social and economic side, though, the group was homogenous. I turned back to Ritchie.

"So you run a nice place."

"Exactly. These men that come in here, they're not just well-adjusted; they're well-connected. That guy's suit over there—no offense, Stefanos—it's probably worth more than your whole wardrobe. I know it's worth more than mine."

"What about these kids?"

"Straight or gay," Ritchie said, "it's irrelevant. These two are street. This isn't their kind of place."

"So how do you think this kid came to get a hold of your matchbook?"

Ritchie shrugged. "Who knows? Maybe they were working the corner outside, working with all those other hustlers. The ones I'm talking about, they come in here, snag matches, bum smokes, sometimes try to hit on my customers. I'm telling you, my clientele's not interested. I know a couple of these hustlers, and some of them are all right. Most of them are country kids. You look at 'em, weight lifters, gym rats, with the sideburns and the pompadours, they all look like young Elvises. But usually, if they're not drinking—and most of the time they're not—I ask them to leave. There've been a couple incidents, and I just don't want those guys in here."

"What kind of incidents?"

"Where some people got hurt. See, the way it typically goes down, the way I understand it, these hustlers make the arrangement with the customer, usually some closeted businessman who works up around the Circle, and then they go down to the woods around P Street Beach. The money changes hands, and after that they do whatever it is they do—giving, receiving, whatever. But what happened last month, a couple of kids were leading those businessmen down there to the woods, then taking them for everything they had."

I dragged on my cigarette. "You know who these guys were?"

"No. 'Course, it never got reported to the cops. But it got around down here fast. What I heard, the other guys out on the street, they took care of the problem themselves. The whole thing was bad for their business."

"Ooordering," came the voice from down the bar.

Ritchie rolled his eyes. "Be back in a minute," he said.

I stood up and finished my beer, slid the photographs back in the folder. I took out my wallet and left money on the bar for the beer, and an extra twenty for Ritchie, with my business card on top of the twenty. Ritchie came back, wiping his hands with a damp rag.

"Thanks for your help," I said.

"Wish I could have done more."

"You did plenty. Any chance you could hook me up with one of those hustlers you were talking about? There's money in it for them—I'd pay for their time."

"I could give it a try, yeah. I don't see why not, if you're talking about money. I don't know what an hour of their time is worth, though. I'm out of that scene, way out. Not that I didn't have my day in the sun. But I've had the same boyfriend for the last five years. When I'm not in here. I'm sitting at home on the couch, watching sports on the tube, like the old fart that I am."

"Stella said you used to be pretty good with a bat."

"Yeah," he said. "I blew out my fucking knees. Now about the only thing I can do is water sports."

"Water sports, huh."

"Don't be a wise guy, Stefanos. I'm talking about swimming laps, down at the Y."

"Sorry." I ran my hand down the lapel of my sport jacket. "So you don't think too much of my threads, huh?"

A light came on in Ritchie's eyes. "Hey, look, don't feel bad. I used to have a jacket just like that."

"Yeah?"

"Yeah," Ritchie said. "Then my father got a job."

"Lucky me. I get to talk to an ex-jock bartender who doesn't drink. And I get a comedian in the bargain."

"I'm crackin' myself up here."

"Take it easy, Ritchie."

"Yeah, you, too. I'll let you know if I can set that thing up."

"Gimme a call," I said. "The number's on the card."

TEN

I HEARD FROM Paul Ritchie, and some others, early on Saturday morning at my apartment. Boyle called first, and he asked about my progress on the case. I told him that up to that point, my few leads had led only to blind alleys. I kept on that tack, and when I was done, I had managed to dig a big hole and fill it to the top with lies. I asked Boyle if the cops had anything new. He told me that an informant in a Southeast project had claimed that Jeter and Lewis were mules for a supplier down that way. I asked them if his people had any details on it and he said, "Nothing yet." We agreed to keep up with each other if something shook out on either end. I didn't like lying to him, and I wasn't exactly sure why I was doing it, but I had the vague feeling that I could see the beginning of some kind of light off in the distance. And it just wasn't in me to give anything away.

Paul Ritchie called next. I thanked him and promised to buy him a beer the next time he was in my part of town. He reminded me that he didn't drink, and I suggested that instead I'd buy myself one and dedicate it to him. Ritchie laughed, but he couldn't help mentioning how good it felt each morning to wake up with a clean head and be able to remember all the details from the night before. I told him I appreciated the testimonial, thanked him once again, and said good-bye.

Later in the morning, the phone rang for the third time that day. I thought it might be Lyla, but instead I heard the excited voice of Jack LaDuke.

"Nick!" he said.

"LaDuke!"

"What do we got?"

"I don't know. Maybe something, maybe not."

"I called you yesterday, Nick. Why you didn't call me back?"

"I was out during the day. And then I had a night shift, got home late."

"Out doing what? Working on the case?"

"Well, yeah. LaDuke, you got to understand, I've got to ease into this, man. I'm used to working alone." He didn't respond. I crushed the cigarette I had been working on in the ashtray. "Listen, LaDuke, I've got an interview with this guy, later today. You want to come along?"

"Damn right I do."

"Okay. I'll pick you up in an hour."

"Uh-uh. I'll pick *you* up."

"What's the big secret? You don't want me to know where you live?"

"I'll swing by in an hour, Stevonus."

"It's Ste*fa*nos, you asshole."

"One hour," LaDuke said, and hung up the phone.

PAUL RITCHIE HAD SET me up with one of the hustlers who worked the corner outside the Fire House, a guy who called himself Eddie Colorado. The name was a phony, but it sung, a canny cross of urban hood and westerner. Over the years, I had seen some of the men who stood around and worked that part of the street, and out of all the butch gimmicks that had passed through town—soldier of fortune, construction worker, lumberjack, and others—the cowboy thing seemed to have more staying power than the rest.

"What have you got goin' on this weekend?" LaDuke said. We were sitting in my Dodge, alongside a small park near the P Street Bridge.

"Dinner with Lyla's folks tomorrow, at their house. What about you?"

"I've got a date with Anna Wang tonight." LaDuke grinned, proud of himself. "I called her up."

"Congratulations," I said, then pointed through the windshield to the bridge. "Here comes our boy."

Eddie waited for the green at 23rd, crossed the street, and headed for my car. Ritchie had told me to look for an unnatural blond, a "skinny rockabilly type with bad skin," and Eddie fit the bill. His orangish moussed hair contrasted starkly with his red T-shirt, the sleeves of which had been turned up, the veins popping on his thin biceps. His jeans were pressed and tight, and he walked with an exaggerated swagger, a cigarette lodged above his ear, a cocky smile spread across his face.

"Look at this guy," LaDuke said with naked disgust.

"Relax," I said, "and get in the backseat. Okay?"

LaDuke got out of the shotgun bucket, left the door open for Eddie, and climbed into the back. Eddie stepped up to the door, took a look around like he owned a piece of the park, pulled a wad of gum from his mouth, and chucked it onto the grass. He leaned a forearm on the frame and cocked his hip.

"You Stefanos?" he said.

"Yeah. Get in."

"Sure thing," Eddie said with a slow accent that had just crawled down off the Smokies. He dropped into the bucket and pulled the door closed.

I looked across the console at Eddie. "Paul Ritchie said twenty-five would buy some of your time."

"A little of it."

"Here." I passed him a folded twenty along with a five. Eddie Colorado pushed his pelvis out and jammed the bills into the pocket of his jeans. He hit my dash lighter, slid the cigarette off the top of his ear, and put the filtered end in his mouth.

"No," LaDuke said from the backseat, "we don't mind if you smoke."

Eddie turned his head, gave LaDuke a quick appraisal, smiled, followed the smile with a tight giggle. "Who's your friend?"

"His name's Jack."

Eddie smiled again, raised his eyebrows, touched the hot end of the lighter to his smoke. He held the cigarette out the window, settled down in his seat, the sun coming directly in on his face. The acne on his cheek looked red as fire in the light.

Eddie stared straight ahead. "Paul told me you wanted me to look at some pictures."

I opened the chrome cover on the center console, took out the photographs of Calvin and Roland, gave them to Eddie. He dragged on his cigarette and blew smoke down at the images in his hand.

"You know them?" I said.

Eddie's mouth twitched a little. He nodded and said, "Yes."

"Were they workin' this area?"

"For a little while, yeah."

"And you and your buddies kicked them out."

"Right."

"What'd they do to make you do that?" I said.

Eddie grinned. "You're getting into somethin' here that might come back to me. It's gonna cost you another twenty-five."

"Bullshit," LaDuke said. "This guy didn't kick anybody out of anywhere, Nick. Look at him."

"Your friend thinks I'm weak," Eddie said. "But I've been

dealing with rednecks all my life, calling me this and that, beatin' me up on the way to and from school. Let me tell you somethin', it ain't no different here in Washington D.C. than in the country. First day I got into town, I went into this burger joint off New York Avenue. This guy says to me, 'Hey, you fuckin' queer.' You wanna know what I did about it? I broke his fuckin' jaw."

I watched a man with matted hair carry a backpack past my car. "So, what, you kicked these two off your turf because they called you a name?"

Eddie shook his head and said, "The twenty-five."

I said, "Give it to him, Jack."

LaDuke pulled his wallet, withdrew the money. He crumpled the bills and dropped them over Eddie's shoulder, into his lap. Eddie smoothed the bills out carefully, folded them, and slipped them into his pocket.

"You say you knew these two," I said. "What were their names?"

"I don't know. Ain't nobody uses his real name down here, anyhow."

"They were doing prostitution down in those woods?"

" 'Doing prostitution'?" Eddie laughed. "If you want to call it that. They were *workin'*, Stefanos, that's what they was doin'."

"Down in those woods?"

"On the edge of the beach," Eddie said. "At first, it didn't bother anybody, 'cause, you got to realize, there's a certain kind of man only goes for boys got dark meat."

"Jesus Christ," LaDuke muttered.

"So," Eddie said, "it wasn't no competition for the rest of us. But then this one here—Eddie put one dirty finger on the face of Roland Lewis—"he took some man's money. I mean all his money. Took more than they agreed to. Just took it."

I said, "You sure he wasn't provoked? Maybe one of these johns threatened him or something, tried to hurt him."

Brown lines of tobacco stain ran between the gaps of

Eddie's toothy grin. "The *johns*, man, they don't hurt us. Most of the time, if there's anything like that to be done, they want us to do it to *them*. Just last week, I had this old man down in the woods, this lawyer works for some fancy firm, down around 19th? He had me slide this rod with little barbs on it right up into his dick. And right before he came, he had me rip it out. Man, you should have seen the blood in his jizz. With all his screamin' and shit, it was hard to tell the pleasure from the pain."

"Goddamn it," LaDuke said, "stick to what we're talking about here."

"Stick to it, Eddie," I said. "We don't need all the extra details."

"All right." Eddie looked in the rearview at LaDuke, back at me. "So anyway, we find out from some of our regulars that this thing has been happening again and again. That these boys are rolling our businessmen on a regular basis, takin' the short road to big money. But there is no short road, see? This is work, like anything else. You don't treat your customers right, they're gonna go somewheres else. So we went and had a meeting with your boys one night, down in the woods."

"You told them to get lost?" LaDuke said.

"It wasn't all that dramatic," Eddie said. "The one who started all the shit said that they were off to something better, that they didn't need this anymore."

"Off to what?"

Eddie stabbed a finger at Roland's picture once more. "He said they were going to get themselves into the movies. Said they met a man who was going to make them a whole lot of money. Big money, man, extralarge."

LaDuke said, "Porno?"

"What do *you* think?" Eddie said.

"This kid you keep pointing to," I said. "Did he seem to be the leader of the two?"

"Appeared to be."

I took a cigarette from the pack on the dash, rolled it unlit between my fingers. "Eddie, did these guys seem like they were into what they were doing?"

"They were into making money," Eddie said. "But what you really mean is, Were they faggots? If I had to make some kind of guess, I'd say the other kid was kinda, I don't know, not sure about anything he was doing. The leader, though, he was definitely into it."

"Into it how?"

"His eyes." Eddie looked in the rearview at LaDuke, held his gaze. "Me and my friends, when things are slow out here, we play this game: Gay, Not Gay. We check out these suit-and-tie boys walking down the street and we make the call. Me, I look at their eyes. And when it comes to knowing what it really is that they're about, I believe I'm usually right." Eddie smirked a little at LaDuke.

"Fuck this," LaDuke said. "I've had enough."

"A couple more questions," I said. "You know anybody in this movie business you were talking about?"

"Uh-uh," Eddie said. "Not my thing. I like the fresh air, Stefanos. Can't stand being cooped up in a small space, under some hot light. I ain't got no ambition to be that kind of star."

"Some of your friends might know something about it."

"Maybe," Eddie said. "I'll ask around. I find out anything, I'll give you a call."

I gave him my card. "There's money in it for you if you come up with something."

"That's the case," Eddie said, "you *know* I'll call."

"We about done?" said LaDuke.

"Your friend needs to relax," Eddie said. "It's not good for him to be so angry."

"See you later, Eddie," I said.

Eddie turned to LaDuke. "Take care of yourself, Stretch."

He got out of the car, and shut the door behind him. I watched him strut across the street and disappear over the hill at the start of the bridge. He lived for money, but he was stupid and he was sloppy, and he had a short attention span. He'd lose my card, or forget my name; I knew I'd never hear from him again.

"*God*damn it," LaDuke said softly from the backseat.

I lit the cigarette that I had been playing with for the last five minutes, took some smoke into my lungs. "Listen, Jack. These kids out here, man, they're going to get into some shit. You didn't think Roland was totally innocent, did you? If you're going to do this kind of work, you've got to stop setting yourself up for disappointment."

"It makes me sick, that's all. To think that Roland comes from a home where his mother raised him with love, and then he ends up down in some woods, having some middle-aged man suck his dick, maybe go butt-up in some porno movie. A kid is confused enough, Nick; he doesn't know shit yet about what he is. To have all these adults doing these things to him... I swear to God, it just makes me sick."

"We're not done yet," I said. "And what we found out here, it could be nothing compared to what we're going to find. Earlier today, I talked to this cop I know. He told me that they've got some information—I don't know how reliable it is—that Calvin and Roland were moving drugs."

"Who were the cops talking to?"

"An informant of theirs, out of Southeast."

"Well, let's find this guy, talk to him ourselves!"

"There's things we can't do, LaDuke. The cops can go into those projects, ask around, because they're cops. We go in there, a couple of white-boy private cops, nobody's gonna talk to us. And it's a good way to get ourselves capped."

"What now, then?"

"We keep doing what we're doing, work with what we know. Here's the thing: Calvin was killed because of something wrong he and his friend got themselves into—there's no doubt about that now. You're going to have deal with it, Jack—Roland might be dead, too."

"*God*damn it," LaDuke said again, and shook his head.

We didn't say much after that. I sat there and smoked my cigarette and checked out the flow of traffic while the bike messengers and the homeless and the hustlers moved about in the park. LaDuke mumbled to himself occasionally, and once he slapped the back of my seat with his palm. Then he picked up a couple of empty beer cans that were at his feet and told me he was going to throw them away.

I watched him walk around the front of the car, moving heavily, shifting his shoulders awkwardly, a tall, gawky guy not entirely comfortable in his own skin, like an adolescent who has grown too fast. There was something else, too, something a little off center and soiled beneath Jack LaDuke's fresh-scrubbed looks. I couldn't put my finger on it that day, and when I did, it was way too late. Eventually, the snakes that were crawling around inside his head found their way out. By then, there was nothing I could do but stand beside him, and watch them strike.

ELEVEN

LYLA MCCUBBIN HAD grown up in a boxy brick house on a street named Bangor Drive, in an unremarkable but pleasant development called Garrett Park Estates in the Maryland suburb of Kensington. Her parents had raised three children there, and they had remained long after Lyla, the last child, had graduated from college and gone out on her own. Lyla said that the neighborhood had changed very little since her childhood: a mixture of starter homes and rentals, none too ostentatious, a comfortable kind of place, where you came to recognize the bark of every dog through the open window of your bedroom as you drifted off to sleep on summer nights.

Lyla's mother, Linda, had practically raised the children herself, as the father, Daniel McCubbin, was usually off at some meeting, organizing the unions or planning the demonstration for his latest cause. The first day I met Lyla, in her office at *D.C. This Week*, I had noticed the photograph of her as a child, standing between her bearded father and straight-haired mother, at a Dupont Circle rally circa 1969. Lyla said that the family never had a dime, but there was some pride in her voice as she said it, never regret. Her father, a fine trial lawyer by all accounts, had managed to resist the advances of the corporate firms in town throughout his career, preferring to use his talents to advance the causes of those individuals whom he considered to be on the side of "right." He wasn't your typical pompous windbag, though. I liked him and I admired him, despite the obvious fact that he was not awfully crazy about me.

We were greeted at the door by Linda McCubbin, who kissed Lyla and then me on the cheek. Linda was Lyla with thirty years added to the odometer, with more silver in the hair than red now and an organic heaviness around the waist and in the hips. Men were always told to look at the mothers, as if that was some kind of test; it never had been for me, but if it had been, then Lyla would have passed.

"Here, Ma," Lyla said, handing Linda a bag containing two liter bottles of white wine. Lyla had insisted we stop for it, though both of us had once again consumed a little too much the night before.

Linda took it, said, "Come on in."

Daniel sat under an overextended air conditioner in the simply furnished living room, in a La-Z-Boy chair, the arms of which had been shredded by the McCubbin cat, a mean tom that someone had ironically named Peace. Lyla bent to her father and kissed him, and then he shook my hand without rising from the chair.

"Don't get up," I said.

"Didn't plan to," he said. "Hot day like this, I'm going to expend as little energy as possible. How's it going, Nick?"

"Good. Good."

Daniel smiled, studied me, and kept the smile until it looked nothing like a smile at all. Maybe I had overdone the aftershave, or maybe it was the unironed khakis or the color of my shirt. Or maybe he liked me just fine, and it was just that I was dating his baby daughter.

"Linda," Daniel said, watching my eyes. "Get Nick here a drink. What'll it be, Nick?"

"Nothing just yet. Too early for me," I said, rocking on my heels.

"Is it?" Daniel said, scratching beneath the white of his beard.

"Well," Lyla said, "*I'll* have one. C'mon, Mom, let's go in the kitchen. I'll help you get ready."

Lyla winked, left me there with her dad. I gave her a brittle smile as she walked away. I had a seat on the sofa, crossed one leg over the other, nervously missed it on the first go-round.

"Where's the rest of the family?" I said.

"They'll be along," Daniel said. "How's the bar business going?"

"Good. Real good."

"You know, I used to go into that place, in the old days, when I was working on the Hill."

"Really."

"Yes, it was called something else back then. You've been there awhile, haven't you? Thought you might own a piece of it by now."

"No, not me. Tough business, that." Real tough.

"And your investigative work?"

"Coming along," I said as I watched my free foot wiggle in the air. "How about you...how's retirement?"

Daniel raised his substantial eyebrows. "Linda says I don't know how to spell the word *retirement.* I guess the difference is, now I don't get paid for what it is I do. Right now, I'm setting up group homes for Haitian refugees. Our church owns these properties, so...I'm helping fix them up."

"Why fix them up?" I said, my foot pinwheeling now, out of control. "You could make more profit by, you know, leaving them the way they are. Crowd a bunch of people in the rooms, I mean—where they come from, they're used to it. Jack up the rents, too, while you're at it."

A smile came into Daniel's eyes. "Of course," he said, "you're ribbing me, aren't you?"

"Just a little."

"You know, you don't always have to work so hard at being cynical around me, Nick. I know that, in your own way, you have a fairly clear idea of what's right and what's wrong. Not all the good that gets done in this world gets done in a church or a meeting hall, I realize that."

"Yeah, well, we make do with what we have, and work with it, you know?"

"Yes, I do."

He stopped giving me the business and picked up the Outlook section of the *Post* that was lying by his chair. I noticed a makeshift bar that had been set up on a mobile cart near a mirrored armoire in the corner of the room. There were bottles of gin and vodka, tonic and ginger ale, an ice bucket, and a sealed bottle of Old Grand-Dad. Apparently, that had been purchased just for me; I had never seen the old man take a drink, and Lyla's mother drank wine, and only with dinner. Something pushed out at the base of the curtains at the bay window and moved along behind them with a deliberate slink: That would be Peace, stalking me as he always did when I came to the McCubbin house for dinner.

I was watching the curtains, thinking of my possible defense against an attack from that lousy cat, when the front door opened and four people stepped inside: Lyla's brother, Mike, his wife, Donna, Lyla's older sister, Kimmy, and Kimmy's husband, Leo. This time, Daniel stood up from his chair, and we all did our back-slapping moves around the living room. A half hour later, we were seated at a cramped table in the dining room, with Daniel McCubbin leading a prayer. During the prayer, our hands were all joined underneath the table, a McCubbin tradition, and my index finger was wiggling around on the inside of Lyla's thigh. Lyla, seated to my right, dug a fingernail into my own thigh, leaving a crescent mark that I discovered an hour later in the bathroom.

"Amen," everybody said, and then Leo, as usual, reached across the table for the first shot at the main course, and started pushing thick slices of roast beef onto his plate.

"Leave some for the rest of the family, Leo," Kim said, only kidding by half.

"Sure, honey," he said, then issued his trademark high cackle, a sound that was always surprising coming from a man as fat as Leo. "You know I can't help it. The Irish love their liquor, and us Greeks love to eat. Right, Nick?"

Daniel McCubbin's eyes flashed on Leo. I nodded weakly, not wanting to appear too anxious to admit to being a member of Leo Charles's ethnic tribe. Leo *was* a Greek—the Charles had been Charalambides before his grandfather stepped off the boat—but he was not a kid my friends or I had known growing up. Leo Charles was also a bigot, and like all bigots, black and white, he was a loser, and he directed his shortcomings and utter lack of self-confidence outwardly and onto the backs of others. Lyla said Kimmy had zero self-esteem and that was why she had married him. And all the time, I'd thought it was his 280-pound frame, all five foot eight inches of it.

"How about those Orioles?" Mike said in the too-gentle way of his that unfortunately suggested a weaker version of his father. Mike ran a volunteer soup kitchen operation out of Le Droit Park. He plopped a mound of mashed potatoes onto his plate and passed the platter to his wife, Donna, a shame-about-the-face public defender with just a killer body. All these do-goodniks at the table, and me. Well, there was Leo, too.

"Yeah, how about 'em, Nick?" Leo said. "Think the bull-pen's gonna take 'em through to the Series?" Leo loved to talk sports but couldn't do a push-up.

"Lookin' good," I said, feeling not so good. I really could

have used a drink. "I'm going up to Camden Yards tomorrow with a buddy of mine, a guy named Johnny McGinnes."

"An Irishman," Leo said, spitting a little ball of mashed potato across the table in the process.

"They love their liquor," Daniel said, but it went over Leo's head, missed him by a mile. He kept right on chewing, breaking down the load that was in his mouth. Lyla's mother laughed a little, and she and Mike exchanged fond looks.

"You didn't tell me you were going to the game," Lyla said.

"Yeah, Johnny won some tickets, sold a million refrigerators last month in some promotion, something like that."

"*That* ought to be interesting," Lyla said, killing the remainder of the wine in her glass. She picked up the bottle off the table and poured herself some more, clumsily trying to fill the glass to the top, spilling some in the process. Daniel looked at her and then at me. Lyla's ears were a little red, her cheeks flushed.

"Anybody want a little more cool in here?" Lyla's mother said. "We could turn up that air conditioner."

"Let me handle this," I said with a wink. "I used to be in electronics—I know how to operate the unit."

I got out of my chair and walked to the window where the air conditioner had been set. As I got to it, I saw something black seem to rise out of nowhere from behind the curtains near my feet, and I heard a woman's voice cry out behind me just as the wail of an animal pierced the air. I felt a slash of pain, pulled my hand back as the crazy tomcat cartwheeled in the air, landed on his feet on the carpet, and took off back across the room, scurrying for his hiding place behind the drapes.

"Fuck!" I shouted, waving my hand, the blood already coming to the surface of the cut. That quieted the rest of them down.

Mike got up and found the cat, carried him back into the room. Lyla tossed me a napkin and went to get a Band-Aid. She returned with it, but by now the cut had stopped bleeding. I put the Band-Aid on anyway, a sympathy play to make my obscenity seem more justified.

"Peace, man," Mike whined, stroking the cat.

"Peace, man," I said, and made a V with my fingers, smiling stupidly at the McCubbin family. Nobody laughed.

"I guess that cat doesn't like you so good," Leo said. "Right, Nick?"

"Leo," Kimmy said, "you've got a piece of lettuce on your cheek."

I sat back down. Lyla patted my thigh under the table. We finished our Sunday dinner.

A COUPLE OF HOURS later, when Lyla's siblings and their spouses had gone and Lyla went to the kitchen with her mother to wash and dry the dishes, I took a beer to the concrete patio out back and had a seat in one of four wrought-iron chairs grouped around a glass-topped table. I lit a cigarette and watched a young father play catch with his son in an adjacent yard. The man rubbed the top of his son's head when they were done, and the boy skipped off toward their house. Then the back door of the McCubbin house opened and Daniel came out and stepped down to the patio.

"Mind if I join you?"

"Of course not," I said. "Have a seat."

He grunted as he settled into a chair across the table. I dropped my lit butt into the top of the beer can and heard it hiss as it hit the backwash. I put the can at my feet.

"How was it?" Daniel said.

"Cold beer on a Sunday in the summer, it's always pretty good."

"Yes, I remember. Watching you today, it took me back to when I was first dating Linda, the times we'd go to her parents' house for dinner. I could have used a drink on those occasions, wanted one desperately, as a matter of fact. It really would have relaxed me, taken the edge off. There's nothing more humbling than dealing with the potential in-laws, no matter how much confidence you have. It's like, all of the sudden, you're a little boy again."

"You guys aren't so bad," I said, and a smile passed between us. "Besides, it's Lyla, so it's worth it."

"You love her, don't you?"

"Yes, sir. I believe I do."

"How much do you love her? Do you love her enough to do what's right for her, even if it means losing her?"

"I don't follow you."

Daniel sat back in his chair, looked into the depths of his own yard. "I told you earlier today that I used to frequent that place you bartend in, when I was on the Hill. I don't know if Lyla's ever told you the...degree to which I frequented those types of establishments."

"No," I said, "she hasn't."

"Well, I was quite a regular in those days, in that place and plenty of others. I wish that I could give you the details, but I don't remember all that much of those years. If it wasn't for photographs, it would be difficult to recall even the faces of my children as they were growing up. All that wasted time. But I can't get it back now, so..." Daniel pulled at the errant edges of his beard. "Anyway, things turned out all right, I think. I got myself into a program, managed to see my children become wonderful adults, with most of the credit for that going to Linda, of course, and I ended up doing a bit of good along the way. So I think you'll understand it when I say, maybe because of the fact that I wasn't always there for them, that I'm rather fiercely protective of my children to this day."

"I understand."

Daniel breathed out slowly, folded his hands on the table, bumped one thumb against the other. "Lyla, she's always taken on my traits, even as a child. I know you think she looks like her mother, and certainly she does. But I'm talking about resemblances in less obvious ways."

I didn't respond.

Daniel kept on: "When Lyla was a teenager, when she used to come home late at night, I could always tell what she had been up to. Her own body, it betrayed her. When she drinks, you know, even now, her ears turn this blazing shade of red. That same thing used to happen to me—in fact, they used to call me 'Red' in some of the bars where they knew me pretty well." Daniel looked me in the eyes. "She's got a problem with it, you know. It's hereditary, I suppose, in a gene I gave her. The researchers, they've been claiming that for quite some time now. She's got the same problem that I had when I was her age. And I see it... I see it only getting worse."

Again, I didn't answer him or respond in any way. A drop of sweat moved slowly down my back. Daniel leaned in, rested his forearms on the table.

"You're an alcoholic, Nick," he said. "You would never admit to it, but that's what you are. You've probably done some binge drinking in your day, but I would say that in general you're what they call a controlled drinker. The worst kind, because it allows you to convince yourself that you don't have a problem, and now you've managed to bury the thought of doing something about it entirely. I've been around enough people like you; I just don't think you're ever going to give it up."

"I know what I'm about."

"Yes, I think you do. But I'm not responsible for you, so that's not good enough. Lyla needs someone strong to tell her what she is and to stand next to her and help her through it. You're just not that person."

I pushed away from the table and stood slowly from my chair. "It's getting late. I better be going."

I began to walk past him, but he wrapped a hand around my forearm. I looked down on him, saw that his eyes had softened.

"I like you, Nick. I want you to know that. I think that you're a good man. You're just not good for *her*."

"Thanks for dinner."

I walked across the patio in the dying light.

"WHAT WERE YOU AND Dad doing out back?" Lyla said. We were driving south on Connecticut, to Lyla's apartment. "What was he, asking about your intentions?"

"Something like that."

"Dad's always been tough on my boyfriends."

"He's only looking out for you," I said.

"I know," Lyla said, and touched the Band-Aid on my finger. "Tough day, huh, Stefanos?"

"Tough day."

I stopped at Lyla's apartment building off Calvert, let the engine idle.

"What, you're not coming up?"

"I better not," I said. "Got something going on early tomorrow on this Jeter thing."

"I should chill out, too. My editor left a message on my machine yesterday. That story I've been working on, the one I finished and turned in after we had lunch the other day, in Chinatown? He wants to meet with me about it in the morning. Sounds ominous."

"You've always been able to control him. You'll do fine."

Lyla leaned across the seat, put her hand behind my head, and kissed me on the mouth. "Love you, Nick."

"I love you too, baby. Take care."

TWELVE

IN D.C., IT'S tough to find a good clean place to catch an art film anymore, and next to impossible to find consistency in repertory. The near-legendary Circle Theater on Pennsylvania Avenue, where many Washingtonians got their film education, is long gone, its "ten tickets for ten dollars" deal a permanent fixture now in the local nostalgia file. Georgetown boasts the Key and Biograph theaters, but Georgetown has devolved into a slum-out for suburban teens, drunks, and tourists—a guy I know calls it a "shopping mall without a roof"—and a lot of in-towners just don't care to bother. Out-of-town bookers place the rest of the films in their corporately designated "art theaters," their unfamiliarity with our city demographics resulting in sometimes laughably illogical bills. It's true that you can catch some cool stuff at the Hirshhorn or at other galleries or museums, but you have to know where to find the listings, and by the time you've gotten around to checking out the art calendars in *City Paper* and *D.C. This Week*, it's often too late.

I have a friend named Gerry Abromowitz, whom I've known since the club days in the early years of the New Wave—music, not film. Gerry owned his own club for a while, a place called the Crawlspace, a venue for harDCore bands and slammers. Off and on, Gerry went by the name of Gerry Louis, Jr., and even looked into having the legal change. But he stopped short of doing it about the time that the Crawlspace closed down after one steaming-hot summer. A personal-injury suit put a lock on the front door, but in truth, the place was a loser from the word go. Now, Gerry Louis, Jr., was back to Gerry Abromowitz and settling into the beginnings of middle age, working as the owner/operator of a movie theater called the Very Ritzy down on 9th.

The Very Ritzy had just been the Ritz, of course, in its original incarnation, but as usual, Gerry couldn't resist fucking around with the name. It started out as a burlesque house, and then it was the last of the burlesque houses, and then it was the last of the porno houses, and when Gerry took it out of mothballs on a short-term lease, his intention was to make it an art house. But he soon found out that it was difficult to outbid the more powerful competition for the bookings, and when he could get a decent film, nobody seemed to be interested in traveling to that part of town after working hours. So he quietly took it back to porno for the matinees and made it straight repertory at night, taking in the spillage and the last-call crowd from the Snake Pit and other clubs in the surrounding area. He seemed to make a living from this novel arrangement, though that was probably due to the fact that his skin-flick matinees were all profit; over the years, Gerry Abromowitz had amassed one of the most extensive privately owned sixteen-millimeter porno collections south of Jersey.

"Ge-roo," I said, shaking his hand. He had agreed to meet me Monday noon at the theater. We stood in the red-carpeted lobby.

"Nick the Stick," Gerry said. "Lookin' good. How about me... I gain much weight?"

About forty, I thought. But I said, "Nah."

"C'mon up. I'm runnin' the projector. My kid's up there; I don't want to leave him alone."

A man in a business suit walked into the lobby, his eyes straight ahead. An usher—long hair, wearing a black T-shirt and ripped black jeans—took the man's ticket, tore it in half, then returned to the paperback he was reading without moving from his stool. The business suit scurried quickly through the lobby to the darkness of the theater. I followed Gerry up a carpeted set of stairs.

We hit a landing and then an office area, where a boy just past toddler played with an action figure that looked to me like the Astro Boy of my youth. All four walls of this room had film cans racked and labeled on wooden shelves, with a large slotted area set aside for one-sheets and stills.

"Gerry junior," Gerry said, tipping his head proudly at the boy.

"Gerry Louis, Jr.?" I said.

"Nick, Nick, Nick," Gerry said.

I turned to his kid. "What's that guy's name?" I said, nodding at his toy.

"Jason the Power Ranger!" the kid said, puffing out his chest and his cheeks. When he did that, the little fats looked a lot like his dad.

"Aw, man," I said, "I wish *I* had one of those." That got Gerry junior excited, and he started running around the room, holding up Jason the Power Ranger in the go-fly position. Gerry senior motioned me up another short set of stairs.

We took seats outside the shut door of the projection booth, close enough to hear if something mechanical went wrong. The air was stagnant and warm, but I was in shorts and a T-shirt, and Gerry was dressed approximately the same way. Gerry's kinky hair had plenty of gray in it, and he had one of those faces that always seemed to be smiling, even when it was not.

"So what's on the bill today?" I said. "*The Sorrow and the Pity*?"

"Not quite. *Crotchless in Seattle.* It's a big title for me this summer."

"I'll bet. So the porno's keeping this place afloat."

"So far. The associations, the exodus of the law firms moving east into the city, that's helped. These guys pay their seven bucks, come in for the first show, fifteen minutes, wack-adoo, wack-adoo"—Gerry contorted his face, made a fist, pumped out a two-stroke jack-off mime—"they're in and out. It's cheaper than a prostie, Nick. And with the plague out there, it's damn sure safer. Everyone thought, with videotape rental, the theatrical was gonna go the way of quadrophonic sound. And that was true to some degree, especially with the pervs. But these married guys, for whatever reason—maybe they're not gettin' enough at home, whatever—they can't pop in a porno tape in their own house. What are they gonna tell junior? 'Keep it down. Daddy's tryin' to watch Stormy Weathers give Ralph Rimrod some head'? Excuse me." Gerry pulled balled Kleenex from his pocket, blew his nose loudly into the tissue. "I'm telling you, this porno thing is a growth market, if you got the right location."

"Yeah, but who cleans up the theater?"

Gerry smirked. "That kid you saw in the lobby, he came to me, said he wanted to learn the exhibition business. I gave him a bucket and mop, said, 'Here, go to school.' Between shows, he does the honors. But it's not as bad as you think, Nick. These business types are very fastidious—they bring their own socks, *Wall Street Journal*s, shit like that. They're better behaved than my nighttime repertory crowd, I'll tell you. But even that's beginning to pick up. Kids are smoking pot again, you know it?"

"Sure," I said, thinking of the stash in my glove box.

"That helps. Helps the 'appreciation of cinema.' Helps

music, and fucking, and everything else, too, right? Anyway, I'm gonna start adding psychotronic midnights on the weekends—"

"Listen, Ger—"

"I know, you don't have all day. You called because you needed some information."

"That's right. I'm looking for a kid, got himself into some local porn action."

"How old?"

"Seventeen."

"What genre?"

"Man on boy, what I can make out. Maybe interracial, if that narrows it down. The kid is black."

Gary scratched behind his ear. "I wouldn't know, directly. Everything I got here is classic, on celluloid, from the archives. The video business is wide open, man; anybody can do it. Let's say you want to make a movie with a school theme. All's you need is a camera, a couple of lights if you want it real clean, some props—a piece of chalk, maybe a blackboard—and you got yourself a real intricate story about a teacher disciplining his student."

"Isn't there any risk? I mean, it's got to be illegal, right?"

"Yes and no. The situation you're describing, if the kid's a minor, yeah, that's illegal, but lookswise he's probably right on the cusp, so who's gonna check? Basically, as long as there're no penetration shots, you're in the clear."

"The business is that scattered."

"Sure. It's done all over the city. Like I say, I wouldn't have any idea where to tell you to start. I'm not in that business."

"Somebody's got to distribute the stuff, though."

Gerry shifted in his seat. "In the man-boy arena? All the homo stuff, and the different varieties of it, everything comes out of this little warehouse around 2nd on K. This guy owns a storefront porno operation. I think it's called the Hot Plate."

"What's his name?"

"Bernard Tobias. Bernie."

"Think he'll talk to me?"

"Not *just* to you, no. Bernie, he's a weird bird. Well, maybe not so weird if you're an amateur psychiatrist. He's a little guy who always needs to be the big magilla. I've met him a few times; he's always bragging about how he only does business with 'executive officers,' never meets with anybody's assistant, like we're talking about Wharton graduates in the skin trade here. I think if you go in with a couple of guys, wear ties, do the dog and pony show, you'll be all right."

"Thanks, Gerry. Appreciate the help."

"Hey, Nick—how'd you end up in this, anyway? I ran into one of my old bartenders from the Crawlspace a few months ago—"

"Joe Martinson."

"Joe, right. He told me what you were doing. The way I remember you, you were this music-crazy guy used to stand in the corner watching the bands, a beer in each hand. Fact, I used to call you 'Nick Two-Beers,' remember?"

"You said it was my Indian name. 'Course, I remember when you insisted everyone call you Gerry Louis, Jr. Things happen to people—you never know where they're going to end up."

"You got that right. That guy in that band Big Black, Durango's his name, remember? He's a corporate lawyer now. I saw his picture in a magazine, little bald guy in a hot-shit suit like every guy you see walking out of Arnold and Porter. So yeah, you never know." Gerry got out of his chair. "Speaking of Jerry Lewis, I'm doing a retrospective next month, kicking it off with *The Nutty Professor*. I can get you a pass."

"I don't think so."

"It's an American classic!"

"So are you, Ger." I shook his hand. "Listen, thanks again, man. Thanks a million."

I USED GERRY'S DIRECTORY before I left, then found a pay phone out on 9th and called Bernie Tobias. I identified myself as Ron

Roget—an appropriately lizardly name I had just seen in the directory—and bullshitted him about my production company out of Philadelphia, which I said did the "man/boy discipline thing" better than anyone "on the East Coast." He said he couldn't meet with me that week, but when I told him that "my associates" and I would be in D.C. tomorrow, and only for one day, he agreed. As Gerry had predicted, the "associates" tag hit Bernie's hot button. We agreed on a time the next day.

I made it to the Spot after the lunch rush had subsided. Mai was behind the bar, bent into the soak sink with a glass load, and Phil Saylor stood at the register counting checks. Anna was by the service bar, arranging her tip change in dollar stacks on the green netting. I spoke to Mai briefly, thanked her for what we had arranged over the phone the day before.

"Hey, Phil," I said, speaking to his back. "I'm taking some time off. Mai and I set it up. That okay by you?"

"I need the shifts, Phil," Mai interjected.

"She told me already," Phil said without raising his head. He didn't add anything, so I went down to the service end of the bar and rubbed the top of Anna Wang's head.

"Hey, Nick."

"Hey, what's up?"

"Got a cigarette?"

"Sure."

I gave her one, lit it for her. She leaned her back against the wall, dragged sharply on the smoke, exhaled just as sharply. "Some woman called you," she said. "Said your uncle wants to see you."

"Costa," I said. "The woman would be his nurse."

"He sick?"

"Cancer," I said. Anna looked at the cigarette in her hand, thought about it, took another drag.

"That's rough."

I nodded. "How'd your date go with LaDuke?"

"Okay, I guess."

I reached out and Anna passed me the cigarette. I took a puff, handed it back. "Just okay?"

"It was fun." Her eyes smiled. "He took me to the Jefferson Memorial last night. We sat on the steps, split a bottle of wine. Or rather, I drank most of it. No guy's ever tried anything so obvious with me. I know it's a corny move, but I got the feeling he didn't think it was, if you know what I mean."

"He's strictly from L-Seven, but genuine."

"Exactly. Most of the guys I meet still in their twenties, they're so ironic, so cynical, you know, I just get tired of it sometimes. Jack's cute, and he's funny, and all those good things, but he's also really square. In some weird way, that's refreshing."

"So why was the night 'just okay'?"

"It always comes down to the big finish, doesn't it?" Anna butted the smoke in an ashtray, looked up. "Well, at the end of the night, I wanted to kiss him, you know? And I'm pretty sure he wanted to kiss me, too. So I took the initiative." Anna grinned. "I gave it to him pretty good, I think. But he was shaking, Nick. I mean, shaking real deep. It's like, I don't know, he was scared to death. And then he just pulled away, and it was like something just seemed to go out of him."

"Maybe it's been awhile for him."

"I guess."

"You gonna see him again?"

"Maybe. I don't know. The guy's carrying something serious around on his back. I'm not sure if I need that right now."

I touched her arm. "Listen, I've got to go."

"Take it easy," she said.

I poked my head into the kitchen, hooked Darnell up as the driver for my appointment the next day. Then I phoned LaDuke from the bar, got him in on it, too. On the way out the door, Phil Saylor grabbed my arm.

"What's your hurry?" he said.

"I'm off to the ball game with a friend of mine. Got to pick him up where he works."

"Don't stay away too long, hear? Mai, she's okay, but after she works a few days straight, she starts jumping all into the customers' shit."

"I thought you were mad at me, Phil."

"You made a mistake. You're allowed one or two."

I moved to shake his hand, but he turned away. The two of us were square again, I guess.

WHEN I WALKED INTO Goode's White Goods in Beltsville, the first thing I saw was Johnny McGinnes, bent into an open refrigerator, blowing pot smoke into the box. During working hours, McGinnes's pants pocket always contained a film canister and a one-hit pipe, which he lit at regular intervals right on the sales floor. After the exhale, he would tap the ashes out against his open palm and drop the pipe back into his pocket in one quick movement. I had worked with him for many years, and to my knowledge, no one, customer or management type, had ever caught him in the act of getting high.

McGinnes saw my entrance, pulled a six of Colt 45 tall boys from the fridge, held them up, winked, and put them back inside. He shut the door and goose-stepped down the aisle back to his customer, a middle-aged woman looking at a dishwasher. As usual, McGinnes was done up synthetic-crisp: navy blue slacks, poly/cotton oxford, and a plain red tie with a knot as pretty as a fist. His thinning black hair slashed down across his high forehead, with only his silver sideburns betraying his age. McGinnes managed to throw me a mental patient's grin as he spoke to the woman; even across the showroom, I could see that he was half-cooked.

Goode's White Goods, one of the few major appliance independents left in the D.C. area since brand-name retailing came to Sears, had managed to carve out a niche for itself as a full-service operation. *White goods* was the industry term for big-ticket appliances, and the company's owner, Nolan Goode—it was inevitable that McGinnes would dub him "No Damn Good"—mistakenly overcalculated the public's comprehension of the wordplay in the store's name. Confusion notwithstanding, Goode's White Goods had managed to survive. And after McGinnes had joined the team, it had actually begun to thrive.

In contrast to the noise common on an electronics' floor, No Damn Good's appliance shop seemed quiet as a museum, orderly rows of silent, shiny, inanimate porcelain aligned beneath wall-to-wall banners. In the center aisle, a young man used an unwieldy buffer to wax the floor, solemnly repeating the phrase "Slippery, slippery," though there were no customers anywhere near him. A man I pegged as the manager—prematurely bald, prematurely overweight—stood behind the counter, hiking his pants up sharply, as if that was the most aggressive act he would attempt all day. On the other side of the counter stood a young, square-jawed guy, smiling broadly, arranging point-of-purchase promotional materials. He had the too-handsome, dim-bulb look of a factory rep, *Triumph of the Will* in a navy blue suit. Out of the corner of my eye, I saw a little guy shoot out of the stockroom and head in my direction, his hand extended all the way out, his hip-on-the-cheap clothing drooping everywhere on his skinny frame.

"And how are we doin' today?" he said as he reached me, his hand still out.

I shook it and said, "Waiting on McGinnes."

"Anything I can do for you while you're waiting?"

"No thanks."

"Well, if you have any questions about a major appliance—"

"The name is Donny," I said.

Donny smiled a little strangely and I smiled back. He scratched his ratty 'fro and walked back down the aisle, slinking behind the counter. I checked McGinnes: He had removed the dishwasher's wash tower—it looked exactly like a vibrator—and was making little jabbing movements with it behind the customer's back, pitching the merits of the machine to her all the while. This was for my benefit, I supposed, or maybe he was just bored. Then a young couple came through the door with buy signs practically tattooed on their foreheads—any salesman worth his salt can tell—and McGinnes excused himself to greet them.

Donny yelled across the sales floor, "Hey, Johnny, you got a call on line one. Guy wants to give you an order," and he pointed to a wall-mounted phone where a yellow light blinked clear as a beacon. McGinnes hesitated, went to take the call. Donny racewalked toward his new customers. Even before I saw McGinnes pick up the phone and make a bitter face, I knew what Donny Boy had done: gotten a dial tone and put it on hold, then used the phony bait to draw McGinnes away from the live ones coming through the door. Johnny should have known; in fact, it was one of the very first tricks he had played on me years ago.

McGinnes closed his deal, though, and Donny did not. Afterward, when I had been introduced to the boys and stood with them around the counter, there seemed to be no residual animosity coming off Johnny. Just another way to grab an up, the memory to be filed away by McGinnes under "payback," to be retrieved the next time a *yom* came walking through the door.

"So, Tim," a very serious Donny said to the factory rep. "You read about Maytag in the paper today?"

"No," Tim said, breathing through his mouth. "What about Maytag?"

"Kelvinator!" Donny said. "Get it? Kelvin...he ate 'er!" Donny cackled, slapped his own knee.

"Ha, ha, ha." Tim's laughter and the brittle smile that went with it failed to mask his contempt.

" 'Course," Donny continued, "that ain't nothin', compared with what the general did."

"What general?" Tim said, and I saw it coming.

"General Electric!" Donny said. "He was Tappan Amana, dig? Put his Hotpoint right on her Coldspot. Know what I'm sayin'?"

Tim began to turn red. McGinnes walked up to the group, a brown paper bag in his hand. He looked at me and smiled.

"You ready, Jim?" he said.

"I'm ready."

"Hold on a second," the manager said.

"What?" McGinnes said.

"I got a belch a few minutes ago," the manager said. "That's what. Customer called, said you stepped him off an advertised single-speed washer to what you claimed was a two speed—an LA three-five-nine-five."

"So?"

"An LA three-five-nine-five is a single-speed washer, too, McGinnes. You told him it had two speeds!"

"It does have two speeds," McGinnes said. "On... and off."

"Off's not a speed, McGinnes!" the manager yelled, but Johnny had already pulled me away, and the two of us were headed for the front door.

McGinnes drew a malt liquor out of the bag and popped the top. He handed the open one to me, found one for himself.

"Off is not a speed!..." The manager's voice trailed off as we pushed through the store's double glass doors.

Out in the lot, McGinnes tensed up his face. "All these complaints. I'm gonna get a sick stomach."

"Had a lot lately?"

McGinnes nodded. "This guy called this morning, all bent out of shape. Says when I sold him his refrigerator, I guaranteed him it was a nice box. And the thing's had three service calls in the last month."

"So? Did you guarantee it?"

"Hell no! I never said it was a nice box. I said it was *an icebox!* The guy just misunderstood me."

"I can't imagine how that happened, Johnny."

"The guy was a putz," McGinnes said. "You know it?"

THIRTEEN

MY FIRST DAY as a stock boy at Nutty Nathan's on Connecticut Avenue, back in 1974, I checked out this pale, speeded-out looking Irishman named Johnny McGinnes and I thought, Who *is* this guy? It didn't take too long to find out. Shortly after meeting him, I watched him volunteer to microwave the frozen dinner of a visiting district manager, and I pegged him as a brownnose. That notion was dispelled a few minutes later when I walked around the display rack and caught him hawking a wad of spit into the DM's food, his chest heaving in suppressed laughter as he carefully mixed it in. By the end of the day, I had witnessed him hit his pipe repeatedly, knock down a steady succession of beers, and swallow two suspicious-looking pills, all the time maintaining his mastery of the floor. Then, at closing time, he laid "Willie the Pimp" on the store's most expensive system, and eighty watts of Zappa were suddenly blowing through a pair of Bose 901s, and Johnny stood atop a vacuum cleaner display, playing air guitar, his bleeding red eyes closed as if in prayer. Even a sixteen-year-old stoner like me could see that Johnny McGinnes was one man who would never grow up.

"You're drinking too slow," McGinnes said, as my Dodge pushed up 95.

"*You're* not," I said. We were nearing Baltimore and the six of tall boys was almost done.

McGinnes gave the radio some volume. "Hey," he shouted, "how you like being a parent?"

I turned the volume down a notch. "I'm not a parent. A kid's parents are who raises them, and I've got nothing to do with that."

"Yeah, but"—McGinnes wiggled his eyebrows foolishly—"you gave her your seed, didn't you?"

"Yes, Johnny, I gave her my seed."

"So, what did Jackie name the boy?"

"Kent," I said, and waited for his comment.

"She named him after a cigarette?"

"It's British or something."

"Her last name's Kahn, isn't it? I thought Kahn was a Jewish name—"

"Shit, Johnny, I don't know. She liked the name, that's all."

I swigged my malt liquor. Some of it ran down my chin. I went to wipe it off and swerved a bit into another lane. Someone reprimanded me with a polite beep and I got the car back between the lines.

McGinnes said, "I don't like it."

"What?"

"The name."

"Why not?"

He raised a finger in the air, like he imagined an academic might do. "You know how kids are. I mean, the other boys, on the playground, they're gonna give him shit about it, twist it all around."

"I don't follow."

McGinnes sighed, exasperated. "You say his name's Kent, right? Nick, the other kids—well, they're gonna call him 'Cunt'!"

"Aw, come on, man..."

"Hey, look!" McGinnes said, pointing through the window excitedly. "Baltimore!"

We stopped in a bar near the stadium, split a pitcher, and watched the first two innings from there. We would have made it for the third, but we got waylaid by the kick-ass food at the concession stands inside the Yards. McGinnes and I both had half smokes smothered in kraut and mustard and two more beers before we got to our seats. By then it was the fourth and the Birds were down by two to the White Sox.

Our seats were in section 330, to the right and way up from home plate. A deaf kid sat alone in front of us, and next to him sat a solid Korean man and his two sons. The Korean ate peanuts the entire game, a mountain of shells at his feet. Behind us a red-bearded, potbellied man loudly heckled the players, with most of his choice obscenities reserved for Sid Fernandez, who that night was truly getting rocked. Near him, a couple of D.C. attorneys in polo shirts talked about how "quaint" the Bromo-Seltzer Tower looked against the open B-A skyline and how D.C. had nothing "like that." It was the kind of boneheaded conversation you heard from transient Washingtonians every time they went to Camden Yards, as if one old building set against a rather ordinary backdrop had any significance at all. Not that I had anything against this city—Baltimore was a fine town, with top-notch food and bars and good people. But Baltimore wasn't mine.

"Hey," McGinnes said, pointing to a vendor. "Let's get a pretzel, man."

"I'd love to," I said. "The trouble is, you gotta put mustard on a pretzel, and I had too much mustard on my half smoke. I feel like it and I don't feel like it, you know what I mean?"

"A couple more beers, then." McGinnes whistled at a guy coming up the steps with a tray of them.

We drank those, and another round, and then it was the sixth. The Sox were taking off behind their suddenly hot bats and the awesome heat coming from Jack McDowell on the mound. McDowell's goateed photograph was up on the telescreen, and McGinnes gestured to it with his head.

"What's with the goatee action?" McGinnes said, loud and a little drunk. "McDowell looks like a Chink! Like he ought to be servin' us dinner and shit."

The Korean looked at McGinnes out of the corner of his eyes and cracked a peanut shell between two thick fingers.

"Johnny, keep it down."

"What," McGinnes said, nodding to the deaf kid, "am I bothering him or somethin'?"

"Listen," I said, changing the subject. "I've got something going on tomorrow, an acting job, for you and a buddy, if you're interested."

"Oh yeah? What's it about?"

After I briefed him, I said, "How about your boy Donny? Think he can handle it?"

"That guy *is* an actor. Sure, it gets on my nerves, I got to listen to him run his cocksucker all day long. But he's all right. Good salesman, too."

"Set it up, then," I said.

McGinnes nodded, then stared sadly at the hot-pretzel man, who was moving our way once again.

"If you want one," I said, "just get one."

"No, that's okay."

"Then what's the problem?"

McGinnes said, "I put too much mustard on my half smoke, too."

McDowell retired the side, three up, three down. We left in the eighth, when the stadium stopped selling booze.

At a liquor store outside the Yards, we stopped for another six, then drank it on the drive back to D.C. McGinnes talked about his girlfriend, Carmelita, and about his "spot" of TB and how the doctors had treated it with INH, which he had taken every morning for a year. Then McGinnes told a very funny joke about an Indian named Two Dogs Fucking, and about that time we killed our last beer and crossed over into PG County. I dropped him at his car in Beltsville, then drove to my apartment, where I fed the cat and paced around listening to records, too drunk to have the sense to go to bed but not drunk enough to pass out. I called Lyla, but she wasn't in, so I left a message on her machine. I thought of Joe Martinson, rang him up.

"Hello."

"Hey, Joe—'Where you goin' with that gun in your hand?'"

"Nick!"

"Thought you might be up for some music."

"I might."

"Snake Pit?"

"Sounds good."

"Meet you in there in a half hour or so."

"Who's playing?"

"What difference does it make, right?"

The Mekons were playing, and the place was jammed. The band had been around forever, but it had still managed to retain its indie status, so the crowd was a mixture of young introductees and veterans like Joe and I. I grabbed two Buds at the door bar and pushed my way back to the right corner of the stage, my usual spot. Joe found me in midset, guitars flailing against the saw of a fiddle, the band just pushing it all the way out, and that's where we stayed until the end of the first show. The Snake Pit can be a drag with its put-on attitude, but on hot summer nights, when the acts are really cooking and the place is drowned in music and sweat, there's still nothing better in D.C.

Out on F, I stumbled into the alley a few doors down from the club to urinate, Martinson filing in behind me, laughing. A lighted office building rose out of the darkness ahead, cutting the symmetry of the brick walls running at my side. I looked into the alley, where rats moved about in the shadows of several green Dumpsters. The picture was odd but strangely beautiful. A smile of relief spread across my face as I stood there, peeing on the stones, and I thought, You know, I really do love this fucking town.

JOE AND I GOT into my Dodge and headed west. Joe found some pot in my glove box and dropped a bud onto the hot end of the lighter from my dash. We took turns snorting the smoke. I pushed a Stereolab tape into the deck and boosted the bass, and we tripped on that as we made our way across town, drinking a couple of beers we had smuggled out of the club. I found a place to park on U at 16th—had to piss again. Did it right on the street.

"Hey, ladies," Joe screamed at some women passing by. "This here is my friend, Nick Stefanos."

Black.

I sat at the full bar at Rio Loco's, Joe Martinson on the stool to my right. There was a bottle of beer in front of me, a shot of bourbon next to that, and a cigarette burning in the ashtray. I sampled all three. A floor waitress I knew, on the heavy side, real sweet, with missile tits and a plain-Elaine face, came by and smiled, and we exchanged a few smart sentences. She drifted, and Joe tapped his bottle against mine.

"I thinks she digs you, man," Joe said.

"Yeah, sure."

"I know she does. What's her name?"

"I think it's Lynn," I said. Or was it Linda?

Joe swigged from his beer. "One thing about you, Stefanos. I wanna get fucked up, I can hook up with you anytime. I know you're never gonna disappoint me, man. With you, it's like it's still 1980. One thing's for sure, I couldn't run with you all the time."

"Yep."

"Okay, so..." Martinson leaned in. "Best tracks, 1990s."

"Best tracks, huh?" I tried to concentrate against the bar noise and the zydeco jump coming from the juke.

"I'll start," Martinson said. "'Get Me'—Dinosaur Jr."

I hit my cigarette. "Dinosaur Jr.? Who does he think he is, Frank Marino or somethin'? You smoke too much weed, Joe."

"Listen to it some time—the kid Mascis can really fuckin' play."

"Okay," I said. "'Summer Babe.' Pavement."

Joe smiled. "'Chapel Hill.' Sonic Youth."

"'Instrument,'" I said. "Fugazi." On that one, Martinson slapped me five.

"Desert island LP," said Joe. "If you had to pick one, what would it be?"

"'Let It Be,'" I said without hesitation.

"The Beatles?" he said, screwing up his face.

"Fuck the Beatles!" I said. "I'm talkin' 'bout the Replacements!"

Joe laughed. I reached for my drink. A lot of time passed, or maybe it did not. I looked to my right, and Martinson was gone. A couple of white boys wearing baseball caps were sitting a few stools down. One of them was looking at me and laughing.

Black.

I sat at a deuce under the harsh lights of last call. Lynn or was it Linda? sat in the chair across the table. She raised her shot glass, tapped it against mine, and smiled. I closed my eyes and drank my goddamned whiskey.

Black.

The sound of an engine turning over, streetlights and laughter and double white lines.

Black.

I was standing in an unfamiliar apartment.

"Where are we?" I said.

"My place," said Lynn or was it Linda? "Adams Morgan."

"What about my car?"

"Out on Belmont," she said with a laugh. "And by the way, you drove great."

I stood in a living room, where a long-haired girl and a long-haired guy were sitting on a couch, cleaning pot in the lid of a shoe box. A singer wailed over some very druggy guitar.

"So what are we listenin' to?" I said to the guy.

"Smashin' Pumpkins," the guy said.

"I want to listen to this kinda shit, I'll dig out some old Sabbath albums. 'Masters of Reality' maybe."

"Yeah?" the guy said. "Well, you had your day, didn't you? Anyhow, your girlfriend's waitin' for you, ace." He and the long-haired girl laughed.

I found my girlfriend in the bedroom, lying on a floor mattress, nude above the waist, her hands locked behind her head. The room was lit by candles, and a stick of incense burned by the bed. I climbed out of my shorts clumsily and pulled my T-shirt over my head.

"I didn't bring anything," I said.

"That's not what I had in mind," she said, pushing her huge breasts together until there was a tight tunnel formed between them. "Come here, Nick."

I straddled her chest and gave her the pearl necklace she was looking for. Our shadows slashed across the wall in the dancing light.

Black.

THE ROOM WAS DARK. Through the slots in the curtains, I could see that the sky had not yet begun to turn. I rose and sat naked on the edge of the bed, listened to the steady snore of the woman next to me, waited for my eyes to adjust to the absence of light. I made my way to the bathroom, put my mouth under the faucet, and drank water until I thought I would be sick. I took a shower, scrubbing my genitals and fingers until I was certain that her smell was gone, then dried off and found my clothes lying in a heap by the bed. I dressed in the light of the bathroom and left the room.

Out on the stoop of her apartment building, I looked down the slope of Belmont, saw my car parked at the bottom of the street. My stomach flipped and I took a seat on a step. I leaned my head against a black iron railing and closed my eyes. A woman and a man argued violently in Spanish not very far away.

Black.

I woke up behind the wheel of my car. My keys were in my hand. The windows were rolled up and the heat was hideous, my hair and clothing wet with the smell of alcohol and nicotine. I turned the ignition and drove northeast into Shepherd Park.

I entered my apartment and looked into my room. Lyla slept in my bed. I fed my cat, took another cold shower, and got under the covers, turning onto my side. Lyla moved herself against me and draped a forearm over my shoulder, brushing her fingers across my chest.

"You okay?" she said drowsily.

"I'm fine."

"I was worried about you."

"I'm here now, baby. Relax."

She drifted off, holding me. I fell to sleep knowing we were done.

FOURTEEN

I SLEPT UNTIL noon and woke with a head full of dust and a stomach full of rocks. Lyla had gone, left some chocolate kisses on top of a note in the kitchen. The note said that she'd call me later and that she loved me.

I ate the chocolate out on my stoop, where I drank the day's first cup of coffee and sat with the worn copy of *D.C. This Week* spread open between my feet. My cat rolled on the grass in the high sun. The phone rang inside my apartment. I went back into the living room and picked it up.

"Nick!"

"LaDuke."

"You sound like you just woke up."

"I'm just sitting here, going through the classifieds in the newspaper. One of the two we found at Calvin's and Roland's."

"Anything?"

"Uh-uh. A few ads, escort services specializing in young

black males, that kind of thing. They could be solicitations for prostitution, but, I don't know, there's more than a few of them, and to me they look too organized, too legit."

"Maybe you're looking in the wrong place," LaDuke said.

"Say what?"

"You're assuming that Calvin and Roland were using the personals to sell themselves, maybe set up prospective johns for some sort of roll. Right?"

"That's what I was looking for, yeah."

"Well, I've been thinking about it—maybe our boys were the buyers, not the sellers. Maybe they read an ad in there, got themselves hooked up as actors in this porno thing."

I pushed my coffee cup around on the table. "You know, Jack, you might not be as dim as you look."

"If that's some kind of compliment, then I guess I better take it."

"You pick me up at my place?"

"In an hour," he said. "Look presentable, okay?"

"Sure thing, Boy Scout. See you then."

After several forced sets of push-ups and sit-ups, I took a long, cold shower. I didn't feel much better, but I felt human. LaDuke swung by right on the button, and I went out to meet him with one of the newspaper copies in my hand. I got into the passenger side of the big Ford and dropped the tabloid on the seat between us. LaDuke wore a starched white shirt with a solid black tie. He had shined his thick black oxfords, the only shoes I had ever seen on his feet. I nodded at the newspaper on the seat.

"Good call," I said. "I was looking in 'Adult Services,' when I should have been looking under 'Wanted.' I found a couple of items in there...could be something. One's a photographer looking for healthy young black males to pose nude. The other one's got a local filmmaker looking for young African-American males for his next production."

"Might be a winner," LaDuke said.

"We'll check it out later," I said. "Let's go."

LaDuke looked me over. "You look like hell, you know it?"

"Thanks for the observation."

"You ought to slow it down a little, Nick."

"Just turn this piece of shit over," I said. "We gotta go pick up Darnell."

At the Spot, Darnell was finishing his load of lunch dishes, so LaDuke and I had a seat at the bar. Boyle sat alone, a beer and a Jack in front of him, two stools away from Mel, who softly sang along to the Stylistics coming from the deck. I ordered a quick beer from Mai, just to steady my hands. It worked. Mai put an ice water on the bar, and I chased the beer with that. LaDuke got up and went to talk to Anna, who was cleaning her tables in the other room. Boyle looked down the bar in my direction.

"Who's your friend?" he said.

"Guy's name is LaDuke," I said.

"I knew that," Boyle said. "Johnson's been talking to Shareen Lewis. She told him all about him—and you."

"So why'd you ask?"

"Just wanted to see how deep you'd go in your lies, Nick. You keep playing me, tellin' me you've got nothing on the case. But you and Boy Detective over there are working on some kind of angle, am I right?"

"I said I'd square it with you when I had something concrete."

"Sure you will."

"How about you? Johnson get any more evidence that Roland and Calvin were moving drugs?"

"I'm done feeding you information," Boyle said. "You're on your own."

"Okay," I said. "Okay."

Darnell came out of the kitchen, rubbing his hands dry on a rag. I left a few bucks for Mai and got LaDuke's attention. He said good-bye to Anna and tossed Darnell the keys to the Ford. The three of us went out the door.

* * *

DARNELL PARKED NEAR THE entrance to Goode's White Goods, and soon afterward McGinnes came goose-stepping out into the lot. He got into the back with LaDuke, introduced himself, said hello to Darnell. Darnell, his hands on the wheel, gave McGinnes an amused smile.

"Where's Donny?" I said.

"He'll be along," McGinnes said, and just as he got the words out, Donny came through the double glass doors. He was wearing some sort of green double-knit slacks and two-inch heeled shoes, with a green shirt and green tie combo to complete the hookup.

"I remember this movie," Darnell said, "when I was a kid. Had Sammy Davis, Jr., in it, playing some cavalry guy, like Sammy was supposed to be Gunga Din and shit."

"*Sergeants Three*," I said.

"With all this green this cat's wearin'," Darnell said, "kind of reminds me of Sammy, tryin' to be Robin Hood."

"Donny's all right," McGinnes said.

Darnell said, "Must be one of those Baltimore brothers, with those threads and shit."

"Here," McGinnes said, passing a few spansules over the front seat, pressing them into my hand. "Eat one of these, man. It'll do you right."

"What is it?"

"Make you go, Jim," McGinnes said.

"Maybe later." I stashed the speed in my pocket.

Donny got in the car, next to McGinnes in the backseat. He shook hands with everyone, gave Darnell a different shake than he gave everyone else. Darnell rolled his eyes and put the Ford in gear.

On the way to the Hot Plate, I gave everyone some background and general instructions. I wasn't worried about McGinnes—I knew he would pick up on the rhythms once we got started. LaDuke sat quietly next to the open window while McGinnes and Donny bantered verbally over who would play what roles when the time came.

"Listen," I said, "we're all supposed to be equal, management-wise—that's the whole point of this thing. This Bernie guy, he likes to feel like he's being courted by a bunch of execs, get it?"

"I get it," Donny said. "But I ain't never run down this kind of game before. Understand what I'm sayin'?"

"Hey, Donny, if you're not comfortable—"

"I'll be all right. It's just that, you know, I don't want anybody thinkin' I'm some kind of *punk*. See what I'm sayin'?"

"We're just businessmen selling this stuff," I said. "So relax."

" 'Cause I ain't no punk," Donny said, unable to give it up. "I ain't never had nothin' back there didn't belong back there. Fact is, I'm so tight, it hurts me to fart."

"Shit," Darnell mumbled.

"Now, women?" Donny continued, moving forward and leaning his arms on the front seat. "I *get* me some women. Had me this girl last night, this freak from Dundalk?"

"Told you he was from Baltimore," Darnell said.

"Anyway," Donny said, "in the beginning, this freak didn't want to come over to my place, on account of I'm on the... slight side. Maybe she thought that meant I was light in other ways, too. See what I'm sayin'? But when I unspooled that motherfucker"—and here Donny imitated the sound of a line being cast—"the freak says, 'Goddamn, Donny, where'd a little man like you get so much dick?' "

"Step on it," LaDuke said, "will you, Darnell?" Darnell gave the Ford some gas.

THE ONLY SIGN OUTSIDE the Hot Plate said NEWSPAPERS, MAGAZINES, BOOKS. The address, however, jibed with the one given to me by Gerry Abromowitz, so Darnell parked the car on K. We left him sitting behind the wheel, reading a paperback on the teachings of Islam, and went inside the shop.

The first section of the store featured racks of daily

newspapers and magazines, weeklies and monthlies, all of the legitimate variety. The clerk behind the counter did not so much as look up when we entered. We went through another open door, into a considerably livelier and more populated section where the real business was being conducted.

A couple of employees—one skinny, one fat, there never seemed to be middle physical ground in places like these—were ringing up sales and keeping an eye on the display floor. Donny immediately went to a rack containing shrink-wrapped magazines whose covers almost exclusively featured women with extralarge lungs. McGinnes seemed more interested in the business aspect of things, wondering aloud how the "profit pieces" were merchandised. LaDuke stood with his hands in his pockets, clearly disgusted at the sight of middle-aged men eye-searching the mags that specialized in man-boy action. Most of the activity seemed to be in that area of the store. I waited for one of the clerks to get free, the pock-faced, skinny one, and announced myself. The kid punched an in-house extension, spoke to someone on the other end, pointed to another open door, and told me we could "go on." I got everyone together and we went through to the back.

We entered a large warehouse arrangement where three men sat in an office area in front of computers, taking orders over the phone. I guessed that the mail-order end of things was Tobias's biggest number, the on-line factor a big element in the company's growth, a way for pedophiles and other pervs to home-shop and network coast to coast without fear of exposure. Progress.

Bernard Tobias stepped out from a row of shelves. He was short and dumpy, but clean, the kind of man who has a wife and kids and a house in Kemp Mill or Hillandale, complete with ashtrays stolen from Atlantic City hotels and clown prints hung on the bathroom walls. He would have told you that he was providing a service, a form of release for those "poor slobs" who "have a problem" with kids, and that maybe, just maybe, it was safer to sell a magazine to a guy who could take it home and jerk off on some boy's photograph, rather than have him out prowling the local video arcade, trying to hand quarters out to someone's son. I hadn't come here to judge him, though, only to get some information: I smiled warmly and shook his hand.

"Ron Roget," I said.

"Bernie Tobias," he said, and looked expectantly at the rest of my group.

"My associates," I said, presenting them with an elaborate swing of my hand. "Mr. Franco, Mr. Magid, and Mr. Jefferson."

The names were characters from the film *The Dirty Dozen*. After a pointless argument on the drive over—McGinnes wanted to be Jefferson, but Donny, of course, wouldn't let him—we had agreed on the aliases.

"I've heard of you guys," Bernie said, scratching his head.

"Of course you have," Donny said. "We're large."

"Follow me," Bernie said, and we all walked through the warehouse aisles to an open area that looked like a small-timer's idea of a meeting room. We took seats around a shiny oval table, with Tobias in the sole chair with arms. There was a desk near the table. Plaques of some sort hung on cinder block. A wooden shelf over the desk contained a row of trophies.

"Thank you for seeing us," I said. "I can see you're very busy."

"Business is good," Bernie said, his fingers locked and resting on his ample belly. "You say you guys are out of Philly?"

"South and Main," Donny said.

"I'd give you a card," I said, "but the truth is, we didn't come prepared for this. We're on a kind of vacation here."

"A retreat," McGinnes said.

"Down south," I said.

"Miami," LaDuke said, probably just wanting to hear his own voice.

"*South* Miami," Donny said, as if he had ever been out of the Baltimore-Washington corridor. "South Beach."

"We got a boat down there," McGinnes said.

"A yacht," said Donny.

"So," I said, "we were passing through town, heading south, and I thought I'd look you up, make an introduction."

Bernie Tobias looked at Donny and McGinnes, back at me. "What exactly is it that you and your associates do, Mr. Roget?"

"Ron," I said.

"What do you do, Ron?"

"Like I told you on the phone, we cater to the NAMBLA crowd—man-boy discipline, that sort of thing."

"In what capacity?" Bernie said.

"We're producers," I said. "We specialize in the type of product you specialize in, on the distribution end."

"And how do you know of me?"

"The network," I said mysteriously, and with a wink.

"But we ain't no punks, now," Donny said.

"It hurts him to fart," McGinnes said, giving a quick head jerk toward Donny.

Bernie Tobias looked oddly at Donny, and then the phone rang on his desk. He excused himself, got up to answer it. LaDuke and I simultaneously shot killer looks at Donny and McGinnes. Tobias raised his voice into the phone, hung it up, and returned to his seat.

"I'm sorry," he said. "I really don't have much time today. There's a lot going on."

"We won't keep you," I said. "But I just wanted to let you in on what we're doing. As far as production values go, we're doing the highest-quality videos for the broadest customer base of anyone else on this coast."

"But I'm very satisfied with what I have," Bernie said. "I deal with only a couple of suppliers. They're local, so there's never any problem in getting merchandise quickly. And they know just what I want—this discipline thing is really taking off for me right now, I'm telling you. It's legal, too—no penetration shots, no actors who are obviously underage."

"Not obviously underage," LaDuke said.

"Well, you have to know how to straddle that line, don't you?"

"Of course," LaDuke said, struggling to form a smile.

"Your suppliers," I said, "they wouldn't be the Brontman Brothers, out of Northwest, would they?" I had seen a sign for Brontman Bakers on a storefront on the way downtown.

"No," Bernie said, distracted by Donny, who had gotten out of his chair and picked up one of Tobias's trophies off the shelf. "I don't even know them. Look, Mr.—"

"Jefferson," Donny said.

"Mr. Jefferson, please put that down, it's my son's—"

"Mr. Tobias," McGinnes said, warming to it now, "you sure you're not getting your product from the Brontmans? Because I know—I *know*—that our product has ten times the value—"

"Sir," Bernie said, "I'm getting most of my product out of Southeast right now, the Buzzard Point area. Some of my stuff comes out of an apartment house in Silver Spring. I mean, I know where my product's coming from."

"We wouldn't suggest otherwise," LaDuke said. "But aside from the fact that we offer the best value for the money, we also offer a steady supply of product. New titles every two weeks."

"I've even got you there," Bernie said. "My suppliers, they shoot one night a week, deliver me new product each Saturday. I couldn't be happier with the situation I've got."

"They shoot on what night?" I said, and saw from the exasperated look on Tobias's face that I had pushed it too far.

He breathed out slowly, let his composure creep back in. "Gentlemen, I know what you're trying to do here. You're trying to pump me for information, gain some kind of competitive advantage so you can come back to me with a program. But that's not the way I do business." Tobias smiled genially. "Listen, the next time you're in town, bring some samples of your product. We'll have a look, sit down, work on some pricing. If I like what I see, who knows, maybe we'll make a deal. In the meantime, I've really got to get back to work."

"Fair enough," I said, and pushed myself up from my chair. My associates followed suit. I shook Tobias's hand.

"Thanks for your time, Mr. Tobias," I said. "We'll be in touch."

"I'm sure you will," Bernie said. "You fellows have an unusual style, by the way."

"We try," I said. "Thanks again."

LaDuke went to shake Tobias's hand. I heard a bone crack, and Tobias jerked his hand back.

"You've got a hell of a grip," Bernie said with a nervous chuckle. "That's my golf hand, you know."

"Sorry," LaDuke said. "I'm stronger than I look, I guess." He smiled, his teeth bared like a dog's. We walked from the room, leaving Tobias staring at his hand.

DARNELL DROVE US BACK to the lot of Goode's White Goods. Donny and McGinnes got out of the car, and I got out with them. The heat rose off the black asphalt of the lot. I put fire to a smoke.

"How'd I do?" Donny said. He looked shrunken in his clothes, his mouth screwed up to one side.

"You did good," I said. "When I get paid on this one, I'll send you and Johnny a little piece of it."

"At your service." Donny looked at Darnell through the open window of the Ford and said, "My brother." Darnell smiled, and Donny stepped across the parking lot, toward the double glass doors.

McGinnes said, "Told you he was all right."

"Thanks, man. Thanks for everything."

"Hey, you and me..." McGinnes shuffled his feet. "Nothing to it." He rubbed at the bridge of his nose. "By the way, No Damn Good's got an opening on the floor. Any interest? You can't keep doing this sideline thing of yours forever."

"It's not a sideline," I said. "It's what I do."

"Right," McGinnes said, unconvinced. "Just thought I'd ask."

"You wouldn't want me to take the food out of your mouth, would you?"

"Wouldn't want that."

"Take it easy, Johnny."

"You too, Jim." McGinnes grinned. "Better get my ass back inside. The little bastard's probably in there stealing all my ups."

He put his hands in his pockets and walked away, whistling through his teeth. I hit my cigarette, dropped it, and ground it under my shoe.

We dropped Darnell back at the Spot, and afterward LaDuke took me back to my place. We sat out front, the Ford idling at the curb.

"Wish we could have gotten more out of Tobias," LaDuke said.

"We got everything we could," I said. "And anyway, I think we got plenty."

"Like?"

"Just a feeling. This thing's getting ready to bust."

"You think?"

"Yeah." I put my hand on the door latch and lightly tapped his arm. "You did all right back there, you know it?"

"I'm catching on."

"I'll call you in the morning," I said. "We'll put it in gear."

"Why not tonight?"

" 'Cause I got to go see somebody right now."

"On the case?"

"No."

"What, then?"

"Look, LaDuke, you don't have to worry. I'm not gonna leave you behind. We're partners, right?"

LaDuke smiled, sat a little straighter behind the wheel. I got out of the car, rapped the roof with my knuckles, and walked toward my apartment as he pulled out from the curb. Some electric guitar and a screaming vocal cut the quiet of the early-evening air. If I hadn't known better, I would have sworn LaDuke had turned his car radio on, and was playing it loud as he drove away.

FIFTEEN

MY UNCLE COSTA is not my uncle. He is not my father's brother, or my grandfather's, or a distant cousin, and I'm fairly certain that there is none of his blood running through my veins. But to Greeks, this is a minor detail. Costa is as much a part of my family as any man can be.

Ten years younger than my grandfather, Big Nick Stefanos, Costa came to this country from a village outside Sparta. Though I've not confirmed it, it's been said that Costa killed his sister's groom over a dowry dispute the night after their wedding and then left Greece the following day. He worked for many years as a grille man in my grandfather's coffee shop downtown and lived above it in a small apartment with his wife, Toula. In the forties, my grandfather hit the number in a big way and staked Costa in his own store, a lunch counter on 8th and K.

Children tend to force assimilation in their immigrant parents, and as Costa and Toula were childless, Costa never fully embraced the American culture. But he loved his adopted country as much as any native-born, and he was especially enamored of the opportunities available for men who had the desire to work. Fiercely loyal to my grandfather, he remained friends with him until Big Nick's death. I saw Costa on holidays after that and spoke to him on the phone several times a year. The last time he phoned, it was to tell me that he had cancer and had only a short time to live.

The beer in my hand wouldn't help Costa, but it would make it easier for me to look at him. I sat in my car on Randolph Street, off 13th, in front of Costa's brick row house. When I had taken the last swig, I crushed the can and tossed it over my shoulder behind the seat. I locked my car and took the steps up to his concrete porch, where I rang the bell. The door opened, and a handsome, heavy-hipped woman stood in the frame.

"Nick Stefanos. I'm here to see my uncle."

"Come on in."

I entered the small foyer at the base of the stairs. The air was still, as it always was in Costa's house, but added to the stillness now was the distinct stench of human excrement. The nurse closed the door behind me and caught the look on my face.

"He's nearly incontinent," she said. "He has been for some time."

"That smell."

"I do the best I can."

I could hear Costa's voice, calling from his bedroom up the stairs. He was speaking in Greek, saying that his stomach was upset, asking for some ginger ale to settle it.

"He wants some soda," I said.

"I can't understand him," she said, "when he's talkin' Greek."

"I'll get it for him," I said, and moved around her.

I went to the kitchen, dark except for some gray light bleeding in from the screens of the back porch. Two cats scattered when I walked in, then one returned and rubbed against my shin as I found the ginger ale and poured it into a glass. There were probably a dozen cats around the house, on the porch or in the dining room or down in the basement. Generations of them had lived here and out in the alley; Costa collected them like children.

The nurse sat in a chair in the foyer as I walked out of the kitchen. She fumbled in her pack for a cigarette. I struck a match and gave her a light.

"Thanks."

"I'll just go on up," I said.

"There's a metal cup by the bed. He probably needs to urinate. You might want to help him out. He won't wear those panties from the hospital. You know I tried—"

"I'll take care of it."

I went up the stairs, made an abrupt turn on the narrow landing, and entered his room. Several icons hung on florid, yellowed wallpaper and a candle burned in a red glass holder next to the door. A window-unit air conditioner set on low produced the only sound in the room. Costa was in his bed, underneath the sheets. Even though he was covered, I could see that he had atrophied to the size of a boy.

"Niko," he said.

"Theo Costa."

I pulled a chair up next to the bed and had a seat. With my help, he managed to sit up, leaning on one knotty elbow. I put the glass to his lips and tilted it. His Adam's apple bobbed as he closed his eyes and drank.

"Ah," he said, his head falling back to the pillow, two bulged yellow eyes staring at the ceiling.

"You gotta take a leak now?"

"Okay."

I found the metal cup on the nightstand, pulled back the covers on the bed. He couldn't have weighed more than a hundred pounds. Pustulated bedsores ringed the sides of his legs and the sagging flesh of his buttocks. Freshly scrubbed patches of brown, the remnants of his own waste, stained the bed. I took his uncircumcised penis in my hand and laid the head of it inside the lip of the cup. Costa relaxed his muscles and filled the cup.

"Goddamn," he said. "That's good."

I put the cup back on the nightstand and pulled the covers over his chest. He left his arms out and took my hand. The American flag tattoo on his painfully thin forearm had faded to little more than a bruise.

"Does it hurt much?" I said.

Costa blinked. "It hurts pretty good."

"That nurse taking care of you?"

"She's all right. Now, the one before, the other one?" He made a small sweep of his hand, as if the hand had kicked her ass out the door. "But this one, she's okay. Has two kids; she's raising them by herself. She's a hard worker. This one, she's okay." Costa licked his blistered lips.

"You want some more ginger ale?"

"I'd like a real goddamn drink, that's what. But I can't. It hurts, after."

"I'll get you one if you want."

"So you can have one, too, eh?"

"What do you mean?"

"You been drinkin' already. I can smell it on you."

"I had a beer on the way over. Can't get anything by that nose of yours."

"You got a nose on you, too, goddamn right."

He laughed, then coughed behind the laugh. I waited for him to settle down.

"You know what?" he said. "I think I had a pretty good life, Niko."

"I know you did."

"I had a good woman, worked hard, stayed here in this house, even after everyone else got scared and moved away. You know, I'm the last white man on this block."

"I know."

"I did a few bad things, Niko, but not too many."

"You talking about your brother-in-law, in Greece?"

"Ah. I don't give a damn nothing about him. No, I mean here, in the old days, with your *papou*, before you were born. We got into some trouble, had a gunfight with some guys. Lou DiGeordano and a Greek named Peter Karras, they were with us. I was thinking of it this morning. Trying to think of the bad things I did. Trying to remember."

"What happened?"

"It doesn't matter. Your *papou*, he stopped that kind of business when you came to him. I stopped, too." Costa turned his head in my direction. "You're going to come into some money, Niko, when I go. You know it?"

"What are you talking about?"

"Your *papou*—everything he had, the money from the businesses, what he made from the real estate, everything, it's going to come to you. I've been taking care of it, just like he had it in his will. I swear on his grave, I haven't touched a goddamn penny."

"I thought it all went to his son in Greece—my father."

"*You* are your *papou's* son. He felt it, told me so many times. He always said that the best Greeks were the ones who got on the boats and came to America. It was the lazy ones that stayed behind. He thought his own son was not ready to inherit his money." Costa grimaced. "He was waiting for you to grow up a little bit before he gave it to you, that's all."

"I don't want his money," I said as a cold wave of shame washed through me.

"Sure you don't," he said. "But money makes life easier. Anyway, when the lawyers get through with it, and Uncle Sam, there's not going to be much left, believe me. So take it. It's what he wanted."

Costa sucked air in sharply and arched his back. I squeezed his hand. He breathed out slowly, then relaxed.

"You better get some rest," I said.

"I got plenty time to rest," he said.

"Go to sleep, Theo Costa."

"Niko?"

"Sir?"

"Enjoy yourself, boy. I can remember the day I stepped off the boat onto Ellis Island. I can still smell it, like I stepped off that boat this morning. It's like I blinked my eyes and now I'm old. It goes, Niko. It goes too goddamn fast."

He closed his eyes. Slowly, his breathing became more regular. Some time later, his hand relaxed in mine and he fell to sleep. Sitting there, I found myself hoping that he would die, just then. But he wasn't ready. For whatever reason, he held on until the fall.

When the light outside the window turned from gray to black, I left the room and walked back down the stairs. I went to the dining room and found the liquor cabinet, near an ornate wall mirror covered with a blanket. Costa's nurse sat at the dining room table, smoking a cigarette. I took a bottle of five-star Metaxa and couple of glasses and had a seat across from her. I poured her a brandy, then one for me. We drank together without a word, beneath the dim light of a chandelier laced with cobwebs and already shrouded in dust.

WHEN I RETURNED TO my apartment, I saw that Lyla had left a message on my machine. I phoned her and she asked if I wanted some company. I told her that it might not be a good idea.

"What, have you got something else happening?"

"No," I said. "I'm just a little tired, that's all."

"Maybe tomorrow night, huh?"

"Tomorrow's looking kind of busy for me."

"Nick, what's going on?"

"Nothing," I said, and shifted gears. "Hey, how'd it go with your editor yesterday?"

"It went all right," she said, and then there was a fat chunk of silence.

"What happened?"

"It was about that day, after we had lunch. In Chinatown?"

"Sure."

"Well, I had a few wines that day, if you remember, and then I went back to the office and finished off this story I was working on. Usually, I wait, go back to it, check it for style and all that. But I was on a deadline, so I turned it in right after I finished it."

"And?"

"It was all fucked up, Nick. Jack gave me an earful about it, and he was right. It was really bad."

"So what's the mystery? You shouldn't be drinkin' when you're writing copy, you know that."

"That's some advice," Lyla said, "coming from a guy who stumbled in this morning after sunup and couldn't even get out of his own pants."

"That's me, baby. It doesn't have to be you."

"Anyway, Jack hit me right between the eyes with it. Said I drink too much, that maybe I've got a problem. What do you think?"

"You said yourself, I'm not the one to ask. All's I know, you wanted to be a journalist since you were a kid. I guess you've got to figure out what you want more. I mean, fun's fun, but the days of wine and roses have to come to an end."

" 'The Days of Wine and Roses'?" she said. "The Dream Syndicate."

"That's my line," I said.

Lyla said, "Yeah, I beat you to it. I knew you were going to say it."

"It only shows, maybe you been with me too long."

"I don't think so, Nick."

"Lyla, I've really got to go."

"You sure there's nothing wrong?"

"Nothing wrong," I said. "Bye."

I had a couple of beers and went to bed. My sleep was troubled, and I woke before dawn with wide-open eyes. I dressed and drove down to the river, looking for a crazy black man in a brilliant blue coat. Nothing. I watched the sun rise, then drove back to Shepherd Park.

After I made coffee, I phoned Jack LaDuke.

"LaDuke!"

"Nick!"

"Get over here, man. Early start today."

"Half hour," he said, and hung up the phone.

I found my Browning Hi-Power, wrapped in cloth in the bottom of my dresser. I cleaned and oiled it, loaded two magazines, and replaced the gun in the drawer. Just as I closed the drawer, LaDuke knocked on my front door.

SIXTEEN

"NOTHIN'!" LADUKE SAID as he hung up the phone in my apartment.

We had just called the first prospect from the classified section of *D.C. This Week*. LaDuke had done the talking, and he had put too much into it in my opinion, his idea of some swish actor.

"What'd he say?"

"Guy turned out to be legit. Some professor at Howard, doing a theatrical feature on street violence in D.C., trying to show the 'other side,' whatever that means. He was looking for young blacks males to play high school athletes sidetracked by drugs."

"All right, don't get discouraged; we've got another one here."

LaDuke put his hand on the phone. "What's the number?"

"Uh-uh," I said. "I'm doin' this one."

I checked the number in the ad—this was the photographer, in search of healthy young black males—and pulled the phone over my way. My cat jumped up onto my lap as I punched the number into the grid.

"Yes?" said an oldish man with a faintly musical lilt in his voice.

"Hi," I said. "I'm calling about an ad I saw in *D.C. This Week*, about some photography you were doing?"

"That's a pretty old ad."

"I was at a friend's place; he had a back issue lying around. I was browsing through it—"

"And you don't sound like a young black male."

"I'm not. But I *am* healthy. And I've done some modeling, and a little acting. I was wondering if you were exclusive with this black thing."

The man didn't answer. Another voice, stronger, asked him a question in the background, and he put his hand over the receiver. Then he came back on the line.

"Listen," he said. "We're not doing still photography here, not really. I mean, you got any idea of what I'm looking for?"

"Yes," I said. "I think I know what you're doing."

"How. *How* do you know?"

"Well, I just assumed from the ad—"

"An assumption won't get you in. And like I said, that's an old ad. You have a reference?"

"I'd rather not say."

"If you know what's going on, then someone referred you. No reference, no audition." I didn't respond. The man said, "If you've got no reference, this conversation's over."

I took a shot. "Eddie Colorado," I said, then waited.

"Okay," the man said. "You come by tonight, we'll have a look at you."

"I don't think I can make it tonight."

"Then forget it, for now. We're shooting tonight, and we only shoot once a week."

"I'll be there," I said. "I'll make it somehow. You're down in Southeast, right?"

"That's right. A warehouse, on the corner of Potomac and Half. The gate looks locked, but it's not. What's your name?"

"Bobby," I said, picking one blindly. "What time?"

"No time. We'll be here all night." The phone clicked dead.

I looked somberly at LaDuke. Then I broke into a smile and slapped his open palm.

"You got something?" he said, standing up abruptly from his chair.

"Yeah. Get your shit, LaDuke. We're going for a ride."

"WHY'D YOU HAVE THE smarts to mention Eddie Colorado?" LaDuke said. We were driving east on M in my Dodge, the morning sun blasting through the windshield. The wind was pushing LaDuke's wavy hair around on top of his square head.

"No other option," I said. "He asked for a reference, and that's the only name that fits with Roland and Calvin. It was a lucky call. Apparently, Eddie's referring potential movie stars to this guy, whoever he is. Eddie's been siphoning it off from both ends."

"Eddie. That mother*fucker*. I'd like to go back there and fuck him up, too."

"Relax, LaDuke. Guys like Eddie dry up and blow away. We've got to concentrate on Roland now."

"You think this is it?"

"Too many other things are falling into place. Bernie Tobias talked about the Southeast location and the-one-night-a-week shoot. This guy I just talked to on the phone, he confirmed it."

"Where we going?"

"Check the place out."

"We goin' in right now?"

"No. Chances are, even if this is the place, Roland's not there yet. I want to see it, then we're gonna find out who owns the warehouse, see if he's got any information on his tenants."

I put a cigarette to my lips, hit the lighter. LaDuke, nervous as a cat, nodded at the pack on the dash.

"Give me one of those things," he said.

"You really want one?"

"Nah," he said. "I guess not."

Past the projects, we cut a right off M and went back into the warehouse district that sits on a flat piece of dusty land between Fort McNair and the Navy Yard. It was midmorning. Trucks worked gravel pits, drivers pulled their rigs up to loading docks, and government types drove their motor-pool sedans back toward Buzzard Point. In the daytime, this area of town was as populated and busy as any other; at night, there was no part of the city more deathly quiet or dark.

"That's it," LaDuke said, and I parked along a high chain-link fence where Potomac Avenue cut diagonally across Half.

The warehouse was squat, brick, and windowless, as undistinguishable from any of the others I had seen on the way in. A double row of barbed wire was strung around the perimeter, continuing at a sliding gate. One car, a Buick Le Sabre, sat parked inside the gate. Across the street was an almost identical building, similarly fenced and wired, with windows only at two fire escapes set on opposing faces. In front of that one, two white vans were parked, advertising LIGHTING AND EQUIPMENT. Next to this warehouse stood a lot containing a conical structure, some sort of urban silo, and an idling dump truck.

"What do you think?" LaDuke said, pointing his chin toward the warehouse where the Buick sat parked.

"That's it," I said. "We know where it is now, and it's not going anywhere. We'll come back tonight."

"Lot of activity around here."

"Not at night. Used to be a couple of nightclubs, ten, fifteen years back, that jumped pretty good. But nothing now." I pushed the trans into drive.

"Where now?" LaDuke said.

"Office of Deeds," I said. "We find out who collects the rent."

* * *

THE OFFICE OF THE Recorder of Deeds sat around 5th and D, near Judiciary Square, the area of town that contained the city's courts and administrative facilities. The building has a funny old elevator that doesn't quite make it to the top floors; to get to where the records are kept, you have to get off the lift and take the stairs the rest of the way. LaDuke and I did it.

There was one disinterested woman working a long line, but I was lucky to see a bar customer of mine, a real estate attorney by the name of Durkin, sitting in a wooden chair, waiting for his number to be called. He also had a copy of the *Lusk's Directory*, a crisscross land reference guide, in his lap. I borrowed it from him and promised him a free warm Guinness Stout—his drink—the next time he was by the Spot. Durkin tipped the fedora that he wore even indoors and gave me the book. By the time my microfiche had been retrieved from the files, I knew enough with the help of the *Lusk's* to have the name of the landlord who owned the warehouse at Potomac and Half. The name was Richard Samuels.

From there, it wasn't a stretch to get an address and phone. If Samuels was like every minimogul/land baron I've met, he could not have resisted putting his name on his own company. He would have told you the ID made good business sense, but it was as much ego as anything else. And his name *was* on the company—Samuels Properties was listed in the first phone book we hunted down, right outside the District Building; the address matched that printed on the deed. LaDuke flipped me a quarter and I rang him up.

"Samuels Properties," said the old lady's voice on the other end.

"Metropolitan Police," I said, "calling for Richard Samuels." LaDuke shook his head and rolled his eyes.

"Let me see if he's on the line." She put me on hold, came

back quickly. "If this is about the fund-raising drive, Mr. Samuels has already sent the check—"

"Tell him it's about his property at Potomac and Half."

"Hold on." More waiting, then: "I'll put you through."

Another voice, deep and rich, came on the line. "Yes, how may I help you?"

"My name is Nick Stefanos—"

"Officer Stefanos?"

"No."

"You're not a cop?"

"Private."

"Well, then, you've misrepresented yourself. I guess we have nothing to talk about."

"I think we do. You might be interested in some activity going on in your property on Half Street in Southeast. And if you're not interested, maybe Vice—"

"Vice?" His tone lost its edge. "Listen, Mr. Stefanos, I'm certainly not aware of any illegal activities, not on Half Street or on any of my properties. But I am interested, and I'm willing to listen to what you've got to say."

"My partner and I would like to see you this morning. The conversation would be confidential, of course."

"That would be fine," Samuels said. He confirmed the address.

"We'll be right over," I said, and hung up the phone.

LaDuke scrunched up his face. "You identified yourself as a cop, Nick. This guy Emmanual—"

"It's *Samuels.*"

"He could turn us in."

"Come on, LaDuke. We're standing at the door. Let's go see what the man's got to say."

THE OFFICE OF SAMUELS Properties was on a street of commercially zoned row houses just north of Washington Circle, in the

West End. We parked the Dodge in a lot owned by Blackie Auger, one of D.C.'s most visible Greeks, and walked to the house. Samuels's office was on the second floor, up a curving line of block steps.

We had expected the geriatric receptionist, but it was Samuels himself who answered the door. He looked to be reasonably fit, a thin, silver-haired man at the very end of his middle years, with prosperity—or the illusion of it—apparent in every thread of his clothes. He wore a nonvented Italian-cut suit over a powder blue shirt with a white spread collar, and a maroon tie featuring subtle geometrics, gray parallelograms shaded in blue to pick up the blue off the suit. His face was long, sharply featured, and angular, except for his lips, which were thick and damp and oddly red, reminding me somehow of a thinly sliced strawberry.

"Mr. Stefanos?" he said in that fine brandy baritone.

"Yes. My partner, Jack LaDuke." The two of them shook hands.

"Please, come in."

We followed him through the reception area, low-lit and deeply carpeted, with stained wood trim framing Williamsburg blue walls. Next was his office, the same cozy deal, but with a bigger desk, walls painted a leafy green, and a window view that gave onto the street. LaDuke and I sat in two armchairs he had arranged in front of his desk. Samuels had a seat in his cushioned broad-backed chair and wrapped his hand around a thick Mont Blanc pen.

"You're all alone," I said.

"Yes," he said. "My receptionist is taking lunch. For one hour each day, I field my own calls."

"It's just the two of you here?"

"It hasn't always been this way. I had a staff of six at one time, including my own in-house real estate attorney. But that was the eighties. And the eighties are over, Mr. Stefanos. The banks went through some tremendous changes near the end of the decade, as you know. When the flow of money stopped, everything stopped—all the growth. But this is a cyclical business that, by definition, adjusts itself. There are signs that the residential is coming back, and the commercial will naturally follow."

"Of course," I said, though I didn't have a clue. LaDuke had tented his hands, his elbows on the arms of his chair, and he was tapping both sets of fingers together at the tips.

"So how can I help you?" Samuels said.

"I'm working on a murder investigation," I said. "As I mentioned to you on the phone, I've been privately retained. Through a series of interviews—I won't bore you with the details—I've come to believe that there might be some criminal activity going on in your warehouse property at Potomac and Half."

"You mentioned that it might be related to Vice."

"For starters. I suspect pornography involving male minors. That kind of business is usually tied to something else."

Samuels frowned. "Let me say first that I'm not cognizant of any such activity in any of my properties. If what you're claiming is a reality, however, it disturbs me. It disturbs me a great deal. You can never anticipate this kind of thing, not totally. All my potential tenants are interviewed, but as long as the rent checks arrive in a reasonably timely manner and there are no major physical problems with the property, you lose touch. Often a tenant will sublet without my knowledge and—"

"We'd like to get in," LaDuke said sharply.

Samuels kept his dignity and his eyes on me. "I pulled the file after you called, Mr. Stefanos." He fingered the edges of some papers on his desk. "The tenants on the lease are using the area both as a silk-screen production house for T-shirts and as a storage facility."

"Would it be possible to get in there and talk to them?"

"Mr. Stefanos, in my business, in any business, in fact, control is very important. If I could both own these properties and run my own profit centers out of them—in other words, if I could control every aspect in the chain, all the way down the line—believe me, I'd do it. But unfortunately, I can't. So essentially I'm in a partnership arrangement with my tenants, for better or worse. And I have to honor that partnership. So you can see why I just can't let you in there, willy-nilly, on the basis of some unsubstantiated accusation."

"But you also wouldn't want the inconvenience, and publicity, of an official police intervention."

Samuels said, "And neither would you. You say you're privately retained—if the cops, in effect, solve whatever it is you're working on, wouldn't that essentially make you unemployed?"

"We're talking about boys," LaDuke said with obvious impatience. "They're being forced against their will—"

"Hold on a second," Samuels said, his voice rising. He turned a framed photograph around on his desk so that it faced LaDuke. In the frame was a family picture—the businessman's favorite prop—of Samuels, his wife, and two children, a teenaged boy and girl. Samuels regained his composure. "You see this? I'm a father, young man. Now, I didn't say I wouldn't help you. I'm only saying that we have to do this properly. Do you understand?"

LaDuke didn't answer. I said, "What did you have in mind?"

"I'm going to speak to my attorney this afternoon. We'll see how we can work this out. I'm thinking maybe by tomorrow, we'll be able to get you in there, or at least get you some kind of answers. How can I reach you, Mr. Stefanos?"

"I'll call *you*, first thing in the morning. And thanks. I appreciate the cooperation."

We all stood then, as there was nothing else to say. Samuels showed us to the door. Out on 22nd, we walked to the Dodge.

"How'd I do?" LaDuke said.

"You gotta learn when to use the muscle and when not to. Samuels, he's not going to respond to that. He doesn't have to.

He's a developer—he probably has a relationship with every member of the city council. He could erase us, man, if we push it too hard."

"You sayin' I almost blew it?"

"You could use a little seasoning, that's all."

"You think he's gonna help us?"

"He'll help us," I said. "He's a smart man. The way I put it to him, he's got no other choice."

I drove to my apartment and cut the engine. LaDuke said that he had something to do, and I let him go. I watched his brooding face as he walked to his Ford, then I watched him drive away. Then I went inside and sorted through my mail, my cat figure-eighting my feet. The red light was blinking on my answering machine. I hit the bar.

A voice that I recognized came through the speaker: "Stefanos, this is Barry. I met you at Calvin Jeter's apartment, at his mom's? I'm the father to his sister's baby.... Anyway, I was headin' over to Theodore Roosevelt Island this afternoon. Up behind the statue, there's a trail, to the left? Down there to the end, where it comes to a T. You go straight in, on a smaller trail, down to the water, facing Georgetown. That's where I'll be. I just thought, man... I just thought you might want to talk. Like I say... *I* don't know. That's where I'll be."

I walked quickly from the apartment, the sound of the machine rewinding at my back.

SEVENTEEN

THEODORE ROOSEVELT ISLAND is a nature preserve, eighty-eight acres of swamp, forest, and marsh in the middle of the Potomac River, between Virginia and D.C. I took the GW Parkway to the main lot and parked beside Barry's Z. A couple of immigrant fisherman sat with their rods on the banks of the Little River, and a Rollerblader traversed the lot, but typical of a midweek day in midsummer, the park looked empty.

I took the footbridge over the river, then hit a trail up a grade and into the woods, to the monument terrace. I crossed the square, walking around the seventeen-foot-high bronze statue of a waving Teddy Roosevelt that sat on a high granite base, and walked over another footbridge spanning a dry moat. Then I cut left onto a wide dirt path that wound through a forest of elm, tulip, and oak and took the path down to where it met the swamp trail that perimetered the island. I stayed straight on in, toward the water. Barry was there, wearing a white T-shirt and shorts, sitting on a fallen tree, beneath a maple that had rooted at the eroded bank.

"Hey, Barry."

"Hey, man."

I sat on the log, my back against the trunk of the maple. Barry watched me as I shook a cigarette out of my deck and struck a match. I rustled the pack in his direction. He closed his eyes slowly and I put the pack away.

Across the channel, the Georgetown waterfront sprawled out, with K street running below the Whitehurst Freeway. Behind it were buildings of varying size, with the smokestack tower of the Power House rising above the skyline. To the right was the Kennedy Center; to the left, Key Bridge; and on the hill beyond, the halls of Georgetown University. Barry stared at the crew-graffitied bulkhead on the D.C. side, transfixed by it, or maybe not thinking of it at all.

"You come down here a lot?"

"Yeah," he said. "This here's my spot. Know what I'm sayin'?"

"Sure." I thought of my own place, the bridle trail off Oak Hill.

"Use to be, I'd ride my bicycle across town, come down here, when I was in junior high and shit, just look up at Georgetown U. Patrick was playin' then, and Michael Graham. I used to dream about going to Georgetown some day, playin' for Coach Thompson. 'Course, I never even thought you had to get the grades, the scores on the tests. Didn't know that shit was all decided for you, even before the first day of elementary school. Just some kind of accident, where you get born, I guess." Barry chuckled cynically to himself. "And you know what, man? I never could play no ball, anyway."

"What about now?"

"Now? I come down here just to get away. You still see some of the city on this island—the drug deal once in a while, and sometimes those sad-eyed old motherfuckers, walking around the trail, lookin' to make contact with some boy. But mostly, over here, it's clean. It makes me feel good, for a little while, anyway. And jealous, too, at the same time. I look across this river, I see the people on the freeway in their cars, and sometimes a plane goes over my head, takin' off from National—everybody but me, *goin'* somewhere."

I blew some smoke down toward the water. A breeze came off the river and picked it up. "You're not doin' so bad, Barry. You've got a steady job, and you're sticking with your family. It means something, man."

"My job. You know how I feel sometimes, workin' there, with these young drug boys comin' in, parkin' their forty-thousand-dollar shit right outside the door, makin' fun of me, of my uniform?"

"I know it can't be easy."

"Then I read the *Post,* these white liberals—so-called—talkin' about this brother, wrote this book, talkin' about how he went into some *Mac*Donald's with a gun, stuck up who he called the 'Uncle Tom' behind the counter, then went to prison, got reformed and shit, became a newspaper writer himself."

"I read about it."

"That man behind the counter, he was no Uncle Tom. He was probably some young brother like me, just tryin' to do a job, maybe pay the bills for his family or have a few dollars in his pocket to take his girl out on Saturday night. And that punk calls *him* an Uncle Tom? And those white boys at the *Post,* print that magazine they got, they be glorifyin' that shit. Makes *him* wanna holler? Man, that shit makes *me* wanna holler!"

"What you're doing," I said again, "it means something."

Barry looked in my eyes. "You really believe that tired shit, don't you?"

"I do."

"I know you do. That's why I called you up. You got this one way of lookin' at things, like it's right or it's not, and nothing in between. I guess, in my own way, that's the way I got to look at things, too. I mean, somebody's got to, right?"

I hit my cigarette hard and ground it under my shoe. "What did you want to tell me, Barry?"

Barry picked up a twig lying at his feet and snapped it in his hands. "About Calvin."

"Yeah?"

"He was mulin' powder."

I felt something twist in my stomach. "For who?"

"I don't know. But I do know this: The powder's for the white man, and the rock is for the niggas. You know it, too. Even got separate laws for that shit."

"Muling it where?"

"Into the projects, man, straight to the cookin' house."

"You got names?"

"Uh-uh," Barry said. "You?"

"No. But I found out he was involved in some other things, too. Prostitution, and pornography."

"That was Roland," Barry said hatefully. "That punk."

"Roland got him into it?"

Barry nodded, spoke quietly against the sound of the current lapping at the bank. "The man in charge, the man with the drugs—whoever he is—he favored boys. Told Roland that if he and Calvin got into this... *movie* shit, they could mule the powder for him, too. Calvin came to me—he wanted the money, man, he wanted to get out of his situation in a big way, like we all do, where we live. He didn't know about that other shit, though. Calvin wasn't no punk. Roland could do it, man, without a thought, 'cause inside he always *was* a bitch. He told Calvin, 'Just do it, man—it's only lips.' I got no thing against a man who *is* that way—understand what I'm sayin'? Matter of fact, I got this cousin like that, over in Northwest, and the man is cool. But Calvin wasn't about that. I told him, 'Don't be lettin' no man suck your dick, not for money or for nothin', not if you don't want to.'"

"Calvin went ahead with it, though, didn't he?"

"The last time I saw him, he was scared."

"When was that?"

"The night he died. He told me they only did this shit once a week, and he had to make his mind up right then, or the mule job, and the money, was out. I told him not to go with Roland that night. He did, though. I got to believe he changed his mind, but too late. I think he tried to get out of the whole thing. And they doomed his ass because of it. They put a gun in his mouth and blew the *fuck* out of that boy."

I said, "And you don't know any more than that."

Barry said, "No."

I lit another cigarette and took my time smoking it, staring across the river. When I was done, I got up off the log and stood over Barry.

"I'm going back," I said.

"You go on," he said.

"Don't you have to work this afternoon?"

"I got a four o'clock shift."

I glanced at my watch. "You better come with me, then."

"Yeah," Barry said, smiling weakly. "Don't want to be late for work."

I put out my hand and helped him up. We took the trail back into the upland forest and walked across the island under a canopy of trees.

I BOUGHT A CAN of beer at the nearest liquor store and drank it on the way home. In my room, I drew the blinds, undressed, and lay down on my bed. I was sick-hot and tired, and my head was black with bad thoughts. I closed my eyes and tried to make things straight.

I woke up in a sweat, lying naked on top of my sheets. The fading light of dusk lined the spaces in my blinds. I took a shower, made a sandwich and ate it standing up, and changed into jeans and a loose-fitting short-sleeved shirt. I listened to my messages: Lyla and Jack LaDuke had phoned while I was asleep. I left a message with LaDuke's answering service, and ten minutes later he called me back.

"Nick!"

"LaDuke. Where you been?"

"I went looking for Eddie Colorado."

"And?"

"I found him."

I had a sip of water and placed the glass down on the table, within the lines of its own ring. "What'd you do to him, Jack?"

"We talked, that's all. I put an edge on it, though. I don't think Eddie's gonna be hanging around town too much longer."

"What'd you find out?"

"Roland Lewis is still alive, and still with them. Calvin tried to get out—that's what got him killed. They're filming tonight."

"I know it. I found out a few things, too. The porno's just a sideshow compared with their drug operation. Calvin and Roland were delivery boys. The cops have been following that angle. I'm not sure if they know anything about the warehouse on Half Street, not yet. We're one step ahead of them there, but it's a short step. They've got informants, and I imagine they're working them pretty good. So we don't have much time."

"Say it, man."

"I know we told Samuels we'd wait till tomorrow. But you and me, we've got to go in there... tonight. We've got to get Roland away from that place before the cops dig deep and bust that operation, put that kid into a system he'll never get out of. We'll get Roland out, get him back home, straighten his shit out then. You with me?"

"You know it."

"You got a gun?"

"The one I held on you that night. And more."

"Bring whatever you got."

"I'll be right over," he said.

"We're gonna need a driver," I said. "I'll call Darnell."

LaDuke said, "Right."

I phoned Darnell at the Spot. I gave him the Roland Lewis story and described the kind of trouble the kid was in.

"You interested?"

"First I got to get to these dishes, man."

"We'll pick you up around ten."

"Bring your boy's Ford," Darnell said. "I'll be standin' right out front."

I went into my room and got my Browning Hi-Power and the two loaded magazines from the bottom of my dresser. McGinnes's benny spansules were on my nightstand, next to my bed; I swept them off the top and dropped them in my pocket. The phone rang. I took the gun and ammunition back out to the living room. I picked up the receiver and heard Lyla's voice.

"Nick."

"Hey, Lyla."

"I've been calling you—"

"I know. Listen, Lyla, I've been busy. Matter of fact, I'm heading out the door right now."

"What's going on with you, Nick?"

"Nothing. I've got to go."

"You can't talk to me, not for a minute?"

"No."

"Don't do this to me, Nick. You're going to fuck up something really good."

"I've got to go."

"Bye, Nick."

"Good-bye."

I hung up the phone, closed my eyes tightly, said something out loud that even I didn't understand. When I opened my eyes, the red of LaDuke's taillights glowed through my screen door as the Ford pulled up along the curb. The clock on the wall read 9:40. I slapped a magazine into the butt of the nine, safetied the gun, and holstered it behind my back. LaDuke gave his horn a short blast. I killed the living room light and walked out to the street.

EIGHTEEN

LADUKE HAD PARKED the Ford under a dead streetlight and was standing with his backside against the car. I went to him, reached into my pocket, and pulled two of the three spansules out. I popped one into my mouth, dry-dumped it, and handed him the other.

"What's this?"

"Something to notch you up. It came from McGinnes, so it's got to be good. Eat it."

"I don't need it. I'm already wired."

"I don't need it, either. But this'll shoot us all the way through to the other end. Eat it, man."

The truth was, I did need it. And I wanted LaDuke right there with me. He looked at me curiously but swallowed the spansule.

LaDuke pushed away from the car, went to the trunk, opened it. The light inside the lid beamed across his chest. I walked over and stood next to him and looked inside. An Ithaca twelve-gauge lay on a white blanket, the edge of the blanket folded over the stock. The shotgun had been recently polished and oiled, but I could see it had been well-used; the blueing on the barrel had been rubbed down where the shooter's hand had slid along with the action of the pump.

"This ain't no turkey shoot, LaDuke."

"I know it."

"Why the Ithaca?"

"Bottom ejection. I don't need shells flyin' up in front of my eyes when I'm tryin' to make a shot."

"What, you think you got to aim that thing? For Chrissakes, just point it."

"I got something else if I want to aim."

"Put everything in the trunk and cover it. We get stopped, we're fucked."

LaDuke dropped to one knee, pulled his snub-nosed revolver from an ankle holster. In the light, I could read the words KING COBRA etched into the barrel—a .357 Colt. He dropped it on the blanket, next to the shotgun. I drew my Browning, whipped the barrel of it against the trunk light, shattered the light. We stood in darkness.

"What the hell did you do that for?" LaDuke said.

"I'll buy you a new bulb. That light was like wearing a billboard. When we get down to Southeast, it's gonna be stone-dark. We don't need the attention."

I put the Browning and the extra clip on the blanket, covered the guns, and shut the lid of the trunk.

"You coulda just unscrewed the bulb," LaDuke said.

"I wanted to break something. Come on."

WE PICKED UP DARNELL outside the Spot. He got behind the wheel, and LaDuke slid across the bench to the passenger side. I got out and climbed into the back. Darnell looked at me in the rearview and adjusted the leather kufi that sat snugly on his head.

"Where to?"

"Half Street at Potomac," I said.

"Back in there by the Navy Yard?"

"Right." I caught a silvery reflection in my side vision, a flash, or a trail. Fingers danced through my hair and something tickled behind my eyes—the familiar kick-in of the speed. Darnell pulled out from the curb.

"This Ford's got a little juice," Darnell said. "I noticed it the other day."

"A little," LaDuke said, tight-jawed now from the drug.

I lit a cigarette and drew on it deeply. "We're gonna go in like we're knocking the place over. You got that, Jack?"

"Why?"

"I'm thinking we're going to make like we're taking the kid hostage, so they think he's got nothing to do with us. They'll probably come after us. But I want to make sure they leave the kid alone."

"How're we going to get in?"

"I'm Bobby, remember? The aspiring actor. I called earlier in the day, spoke to the man in charge... like that. Assuming I get that far, you step around the corner, show your shotgun to whoever it is we're talking to, let him know what it means. After that, we'll improvise."

"Improvise?"

"You'll get into it. And... LaDuke?"

"What?"

"We get in there, don't call me by my name."

Darnell pushed the Ford down M, made a right onto Half. Off the thoroughfare, the street darkened almost immediately.

"I'm thirsty," LaDuke said quickly. "I need something to drink."

"We'll have a drink," I said. "Let's just get this done now. Then we'll drink."

"Up around there?" Darnell said.

"That's the place," I said. "Drive slow by it, then drive around the block."

The perimeter was lighted by floods. Three cars, including the Le Sabre, were parked in the surrounding lot. A heavy chain connected the gate to the main fence. As we passed, I could see a padlock dangling open on one end.

Darnell drove slowly around the block and stopped the Ford along the fence of the warehouse across the street, where the white LIGHTING AND EQUIPMENT vans were parked. I took the last spansule from my pocket and broke it open. I leaned over the front seat.

"Make a fist, LaDuke, and turn it."

He did it, his eyes pinballing in their sockets. I poured half the spansule out on the crook of his hand, then poured the other half, a tiny mound of shiny crystal, on mine. I snorted the powder off my hand and up into my nose, feeling the burn and then the drip back in my throat. LaDuke did the same. His eyes teared up right away.

"Goddamn," LaDuke said.

"Let's go," I said.

Darnell gave me one last look, and then we were out of the car. LaDuke popped the trunk, reached inside, pulled back the blanket. He holstered the revolver on his ankle, picked up the shotgun, cradled it, dropped extra shells in his pocket. I found the Browning, switched off the safety, and put one in the chamber. I slid the gun, barrel down, behind the waistband of my jeans, covered it with the tail of my shirt. We crossed the street.

The gate was a slider. I pulled the chain through the links. LaDuke pushed the gate along a couple of feet and the two of us slipped inside.

We moved quickly across the lot, over to the side of the building, where there was a steel door behind a flatbed trailer. Above the door, a floodlight blew a triangle of white light onto a two-step concrete stoop. LaDuke and I flattened ourselves against the brick side of the building, outside the area of the light. LaDuke rested the butt of the Ithaca on his knee.

"I'm all right," he said, though I hadn't asked him.

"Good," I said. "I'm going to go up on that stoop now, ring the bell."

"I wanna *move*, man."

"That's good, too. LaDuke?"

"Yeah."

"This goes off right, you won't have to use that shotgun. Hear?"

"Let's do this thing," he said.

I stepped up onto the stoop, rang a flat yellow buzzer mounted to the right of the door. I rang it once, then again, and waited. Moths fluttered around my head. My bottom teeth were welded to my top and it felt as if someone were peeling back the top of my head. A lock turned from behind the door and then the door opened.

A wiry white man stood before me, his long brown hair tied back, knife-in-skull tattoos on thin forearms, the veins throbbing on the arms like live blue rope. He had a slight mustache and a billy-goat beard, and almond-shaped, vaguely inbred eyes.

He looked me over and said, "What?"

"Hi," I said. "I'm Bobby."

And then LaDuke, wild-eyed and chalk white, jumped into the light, a frightening howl emanating from his mouth. I stepped aside and the man stepped back, reaching beneath the tail of his shirt. The almond eyes opened wide and he made a small choking sound; he knew it was too late. LaDuke swung the shotgun like he was aiming for the left-field bleachers. He hit it solid, the stock connecting high on the wiry man's cheek. The man went down on his side, all deadweight hitting the floor, no echo, no movement. When he found his breath, he began to moan.

LaDuke pumped the shotgun, pointed it one inch from the man's face.

"Don't talk unless I tell you to talk," LaDuke said. The man closed his eyes slowly, then opened them. He stared blankly ahead.

We were in a long hall that had thin metal shelving running along either side. Paints and hardware sat on the shelves. I found a rag and dampened it with turpentine. Then I went to an area where there appeared to be several varieties of rope and cord. I took a spool of the strongest-looking rope and walked back to LaDuke, picking up a cutting tool—a retractable straight-edged razor used by stock boys and artists—along the way.

"What now?" LaDuke said. He was sweating and his knuckles were white on the pump.

"Go ahead and ask the man some questions." The man's face had swelled quickly; I wondered if LaDuke had caved his cheekbone.

"What's your name?" LaDuke said.

"Sweet," the man said.

"Okay, Mr. Sweet," LaDuke said, "this is a robbery. We know about the business you're running here. We'd like all the cash money you have on hand. First we want to talk to your associates. Where are they?"

The man closed his eyes. "Straight down the hall"—he winced at the movement in his own jaw—"Straight down the hall, then right. To the end, last door on the right. Metal door."

"How many in the room?"

"Four."

"How many guns?"

"One."

I cut a long length of rope, then a shorter one. I tied Sweet's hands to his feet, behind his back. Then I stuffed the rag into his mouth and wrapped the short length of rope around his face. I tied it off behind his head and slipped the razor in the seat pocket of my jeans.

LaDuke sniffed the air. "What's that, paint thinner?"

"It won't kill him," I said. "It'll make him too dizzy to move much, though. Come on."

LaDuke took the barrel away from the man's face, rested it across his own forearm. I pulled my Browning, picked up the spool of rope, and gave LaDuke's shirt a tug.

We walked quickly down the hall, our steps quiet on the concrete floor. At the end, we made a right and went down a hall no different from the first. I had to jog a few steps to keep pace with LaDuke.

"I could run right through a fucking wall," he said.

"You're doing fine," I said. Just as I said it, we reached the last metal door on the right.

We stood there, listening to male voices behind the door; under the voices, the buzz of a caged lightbulb suspended above our heads. I looked at LaDuke and placed the spool of rope at my feet. LaDuke managed a tight smile.

I stood straight, knocked two times on the door.

Footsteps. Then: "Yes?"

"Sweet," I said with an edge.

The knob turned. When the door opened a crack, I put my instep to it and screamed. Something popped, and the man behind the door went down. LaDuke and I stepped inside.

"This is a robbery," LaDuke said.

I made a quick coverage. The man on the floor: heavy, bald, and soft, holding his mouth, blood seeping through his fingers, repeating, "Oh, oh, oh..." A black man, mid-thirties, sat on a worktable set against a cinder-block wall. He watched us with amusement and made no movement at all. Two shirtless actors stood in front of a tripoded camera, in the center of a triangular light arrangement, a spot and a couple of fills. The first actor, who wore a tool belt around his bare waist, could have been the star of any soap, some housewife's idea of a stud, all show muscles, his plump mouth open wide. The second actor, the only one of them with the nerve or the stupidity to scowl, was a young black man, thin and long-featured—Roland Lewis, no question.

LaDuke motioned the barrel of the shotgun at the pretty

actor. "First, you get down, lie flat, facedown. Don't hurt yourself, now."

"Better do it, Pretty Man," the black man said.

"This isn't what you think," Pretty Man said. "This is just a job. You think I'm some kind of faggot? I have a girlfriend...."

The black man laughed. I kept my gun dead on him.

"Get down," LaDuke said, "and put your face right on the concrete." Pretty Man got down.

"You have a gun," I said to the black man. "Pull it slow, by the barrel, and slide it to the end of the table."

"Now what makes you think that I have a gun?" the black man said.

"I talked to your friend Sweet. He talked back."

"Sweet?" The black man smiled. "I thought you were Sweet. You said you were Sweet, just before you came in."

"No," I said. "I'm not Sweet."

"Then where's Sweet?" said the black man.

"We put him to sleep," said LaDuke.

"He ain't gonna like that, when he wakes up."

"Pull it," LaDuke said. He had his shotgun on the black man now, too. I had an eye on Roland, who had not yet spoken but who stared at us hatefully.

"You know," the black man said to LaDuke, "you kinda pretty, too. Maybe you and Pretty Man here ought to get together and—"

"You shut your mouth," said LaDuke.

"Relax," I said, looking at the black man but speaking to LaDuke.

"You boys are higher than a motherfucker," the black man said, studying us with a hard glint in his eye. "You ought to cool out some. Maybe we can talk."

"Pull it!" LaDuke screamed.

"You're the man," the black man said, "for now." He put one hand up and reached the other behind his back. For a moment, I thought Roland might make a move—he was balling and unballing his fists, and he was leaning forward, like he was in the blocks—but then the black man's hand came around, dangling an automatic by the barrel. He tossed it on the work-table and it slid neatly to the end. I went and picked it up, slipped it behind my back.

"All right now," LaDuke said. "The money."

"You've broken my crown," the plump man whined, still on the floor, his hand and face smeared with blood. "You've broken it! Are you satisfied?"

The black man laughed.

Pretty Man raised his head from the floor, tears on his face. He looked at LaDuke.

"Put your head down," LaDuke said.

"Please don't make me put me head down," Pretty Man said, his fat lip quivering like a piece of raw liver. "Please."

LaDuke pushed the muzzle of the shotgun against Pretty Man's cheek, forced his head to the floor. Pretty Man's back shook as he sobbed, and soon after that, the stench of his voided bowels permeated the room.

"Whew," the black man said.

"Don't be givin' up no cash money, Coley," Roland said to the black man.

"Shut up," LaDuke said.

"Yeah," Coley said, "you really ought to shut your mouth, Youngblood. 'Specially when a couple of crazy white boys are holdin' the guns. You ought to just shut the fuck up and shit. Understand what I'm sayin'?"

But Roland did not appear to agree. He went on staring at LaDuke and I as if we were stealing his future. Then Coley got off the table, went to a metal desk that adjoined it, and opened a drawer. He withdrew a cash box, the type used in restaurants and bars, placed it on top of the desk, and opened it.

"It's not all that much," he said with a flourish and a wave of his hand. "Take it and go."

I wrist-jerked the Browning in the direction of the table,

and Coley went back to it and took his seat. He was tall and lean, and he moved with an athletic confidence. He would have been handsome, if not for his pitted complexion and his left ear, which had been removed to the drum. I grabbed the money from the cash box—three banded stacks of hundreds and fifties—and stuffed it into my jeans.

I said to LaDuke, "I'm gonna get the rope."

The spool was right outside the door. I came back in with it, tied Pretty Man's hands to his feet, tried not to gag at his smell.

"Yeah," Coley said, "Pretty Man done shit his drawers. Kinda funny, tough man like him, needin' diapers and shit. See, in the movie we're makin', he's supposed to be some kind of carpenter. Guess you can tell by that tool belt he's wearin'. And Youngblood here, he's like the apprentice, come in for his lesson. The way the story line goes—what we call the *screen treatment*—the carpenter's gonna teach the apprentice a thing or two about showin' up late for his lesson—"

"Oh no," the plump man said. Blood and saliva pooled on the concrete where it had splashed from his mouth.

"This here's our director." Coley gestured to the plump man with a contemptuous limp wrist and a flick of his fingers. "Maybe I ought to let him tell you about tonight's film."

"My crown," the plump man said.

"Everybody," LaDuke said, "keep your mouths shut."

I tied the plump man up, then pointed my chin at Coley. "Put the shotgun on him," I said.

I told Coley to roll over onto his stomach and lie facedown on the table. He did it without protest, and I bound him in the same manner, but more tightly than the others. I cut the excess with the razor and slipped the razor back in my jeans.

I looked at Roland. "All right. You, come here. You're next."

"No," LaDuke said. "We're taking him with us."

"Why?" I said.

"Insurance," LaDuke said.

"*Fuck* no," Roland said. "I ain't goin' nowhere with you motherfuckers—"

"You're coming with us *now*, Roland!" LaDuke said, and then he looked at Coley, who had rested his cheek on the worktable. "If you try and follow us, we'll kill him. You understand?"

"I understand everything just fine," Coley said, a thread of a smile appearing on his face. His eyes moved to mine. "That gonna do it for you boys?"

"No," LaDuke said. "I don't think so."

LaDuke walked over to the spotlight. He raked the barrel of the shotgun sharply across the bulb. The bulb exploded, glass chiming, showering the plump man's head. LaDuke went to the fills and did the same. The stands fell to the floor, sparking on contact. The color of the light changed in the room.

"That about how you did the one in my trunk?" LaDuke said, his eyes wide and fully amphetamized.

"Something like that," I said, knowing he wasn't done.

LaDuke said, "Watch this."

He turned, pointed the shotgun at the video camera. Roland hit the floor and Coley closed his eyes.

"Hey," I said.

LaDuke squeezed the trigger. There was a deafening roar, and then the camera was just gone, disintegrated off its base.

"Oh no," the plump man moaned, against Pretty Man's steadily rising sob. "Oh no."

My ears stopped ringing. I checked the rest of them—no one appeared to have been hit.

LaDuke pumped the Ithaca, smiled crazily, walked through the smoke that hovered in the room. "All right," he said. "All right."

He picked up a T-shirt that was draped over a chair and dropped it on Roland's bare back. Roland got to his knees shakily and put the T-shirt on. LaDuke grabbed him by the arm, pulled him up. He hustled him toward the door and the two of them left the room. I walked backward, the Browning at my side.

"You made a mistake tonight," Coley said in a very easy way. "Now you're fixin' to make the biggest one of your life."

"That right," I said, the speed riding in on the blood that was pumping through my head.

"Yeah. You're gonna walk out of here and let us live. When really, what you ought to do—if you really think about it—is kill us all." His eyes were dead as stone. "I mean, that's what *I* would do."

"I'm not you," I said.

I backed away and left him there, moved into the hall. LaDuke and Roland had already turned the corner. I followed them, caught them at the end of the next hall, near the outside door. Sweet was lying there, unconscious and bound, his face ballooned out and black. We stepped around him and walked out to the lot.

LaDuke pushed Roland toward the gate. Darnell kept the headlights off and pulled the Ford along the fence. We slipped out, then put Roland in the backseat. I gave LaDuke my Browning and the extra clip, along with Coley's automatic. He dumped them and his own hardware into the dark trunk. He went around and got into the front seat and I climbed into the back with Roland. Roland looked at the back of Darnell's head, then at me.

"I don't wanna die," Roland said, looking suddenly like the teenaged kid he was.

"Boy?" Darnell said. "These two just saved your dumb life."

I reached over the front seat and found a cigarette in the visor. LaDuke grinned and clapped my arm. I sat back, struck a match, and took in a lungful of smoke. Darnell pulled out into the street and headed north. He switched on the lights and gave the Ford some gas.

"Where we goin'?" Roland said, the toughness back in his voice.

"We're takin' you home," I said.

None of us said anything for some time after that.

* * *

DARNELL GOT US OUT of the warehouse district and kept the Ford in the area of the Hill, driving down the business strip on Pennsylvania and then into the surrounding neighborhoods. It was near midnight, and most of the shops were closed, but people still moved in and out of the doorways of bars, and on the residential streets the atmosphere was thick and still.

"Pull over," LaDuke said, pointing to a pay phone standing free in the lot of a service station. Darnell drove the Ford into the lot.

"What we gonna do now?" Roland said.

"Call your mom," said LaDuke.

"Shit," Roland said.

LaDuke left the car and made the call, gesturing broadly with his hands, smiling at the end of the conversation. He returned and settled back in the front seat.

"Let's go," LaDuke said to Darnell. "His mother's place is in Northeast, off Division."

"I ain't goin' home," Roland said. "Anyway, we got some business to discuss."

"What kind of business?" I said.

"That money you took, it must have been ten, maybe more. I can turn that ten into twenty."

"Forget about the money."

"I only want what's mine. I worked for it. On the real side, man, that shit is mine."

"Forget about it," I said.

LaDuke pointed to the shifter on the steering column. "Put it in gear," he said.

"I told you," Roland said, "I ain't goin' nowhere."

I shifted in my seat, turned to Roland. "Maybe you'd like just to sit here and talk."

"About what?"

"We could start with what happened to Calvin."

Roland licked his lips and exhaled slowly. "Man, *I* don't know. Calvin just left—see what I'm sayin'? He didn't want to come along. The next thing I knew, I was readin' about that shit my own self, in the papers."

"You must have been real broken up about it," I said. "You didn't even go to his funeral."

"Look, Calvin was my boy. But I had my *own* thing to take care of."

"Get going," LaDuke said to Darnell.

Roland said, "I ain't goin' nowhere, not till we settle up on my cash money."

Darnell's eyes met mine in the rearview. "You thirsty, man? You look kinda thirsty."

"Yes," I said. "I'm thirsty."

"Why don't I just drop you off, maybe the two of you could have a beer. I'll swing back, pick you up."

"What're you going to do in the meantime?"

"Me and Roland here," Darnell said, "we're gonna drive around some. Have ourselves a little talk."

DARNELL PUT US OUT on Pennsylvania. LaDuke and I went into the Tune Inn, noisy and packed, even at that hour, with Hill interns and neighborhood regulars. We ordered a couple of drafts from one of their antique bartenders and drank the beers standing up, our backs against a paneled wall. LaDuke and I didn't say a word to each other or anyone else the entire time. At one point, he began to laugh, and I joined him, then that ended as abruptly as it had begun. I was killing my second beer when the Ford pulled up on the street outside the bar window.

We drove across town and over the river, deep into Northeast. Roland sat staring out the window, the streetlights playing on his resigned face, his features very much like his mother's in repose. I didn't ask him any more questions; I was done with him for now.

We pulled up in front of the Lewis home, Darnell letting the engine run on the street. On the high ground, where the house sat atop its steep grade, I saw Shareen in silhouette, sitting in the rocker sofa on her lighted porch. She got up and walked to the edge of the steps. Roland stepped out of the car, moving away from us without a word of thanks. We watched him take the steps, slowly at first, then more quickly as he neared his home. As he reached his mother, she embraced him tightly, and even over the idle of the Ford, I could hear her crying, talking to her son. Roland did not hug her back, but it was more than good enough.

"Let's get out of here," I said.

"Sure," Darnell said.

LaDuke did not comment. He smiled and rubbed the top of his head.

We dropped Darnell at his efficiency near Cardoza High, in the Shaw area of Northwest. I thanked him and peeled off a couple of hundreds from the stack. He protested mildly, but I pressed it into his hand. He shrugged, pocketed the cash, and walked across the street.

"I could use a drink," I said.

"Yeah," LaDuke said, surprising me. "I could use one, too."

NINETEEN

STEVE MAROULIS SHOUTED, "*Ella*, Niko!" as LaDuke and I entered his bar.

Maroulis was the tender at May's, below Tenleytown on Wisconsin, a liquorized pizza parlor and hangout for many of the town's midlevel bookies. Though quantities of cocaine had moved through the place for a brief time in the eighties, gambling remained the main order of business here, a place where men in cheap sport jackets could talk with equal enthusiasm about Sinatra's latest tour or the over/under on the game of the night. LaDuke and I had a couple of seats at the bar.

Maroulis lumbered our way, put a smile on the melon that was his face. "Way past last call, Nick. Drinks got to be off the tables in a few minutes."

"Put four Buds on the bar, will you, Steve? We'll leave when you say."

"Right."

He served them up. I grabbed mine by the neck and tapped LaDuke's bottle, then both of us drank. Tony Bennett moved into Sam and Dave on the house system, a typical May's mix of fifties pop and sixties frat. I shook a cigarette out of my pack, struck a match, and put the flame to the tobacco.

"How'd you think it went tonight?" LaDuke said.

"We got Roland out of there."

"You didn't push it too hard with him."

"I'll talk to him again."

LaDuke motioned to my pack of smokes. "Give me one of those things."

"You really want one?"

"I guess not. No."

I dragged on mine, flicked ash off into the tray.

LaDuke said, "Those guys at the warehouse—Sweet and Coley. You think they had anything to do with Calvin's death?"

"I'm not sure yet. But I'd bet it."

"Why didn't you press Coley?"

"Calvin's dead. Gettin' another kid killed isn't going to even anything up. The object was to get Roland the fuck out of there. We did that. It's only over for tonight. That doesn't mean it's done."

"Why you figure it was Sweet and Coley?"

"It was a black man and a white man killed Calvin."

"How do you know that?"

I hit my cigarette, watched myself do it in the barroom mirror. "Because I was there."

LaDuke whistled through his teeth. "That's not what you told me."

"I know what I told you. I wasn't hired by Calvin's mother. I stumbled right up on that murder, man. I got drunk, real drunk that night, and I ended up down by the river, flat on my back and layin' in garbage. I heard the voices of a black man and a white man; they were dragging someone to the waterline. I heard them kill him, man, but I couldn't even raise my head. I was just fucked up, all the way fucked up, understand?" I rubbed at my eyes, then killed the first bottle of beer. I pushed that one away with the back of my hand. "That's the way this thing started—with me on a drunk."

I picked up the fresh beer, drank some of it off. LaDuke looked at the bottle in my hand.

"You better be careful with that stuff," he said. "You fall in love with it too much, there's no room for anyone else."

"I know it," I said, closing my eyes as I thought of Lyla.

"How is she, anyway?" LaDuke said.

"Who?"

"You know who. You haven't mentioned her much these last few days."

"It's over," I said, hearing the words out loud for the first time. "I've just got to work out the details. I'm doing it for her, man. She's going nowhere fast, hanging out with me."

"Self-pity, Nick. Another curse of the drinking man."

"Thanks for the tip, Boy Scout."

"I'm only talking about it because I know. My mother left us when I was a kid. She liked the bottle better than she liked raising a family."

"Your father raised you?"

"Me and my brother, yeah."

"Where you from, anyway?"

"Frederick County, not far over the Montgomery line. Place about forty minutes outside of D.C."

"Your father still alive?"

"Yeah," LaDuke said, and a shadow seemed to cross his face.

"What's he do?"

"Country veterinarian. Horse doctor, mostly." LaDuke swigged at his beer, put it back on the bar. "What are you, writin' my life story?"

I shook my head. "It would take way too long. You're a work in progress, LaDuke." I got off my bar stool, grabbed my beer. "Be right back. I gotta make a call."

I went back to the pay phone outside the rest rooms. A couple of kitchen guys were working a video game nearby, and someone was puking behind the men's room door. I sunk a quarter in the slot, dialed Boyle's number at the station, and left a taped message directing his Vice boys to the warehouse on Potomac and Half.

LaDuke was finishing his beer when I returned to the bar. Maroulis had brought the white lights up, and he had put on "Mustang Sally," the traditional "clear out" song for May's. Most of the regulars had beat it. I ordered a six to go, and Steve arranged them in a cardboard carrier. I left thirty on eighteen, and LaDuke and I headed out the door.

We drove southeast, all four windows down and the radio off. The streets were empty, the air damp and nearly cool. I lit a cigarette, dangled the hand that held it out the window, drank off some of my beer. The speed had given me wide eyes and a big, bottomless thirst; I could have gone all night.

I had LaDuke stop at an after-hours club downtown, but even that had closed down. We sat on the steps of it, drank a round. Then we got back into the Ford and headed over to the Spot. LaDuke urinated in the alley two doors down while I negotiated the lock and got past the alarm. He joined me inside and I locked the door behind him. The neon Schlitz logo burned solo and blue. I notched up the rheostat, the conicals throwing dim columns of light onto the bar. My watch read half past three.

LaDuke had a seat at the bar and I went behind it. I iced a half dozen bottles of beer and put two on the mahogany, along with the bottle of Grand-Dad from the second row of call. I placed a couple of shot glasses next to that, an ashtray, and my deck of smokes.

"You with me?" I said, my hand around the bottle of bourbon.

"Maybe one," said LaDuke.

I poured a couple, lifted my first whiskey of the night. It was hot to the taste and bit going down. My buzz went to velvet, as it always did with the first sip. I moved down to the deck and put on some Specials. Then I came back and LaDuke and I had our drinks. We chased them with beer and listened to the tape for its duration without saying much of consequence. I stayed in the ska groove and dropped a Fishbone mix into the deck. Walking back, I noticed that my watch read 4:15. I poured LaDuke another shot, then one for me. LaDuke sipped at it, followed it with beer.

I took the stickup money from my pockets, dumped it all on the bar. LaDuke didn't comment, and neither did I. I lit a cigarette, gave it a hard drag, looked at the long night melting into LaDuke's face.

"You're hangin' pretty good for a rookie," I said.

"I'm no rookie," LaDuke said. "I just haven't done anything like this for a while, that's all."

"You gave it all up, huh?"

"Something like that. The funny thing is, after all that time off it, I don't even feel that fucked up. I could drink whatever you put on this bar tonight, I swear to God. And I could keep drinking it."

"The speed," I said. "You'll feel it in the morning, though, boy. You can believe that shit."

"I guess that's what got me going back there, too."

"You blew the fuck out of that camera, LaDuke. I could have done without that."

"I wanted to break something."

"I know."

"Anyway, it's not like I don't know how to handle this stuff. You rib me all the time, Stevonus, 'Boy Scout' this and 'Boy Scout' that. Shit, I was like any teenager growing up when I did—I tried everything, man. The difference between you and me is, I grew out of it, that's all."

"So when'd you stop?"

LaDuke said, "When my brother got killed." He pointed his chin at the pack of smokes on the bar. "Give me one of those, will ya?"

"Sure."

I rustled the deck, shook one out. LaDuke took it and I gave him a light. He dragged on it, held the smoke in, kept it there without a cough. He knew how to do that, too.

I put one foot up on the ice chest, leaned forward. "What happened?"

"My brother and I, we were both up at Frostburg State. I was in my senior year and he was a sophomore. It was Halloween night; there were a lot of parties goin' on and shit, everybody dressed up in costume. I was at this one party; all of us had eaten mushrooms, and the psilocybin was really kicking in. Just about then, a couple of cops came to the door, and of course everybody there thought they had come to bust the shit up. But they had come to get *me*, man. To tell me that my brother had been killed. He had been at this grain party, up over the Pennsylvania line. Driving back, he lost it on a curve, hit a fuckin' tree. Broke his neck."

I hit my cigarette, looked away. The tape had stopped a few minutes earlier. I wished it hadn't stopped.

"So anyway," LaDuke said, "they took me to identify the body. So I was in the waiting room, and there was this big mirror on one wall. And I looked in the mirror, and there I was: I had dressed up like some kind of bum that night, for the party, like. I had bought all this stupid-lookin' shit down at the Salvation Army store, man. None of it matched, and goddamn if I didn't look like some kind of failed clown. I looked at myself, thinkin' about my brother lying on a slab in the other room, and all I could do was laugh. And trippin' like I was, I couldn't stop laughing. Eventually, they came and put me in another room. This room had quilted blankets on the walls—the kind moving guys use to cover furniture—and a table with a pack of Marlboro Lights in the middle of it, next to an ashtray. And no mirrors. So that was the night, you know? The night I decided, It's time to stop being some kind of clown."

I stabbed my cigarette out in the ashtray, lit another right behind it.

"That's rough, Jack," I said, because I could think of nothing else to say.

"Sure," he said. "It was rough." He rubbed at the tight curls on top of his head, looking down all the while. I drew two beers from the ice, put them on the bar.

"How'd your father handle it?" I said.

"My father," LaDuke muttered, savagely twisting the cap off the neck of the bottle.

I watched him tilt his head back and drink.

"What's wrong with you, man?" I said.

LaDuke tried to focus his eyes on mine. I could see how drunk he was then, and I knew that he was going to tell it.

"My father was sick," LaDuke said. "*Is* sick, I guess. I haven't seen him for a long time. Not since my brother's funeral."

"Sick with what?"

"His problem."

"Which is?"

LaDuke breathed out slowly. "He likes little boys."

"Shit, Jack."

"Yeah."

"You tellin' me you were abused?"

LaDuke drank some more beer, put the bottle softly on the bar. "I was young...but yeah. When I finally figured it out—when I figured out that what he was doing, when he was coming into my room at night, handling me that way—when I figured out that it was wrong, I asked him about it. Not a confrontation, just a question. And it stopped. We never even talked about it again. I spent the rest of my childhood, and then my teenage years, making sure the old man stayed away from my little brother. When my brother died, man, my life was finished there. I got through college and then I booked."

"Booked where?"

"I went south. I never liked the cold. Still don't. Lived in Atlanta for a while, Miami after that. I had a degree in criminology, so I picked up work for some of the security agencies. But, you know, you tend just to come back. I've been looking for answers, and I thought I might find out more about myself the closer I got to home."

"You've talked to your father?"

"No." LaDuke took in some smoke, crushed the cherry in the ashtray. "I guess you think I ought to hate him. But the truth is, I only hate what he did. He's still my old man. And he did raise me and my brother, and it couldn't have been easy. So, no, I don't hate him. The thing is now, how do I fix my own self?"

"What do you mean?"

"I don't believe in this victimized-society crap. All these people pointing fingers, never pointing at themselves. So people get abused as kids, then spend the rest of their lives blaming their own deficient personalities on something that happened in their childhoods. It's bullshit, you know it? I mean, everybody's carrying some kind of baggage, right? I know I was scarred, and maybe I was scarred real deep. But knowing that doesn't straighten anything out for me." LaDuke looked away. "Sometimes, Nick, I don't even know if I'm good for a woman."

"Oh, for Chrissakes, Jack."

"I mean it. I don't know what the fuck I am. What happened to me, I guess it made me doubt my own sexuality. I look at a man, and I don't have any desire there, and I look at a woman, and sometimes, sexually, I don't know if it's a woman I want, either. I'm tellin' you, I don't know *what* I want."

"Come on."

"Look here," LaDuke said. "Let me tell you just how bad it is with me. I go to the movies, man. I'm sitting there watching the man and the woman makin' love. If it's really hot, you know, I'll find myself getting a bone. And then I start thinking, Am I getting hard because I wish I was him, or am I getting hard because I wish I was her?"

"Are you serious, man?"

"I'm not joking."

"Because if you're serious, LaDuke, then you are one fucked-up motherfucker."

"That's what I'm trying to tell you!" he said. "I am one seriously fucked-up motherfucker."

Both of us had to laugh a little then, because we needed to, and because we were drunk. LaDuke's eyes clouded over, though, and the laughter didn't last. I didn't know what to do for him, or what to say; there was too much twisting around inside him, twisting slowly and way too tight. I poured him another shot of bourbon, and one for myself, and I shook him out another smoke. We sat there drinking, with our own thoughts arranging themselves inside our heads, and the time passed like that. I looked through the transom above the front door and saw the sky had turned to gray.

"You know, Jack," I said, "you were right about everybody having some kind of baggage. I never knew my mother or father; they sent me over from Greece when I was an infant. I got raised by my grandfather. He was a good man—hell, he *was* my father—and then he died, and my marriage fell apart, and I thought I was always gonna be alone. And now I'm fixing to blow the best thing that's ever come my way. But, you know, I've got my work, and I've got this place and the people in it, and I know I can always come here. There's always someplace you can go. There's a whole lotta ways to make a family."

"So, what, you're sayin' this place is like your home?"

"I guess so, yeah."

"But it's a shithole, Nick."

I looked around the bar. "You know somethin'? It *is* a shithole." I smiled. "Thanks for pointing that out to me."

LaDuke smiled back. "Yeah, you gave it a good try."

We had some more to drink, and after awhile his eyes made their way over to the money heaped on the bar. I watched him think things over.

"It's a lot of cash," I said, "you know it?"

"Uh-huh. What are we gonna do with it?"

"I don't know. You want it?"

"No." LaDuke shook his head. "It's dirty."

"It's only dirty if you know it's dirty."

"What's your point?"

"I was thinkin'... why not just take this money, put it in an envelope, and mail it off to Calvin's mother. I've been to her place, man, and she sure could use it. There's a couple of babies there—"

"What, just put it in the mail?"

"I've got an envelope around here somewhere."

LaDuke shrugged. "All right."

I found a large manila envelope in Darnell's kitchen. There was a roll of stamps back there, too, in a file cabinet next to Phil Saylor's logbook. I ripped off a line of stamps and took them and the envelope back to the bar. Then I grabbed a D.C. directory that was wedged between the cooler and the wall and put that on the bar, as well. I looked through the Jeter listings while LaDuke stuffed the money into the envelope.

"There's a shitload of Jeters," I said.

"You know the street?"

"I think so."

"You think so? We're gonna mail out ten grand on an 'I think so'?"

"Here it is," I said. "Gimme the envelope."

I used a black Magic Marker to address it, then applied the stamps and gave it a seal. LaDuke had a look at my handiwork and laughed.

"It looks like a kid did this," he said. "Like it's first grade, and you just learned how to write and shit."

"What, you could do better?"

"Man, I can barely see it."

"Come on," I said. "Let's go."

I set the alarm, locked the place up. The two of us walked out the door. Dawn had come, the sun was breaking over the buildings, and the bread men and the icemen were out on the streets.

"Shit," I said, shaking my head as we moved down the sidewalk.

"What?" LaDuke said.

"I was just thinking of you sittin' in a movie theater, not knowing if it's the man or the woman givin' you a hard-on. I mean, it's really hard to believe."

"I guess I shouldn't have told such a sensitive guy like you. I know you're never gonna let me forget it. But believe it or not, you're the first person I ever unloaded this on. And I gotta tell you, just letting it out, I do feel a little better."

"You'll get through it, LaDuke."

"You think so, huh."

"It'll pass. Everything does."

I dropped the envelope in the mailbox on the corner. LaDuke slipped, stepping off the curb. I grabbed him by the elbow and held him up. We crossed the street and headed for the Ford, parked in a patch of clean morning light.

TWENTY

I WOKE UP a little after noon. I was spread out on top of the sheets, soaked with sweat, still dressed right down to my shoes. My cat was lying sphinx-style on my chest, kneading her claws through my shirt, her face tight against mine. Starved for food or attention, it didn't matter which. I got up and opened a can of salmon and spooned it into her dish. The smell of the salmon tossed my stomach and I dry-heaved in the kitchen sink. I stripped, climbed into the shower, stood in the cold spray, going in and out of sleep against the tiles. When I stepped out, the phone was ringing, so I went into the living room and picked up the receiver. Boyle was on the line, thanking me for the previous night's tip.

"You get anything?"

"Nothing human," Boyle said. "All the warm bodies were long gone by the time Vice secured the warrant. They found a whole bunch of tools, some lighting and equipment, a camera that had been blown to shit. Looked like someone had quite a party in there, from what I understand. I guess they were in a hurry clearing out."

"I guess."

"You sound a little tired," Boyle said.

"It's hot in here, that's all."

"Heat wave moved in this morning. Say it's gonna be up around a hundred the next few days."

"I'm working a shift this afternoon, so I'll be out of it."

"Uh-huh." Boyle cleared his throat. "The porno operation in that warehouse—that have anything to do with the Jeter murder?"

"No. I thought it did, but it didn't. I got in there, saw what was going on, and got out. Then I called you."

"Right," Boyle said after a meaningful pause. "Well, I guess that's it. Take it easy, Nick."

"You, too."

I hung up the phone, got myself into shorts and a T-shirt, and headed down to the Spot.

Mai was behind the stick when I walked in. She gave me a wave, untied her apron, and walked out the front door. I stepped behind the bar. Happy, Buddy, Bubba, and Mel were all in place, snuggled into their stools, drinking quietly under the buzz of the air conditioner and the Sonny Boy Williamson coming from the deck. Buddy asked for another pitcher, his lip curled in a snarl. I drew it for him, placed the pitcher between him and Bubba. Happy mumbled something in my direction, so I fixed him a manhattan. I placed the drink on a bev nap in front of him, and he burped. The smell of Darnell's lunch special drifted my way. I replaced the blues on the deck with an Impressions compilation, and the intro to "I've Been Trying" filled the room. Mel closed his eyes and began to sing. Looking through the reach-through to the kitchen, I could see Ramon doing some kind of bull-jive flying sidekick toward Darnell, Darnell stepping away from it with grace, the two of them framed beneath the grease-stained Rudy Ray Moore poster thumbtacked to the wall. I knew I was home.

Anna Wang came in from the dining area, leaned on the service bar, and dumped out her change. She began to count it, arranging it in sticks. I poured a cup of coffee for myself, added some whiskey to the cup, and took it over to Anna. She reached into the pocket of my T and found a cigarette. I gave her a light. She exhaled and shook a bunch of black hair out of her face.

"Welcome back."

"Thanks."

She grinned. "How you feelin', Nick?"

"Better now," I said, holding up the cup. And I did, too.

"Phil came in first thing this morning. Said there were enough Camels in the ashtray to service the Egyptian army."

"Yeah, that was me. And LaDuke. Was Phil pissed?"

"Not really. At least you set the alarm this time."

Anna pushed the stacks of change across the bar. I went to the register, turned the coin into bills, took the bills back and handed them to Anna. She folded her take and stuffed the money in the pocket of her jeans.

She said, "So how's Jack?"

"He's fine."

"Tell him I said hey, will you?"

"Sure, Anna, I'll tell him."

Happy hour was on the slow side, but I had plenty to do, restocking the liquor and arranging the bottles on the call shelf to where they had been before I left. Evening came and my regulars drifted out like pickled ghosts, and then it was just me and Darnell. I locked the front door and drove him back to his place through the warm, sticky night. He didn't mention the warehouse affair, and neither did I.

Back at my place, Lyla had phoned, so I phoned her back. She wanted to come over and talk. I said that it was probably not a good idea, and she asked why. I said it was because I didn't want to see her. She raised her voice and I raised mine back;

things just went to hell after that. The conversation ended very badly, and when it was done, I switched off the light and sat at the living room table and rubbed my face. That didn't amount to much, so I went to the bedroom and lay down in the dark and listened to the purr of my cat somewhere off in the apartment. It seemed like a long time before I fell asleep.

Jack LaDuke phoned early the next morning. Roland Lewis had been found dead beneath the John Philip Sousa Bridge: one bullet to the head.

TWENTY-ONE

THE AUTOPSY DELAYED the funeral, so it wasn't until Monday that Shareen Lewis put her son in the ground. Roland made the Roundup in Saturday's *Post*, with a corresponding death notice in the obits giving out the funeral home's location and burial particulars. There had been a dozen gun kills that weekend, so column-inch space was at a premium, and even for a young black male, Roland's death received very little ink. He had spent his whole life wanting to be large, but in the end his public memorial was two generic sentences buried deep in Metro; he was simply erased.

I retrieved my one suit, a charcoal three-buttoned affair, from out of the cedar closet on Monday and made it over to the service at a Baptist church off East Capitol Street. The attendees were racially mixed—the whites representing fellow employees from Shareen's law firm; the blacks representing family and friends. This was not a gang-death funeral, so there was not the traditional garb worn by crew members to honor their fallen comrade. In fact, there were very few young people in attendance at all. LaDuke, in his black suit and black tie arrangement, stood near the front, at the end of a pew. I watched him from the back of the church, his hands tightly clasped in front of him, as the beautiful voices of the choir resonated in the room.

They buried Roland in a cemetery off Benning Road in Marshall Heights. I brought up the rear of the procession and watched the ceremony from a distance, leaning against my Dodge, smoking a cigarette in the shade of an elm. An unmarked car pulled up behind mine and Boyle stepped out of the passenger side. He came and stood next to me, his face hard and grim.

"Nick," he said.

"Boyle."

"Thought you might be here."

"You were right on the money, then. I always said you were a good cop."

"Turn around," Boyle said, "and look at the car I just got out of."

I did it, looked through the tinted windshield, saw no one identifiable, just the featureless outline of a suit-and-tie black man behind the wheel.

"That good enough?" I said.

Boyle nodded. "That's Detective Johnson, assigned to the case. I told you about him. He just wanted to get a good look at you in case he gets proof that you been holding out on us with this one. If that's true, he's gonna want to talk to you again."

"Fair enough," I said.

"The ME's report came in. The shooter used a silenced twenty-two on Roland Lewis. Same markings as on the Jeter murder. Same gun. But I guess you knew that."

I dragged on my cigarette, dropped it under my shoe. "I don't know anything."

"You pulled the Lewis kid out of the warehouse on Potomac and Half, I'm pretty certain of that. His prints were all over the place. If you had turned him in to us, he'd be alive right now. He would have talked, too, and we'd probably have this whole thing wrapped up by now." Boyle put his face close to mine. I could smell the nicotine on his breath and the previous night's alcohol in his sweat. "You got this kid killed. Think about that, hotshot."

"Take it easy, Boyle."

"Yeah," he said. "Yeah, sure."

I listened to his footsteps as he walked away, and to the sound of the door shutting and Johnson putting the car in gear. I stared straight ahead, at the black pool of mourners huddled against the rolling green grounds. Low-slung sheets of flannel-colored clouds were moving in from the northeast. I reached into my jacket for another cigarette and fumbled through my pockets for a light.

THE BAPTIST'S VERSION OF a wake was held at Shareen Lewis's house off Division, directly following the burial. I dropped by, then stood around uncomfortably and wondered why I had. Shareen attended to the food table, a mix of fried chicken and cold cuts and some sort of dry punch, in a fragile but efficient manner, and Roland's sister helped her, passing me several times without acknowledgment, trays and bowls balanced in her hands. LaDuke stood across the room talking to Blackmon, the bondsman who had turned him on to the case. LaDuke met my eyes only once, giving me an abbreviated nod with his chin, his own eyes drawn and red. I jiggled the change that was in my pocket and smiled when someone smiled at me, and after a while I left the house and walked outside to have a smoke.

I went to the edge of the porch and looked down to the cars, shiny and wet, lined along the curb below. The rain had come in steady, quiet waves, clicking against the leaves, drumming on the aluminum awning of the porch. The rain brought steam up off the street, and woke the green and living smells of summer. I lit a cigarette, flipped the spent match off the porch, toward the grass.

"You have an extra one of those?" said a woman's voice behind me.

I turned around. The voice belonged to Shareen Lewis. She was sitting on the rocker sofa in front of the bay window.

"Sure," I said. I went to her and shook out a cigarette, struck a match and gave her a light. She wore a simple black dress, black stockings, and black pumps. An apricot brooch closed the dress at the chest. Her nails were painted apricot, with her lips the color of the nails.

She took some smoke into her chest, kept it there, closed her eyes as she let it out. "Sit down with me. Please."

"All right."

The springs creaked as I took a seat, and the sofa moved back and forth on its track. It settled to a stop, and then there was just the clicking on the leaves and the drumming on the awning. Shareen flicked some ash to the concrete of the porch and I did the same.

"Thank you," she said.

"It's okay," I said.

"Thank you for bringing my son back to me."

"It's okay."

Shareen put her lips to the cigarette, dragged on it, blew a stream of exhale. The smoke jetted out, then slowed and roiled in the stagnant, heavy air.

"You know," Shareen said, "I only had him for that one night. He left the next day."

I flicked a speck of lint from my trousers.

"Before he left," she said, "I made him his favorite lunch: a grilled cheese sandwich on white bread, with tomato right out of my garden, and a little mustard. Mustard on the bottom *and* the top slice of bread. The way he liked it, from when he was a little boy. He'd come in after the playground, come runnin' through that screen door there—don't you know he'd always slam that screen door—and he'd say, 'What's for lunch, Mom?' And I'd say, 'Grilled cheese, honey.' And he'd say, 'All right!'" Shareen flipped her hand in an excited, childish gesture, the way her son might have done.

I hit my cigarette and looked down at my shoes. One foot was moving metronomically, left to right and back again.

"After he had lunch on Thursday," Shareen said, "he said he had to go out, and out he went. He slammed that screen door, too. You know that, Mr. Stefanos?"

"Mrs. Lewis—"

"Then they called me on Friday and asked me to come down to the morgue. And I went in there to identify him; they pulled back the sheet, and there he was. And for a moment there, you know, I just didn't believe it was him. I mean, intellectually, I knew it was my son. But it just wasn't *him*. You understand? This was just a dead thing lying on a piece of cement. Not my son. Just something dead."

Shareen took in some more smoke, then dropped the cigarette and crushed it with the toe of her pump. She stared off into her front yard and flattened her hands in her lap.

"When he was first starting out school, he hated it, you know. As many times as I'd call upstairs to him in the morning, try to get him to wake up, he'd never answer. He'd just keep pretending that he was asleep, 'cause he didn't want to go to school. So I had this thing: I'd go into his bedroom and shake him and shake him and shake him. And finally, I'd put my index finger up into his armpit, just touch it, you know. And Roland, ticklish as he was, he'd still have his eyes closed, but he couldn't help but crack a smile. We did that every morning, Mr. Stefanos, when he was a boy. That was our routine. It was the only way I could get him up to go to school."

"Mrs. Lewis, maybe we better go on inside."

"Down in the morgue on Friday, I put my finger there, underneath his arm. Don't you know, that boy didn't even crack a smile!" Shareen grinned, the grin horrible and artificial. "I could have put my mouth right up to his ear and screamed to

God in heaven. It wouldn't have made any difference. And that's when I knew—I *knew*—that the boy in there on that slab, that boy was not my Roland. 'Cause Roland, when I touched him there? My Roland would have smiled."

"Mrs. Lewis," I said.

Her grin slowly went away. I put my hand on top of hers. The hand was cool and thin, wormed with veins across its back. She looked at me, then through me, her eyes hollow and all the way gone. We sat there and listened to the rain. After a while, she rose abruptly and walked back into her house. I got up off the rocker, crossed the porch, and took the steps down to my car.

I HAD ANOTHER EVENING shift at the Spot, and I worked it without saying much of anything to anyone, not even Anna or Darnell. The regulars made comments on my attire between calling for their drinks, and I let them, and when the bar fell silent for long periods of time, they reminded me to change the music on the deck. I started drinking in the middle of happy hour, one beer after another, buried in the ice chest to the neck. By the time I closed the place down, I had a beer buzz waiting on a shot of liquor to keep it company, so I poured two ounces of call bourbon into a glass.

Darnell shut off the light in the kitchen, stopped to get a good look at me, and walked out the front door. He didn't even bother asking for a lift uptown. I had a couple more rounds and somewhere around eleven I heard a knock on the front door. I turned the lock and LaDuke stepped inside.

"Hey," I said, clapping him a little too roughly on the shoulder.

"Nick."

He was still in his suit and tie, jacket on in the heat, the tie's Windsor knot centered and tight.

"Come on in, Jack, have a drink with me."

"I don't think so," he said.

"Suit yourself."

I went back behind the bar. LaDuke stayed where he was, at the top of the two-step landing, leaning against the entranceway's green wall. I had a sip of bourbon and put fire to a smoke.

LaDuke said, "You're wasting time with that shit. We've got work to do."

"Maybe tomorrow," I said. "Tonight I'm gonna drink."

"Tonight and the next," he said, "and the one after that. You're no good that way."

"Thanks for the lecture, Boy Scout."

"We've got to finish what we started."

"I am finished," I said. "I don't want to see any more death. They kill and we kill and it doesn't stop and nobody wins. I'm tellin' you, man, I'm through with it."

"Well, I'm not through," he said, his voice cracking. "Roland's dead because of me. I've got to fix it now."

"Roland offed himself. He went back to them because of greed, flat out. They killed him, Jack, not you."

"No, Nick. It was me. That night in the warehouse, I called him by his name. You remember? I said, 'You're coming with us, Roland!' The one named Coley, he must have picked up on it. It made it look like Roland was in on the robbery, in on it with us. You understand, Nick? It was *me*."

"Roland was headed that way all along. You had nothing to do with it, hear?"

LaDuke pushed off from the wall. "I'm not done. Come along or don't come along—it makes no difference to me."

"Come on." I smiled and raised my bottle of beer. "Come on over here, Jack, and sit down with me. Sit down with me and have a drink."

He looked me over slowly, his eyes black with contempt.

"The hell with you," he said.

LaDuke walked from the room. I listened to the door close, then the silence. My shot glass sat empty on the bar. I reached for the bottle and poured myself a drink.

TWENTY-TWO

CASES BREAK, AND major changes get put in motion, in seemingly innocuous ways.

My ex-wife and I met in a bar, on a night when I decided to go out for a late beer at the incessant goading of an acquaintance whose name I don't remember. Similarly, I got my start in the sales business when, as a teenager, I happened to be hitching down Connecticut Avenue and found myself standing in front of the Nutty Nathan's plate-glass window, staring at a HELP WANTED sign. And then there was my friend Dimitri, a Greek boy out of Highlandtown, who got into a car he didn't know was stolen, then died after a high-speed chase at the age of seventeen. I often wonder how my life would have turned out had I not gone out for that beer, or had I been picked up hitchhiking farther north on the avenue that day. And I think about Dimitri, an innocent smile on his face as he climbed into that car, and I think of all the things my friend has missed.

The Jeter case was like that, too. The Jeter case might have ended with me and LaDuke parting company on a hot summer night. It might have ended, but it did not. The very next morning, I took a different route to work than I normally take, and everything got heated up again and boiled over in a big way.

My normal path out of Shepherd Park is 13th Street south, straight into downtown. From Hamilton Street on down, there was some road repair that morning, forcing a merge into one lane. I got into the lane and inched along for a while, but my hangover was scraping away at my patience. So I cut right on Arkansas, with the intention of hitting Rock Creek east of 16th.

I wasn't the only one with that plan, however, and the traffic on Arkansas was as backed up as it had been on 13th. After Buchanan Street, the flow ebbed considerably, and just before Allison, things came to a complete stop. I was idling there, looking around absently and trying to clear my head, when I noticed the brick building of the Beverley ice company on my right. Some employees were walking out of the rear door of the icehouse, on the way to their trucks. The temperature that morning had already climbed to ninety-plus degrees, the sun blazing in a cloudless sky. Sitting in my car, I could feel the sweat soaking into my T-shirt; the men walking out of the icehouse wore winter coats.

I landed on my horn. The guy ahead of me moved up a couple of feet, enough for me to put two wheels on the sidewalk and get the car onto Allison. I punched the gas and got it on up to 14th, parking in front of a corner market. There was a pay phone outside the market, with a directory, miraculously intact, beneath the phone. I opened the book, flipped to the *I*'s. I found plenty of wholesale ice merchants, most of them located in Northeast. There was only one located in Southeast: a place called Polar Boys, northwest of M, not too far from the Anacostia River—not too far from the river and only a short walk from the John Philip Sousa Bridge.

I dropped a quarter in the slot, woke Mai at home, and asked if she could work my shift.

"I'll do it," she said after the obligatory mild protest. "But I still want my whole two shifts tomorrow. And you owe me now, Nicky."

"I'll cover for you, Mai, anytime. Thanks a million, hear?"

She said good-bye. I ran down the sidewalk to my car.

MOST DETECTIVE WORK CONSISTS of watching and waiting. The job requires patience and the ability to deal with boredom, two character traits I do not possess. It's one of the reasons I don't take tail gigs anymore, following errant wives and hard-dick husbands to motel parking lots, waiting for them to walk out the door of room 12 so I can snap their pictures. The tip jar from the Spot not only keeps me solvent, it also allows me the luxury of selectivity.

I was thinking of the waiting game as I sat across the street from Polar Boys off M. I had parked near a store called Garden Liquors, though there appeared to be no garden or greenery of any kind in the general vicinity. The projects were located one block over, and some vampire was doing landmark business out of the store, selling forties and pints and lottery tickets at 11:30 in the morning. I sat behind the wheel of my Dodge, alcohol sweat beaded on my forearms, my ravaged stomach and my own smell making me sick. I could have used a beer myself, and another one after that.

A half hour later, some men began to filter out of the steel door of Polar Boys, removing their jackets in the sun as they walked across the broiling brown grass, some toward the liquor store, others toward a roach coach parked by the loading dock. Soon another man walked out alone, a bearded man approaching middle age, with a pleasant face framing quiet, serene eyes. He wore khaki pants, thick-soled boots, and a brilliant blue coat. I felt my pulse quicken as I stepped out of my car, then a chemical energy as I crossed the street.

"How's it going?" I said, blocking the man's path on the sidewalk.

"Very well," he said, "thank you." He went to move around me. "Excuse me, please."

I stepped in front of him, keeping a friendly smile on my face. "Kind of hot to be wearin' that coat, isn't it?"

"Hot? Yes, I suppose it is." He tried again. "Excuse me."

I withdrew my wallet from my back pocket, flipped it open. "My name is Nick Stefanos. I'm a private investigator." He glanced at my license despite himself.

"Yes?"

"There was a murder down by the river a couple of weeks ago. A young man was shot in the mouth."

He waited, spoke carefully. "I read about it in the papers, I think. Yes, I seem to recall it."

"I'm working on that case. I'm going to be blunt with you, because I don't have much time. I believe you witnessed the murder."

"You're mistaken," he said. "Or misinformed. Now if you'll excuse me, I only have one hour for lunch."

"I'll just talk to your employer, then. And maybe after that I'll go over to that pay phone, give the police a call. Since this is just a misunderstanding, you won't mind clearing things up with them, right? Upstanding citizen like you—"

"Now wait a minute," he said, his shoulders relaxing. "What is it that you want?"

"An hour of your time, an answer or two. And then I'll go away."

He looked back at the icehouse, then at me. "You have a car?"

I jerked my chin toward the Dodge. Something came into his eyes, passed just as quickly. The two of us crossed the street. I opened the passenger door, looked at him as he began to climb inside.

"You know?" I said. "You don't look too crazy to me."

"Crazy?" he said, glancing up at me as he settled into his seat. "Why, Mr. Stefanos, of course I'm crazy. As crazy as Ahab, or Lady Macbeth, or the quiet man who trims your neighbor's lawn. We're all a little bit crazy, in our own way. Don't you agree?"

I GOT BACK ON M and took the 11th Street Bridge over the river, heading toward Anacostia. On the bridge, I caught him glancing over the rail, at the marinas and the clearing and the sunken houseboat below.

"What's your name, anyway?" I said.

"William Cooper."

I pushed in the dash lighter and put a cigarette to my lips. "I read a short story collection last year that I really liked. The stories were all set in D.C., written by a local guy. Guy's name was William C. Cooper."

"William C. Cooper," he said, "is me."

Cooper directed me to a short street off the east side of the bridge. We parked in front of his place, a clapboard row house fronted by a shaky wood porch, and went inside. I sat in a dark, comfortable living room while Cooper went off and built a couple of sandwiches and made a pitcher of iced tea. Books lined the shelves along the wall and were stacked on tables and beneath chairs throughout the room. I stood in the icy cool of the air conditioning and read the titles of the books, and after awhile Cooper, still wearing his coat, reentered the living room with lunch on a tray.

"You ever take that coat off?" I said between bites of a sandwich of sliced chicken on French bread with creole mayonnaise.

"I wear it from the time I leave every morning to the time I return from work."

"It's cold enough in the icehouse, and it's definitely cold enough in here. But why outside, in this heat?"

Cooper shrugged. "I've worked in that icehouse for many years and my body has just adjusted. I found that I was getting ill very often in the beginning, taking my coat off outdoors, putting it on again when I went back inside. My body temperature is kept constant this way, I suppose. These days, I rarely get sick. I guess you could say that this old coat has contributed quite nicely to my continued good health."

"You talk kinda funny, you know it?"

Cooper smiled tolerantly. "You mean, for a black man, don't you?"

"Partly," I admitted, "yeah. But to tell you the truth, I don't know many white folks who talk like you, either. And zero Greeks."

"It's not the world you travel in, that's all. I'm hardly a blue blood. I was raised in Shaw, but my higher education was extensive, and strictly Ivy League. It's not an affectation, I can assure you of that. It's simply where I spent my adult life."

"So a guy like you... why an icehouse?"

Cooper had a long drink of his tea. "I wore the white collar and the rep tie and the Harris tweed and found that the life of an academic bored me. The politics, and the people, all of it was utterly bloodless, and ultimately quite damaging to my work. I took the job in the icehouse so that I could once again have the freedom to think. It might appear to the outsider that I'm doing menial labor, but what I'm really doing, all day, is composing—writing, in effect, in my head. And the amount of material I soak up in that place, it's tremendous. Of course, I need the money, as well."

"What about your morning routine, under the bridge. The boatyard workers, they all pegged you as a headcase."

Cooper smiled. "And I did nothing to dispel their suspicions. That was always my time to be alone, and I preferred to keep it that way. I'd wake up in the morning, walk across the bridge, take my book and my cup of coffee, and have a seat under the Sousa. Sometimes I'd read, and oftentimes I'd sing. I'm in the choir at my church, you know, and the acoustics beneath that bridge are outstanding."

"Were you there the morning that boy was killed?"

"Yes," Cooper said with a nod. "And so were you. Your car was parked in the wooded area, to the right of the clearing. I recognized it as soon as you pointed it out to me."

"I didn't see anything, though. What did *you* see?"

"Not much. I heard a muted gunshot. Then a car drove by me, turned around at the dead end, and drove by once again."

"You see the driver or the passenger?"

"No."

"You read the plates?"

"No."

"What kind of car?"

"One of those off-road vehicles—I don't recall the model or make. A white one."

"Anything else to identify it?"

Cooper looked in my eyes. "A business name was printed on the side. 'Lighting and Equipment,' it said. Does that help you?"

I sat back in my chair. "Yes."

We finished our lunch in silence. He picked up the dishes and took them back into the kitchen. When he returned, I got up from the table.

"That do it?"

"One more question," I said. "Why didn't you go to the police?"

"I'm no one's hero, Mr. Stefanos. And I had no wish to become involved. My anonymity and my solitude are my most prized possessions. I don't expect you to understand. I'm sorry if you don't."

"I'm the last guy qualified to judge you."

"Then I guess we're through."

"Yes. I never met you and you never met me."

"Agreed," he said. "Though don't be surprised if you end up in one of my stories."

"Make me handsome," I said. "Will you?"

Cooper laughed and looked at his watch. "I'd better get going. Will you drop me back at work?"

"Yeah. I've gotta get to work, too."

I HIT THE FIRST pay phone past Polar Boys and called LaDuke. I got his machine, and left a message: "Jack, it's Nick. It's Tuesday, about one-thirty in the afternoon. I found the witness to the Jeter murder. The shooters drove a white van, said 'Lighting and Equipment' on the side—the van came from the lot of the warehouse on Potomac and Half, across the street from the warehouse we knocked over last week. The killers didn't leave town, Jack, they moved across the fucking street. Anyway, I'm headed home. Call me there when you get in; we'll figure out what to do next. Call me, hear?"

BUT LADUKE DIDN'T CALL. I waited, did some push-ups, worked my abs, and then took a shower. I dried off and put some Hüsker Du on the platter, then a Nation of Ulysses, and turned the volume way up. When the music stopped, I left a second message for LaDuke and sat around for another hour. Then I got my ten-speed out and rode it a hard eight miles, came back to the apartment, and took another shower. I dropped a frozen dinner in the oven, ate half of it, threw the rest away. I made a cup of coffee and lit a cigarette and smoked the cigarette out on my stoop. By then, it was evening.

I dressed in a black T-shirt and jeans, put an old pair of Docs on my feet, laced them tightly. I went into my bedroom and opened the bottom dresser drawer, looking for my gun. The gun was gone; I had dumped it in the trunk of LaDuke's Ford after the warehouse job. I thought about my homemade sap and a couple of knives I had collected, but I left them alone. I went back out to the living room, looked through the screen door. The night had come fully now, the moths tripping out in the light of the stoop. My cat came from the kitchen and brushed against my shin. I picked up the phone and dialed LaDuke.

"Jack," I said, speaking to the dead-air whir of his machine, "I'm going down there, to the warehouse. "It's..." I looked at my watch, "It's nine-forty-five. I've got to go down there, man. I've gotta see what's going on."

I stood there, listening to the quiet of my apartment and the rainlike hiss of the tape. My heart skipped and my hand tightened on the receiver.

"LaDuke!" I shouted. "Where the fuck *are* you, man?"

TWENTY-THREE

I STARTED THE Dodge and headed downtown. On North Capitol, between Florida and New York avenues, the people of the neighborhood were out, sitting on trash cans and stoops, their movements slow and deliberate. Later, passing through the Hill, the sidewalks were empty, the residents cocooned in their air-conditioned homes. Then in Southeast, by the projects, the people were outdoors again, shouting and laughing, the drumbeat of bass and the sputter of engines and the smell of reefer and tobacco smoke heavy in the air.

I turned onto Half and drove into a darkened landscape of line and shadow, animation fading to architecture. And then it was only me, winding the car around short, unlit streets, past parked trucks and fenced warehouses and silos, to the intersection of Potomac and Half.

I pulled behind a Dumpster and killed the engine. There was the tick of the engine, no other sound. A rat ran from beneath the Dumpster and scurried under the fence of an empty lot. I lit a cigarette, hit it deep. I had a look around.

The knock-over warehouse sat still and abandoned, no cars in the lot, a police tape, wilted and fallen, formed around the concrete stoop.

Across the street, near the steel door of the second warehouse, two LIGHTING AND EQUIPMENT vans and the Buick Le Sabre were parked behind a fence topped with barbed wire.

I looked up at the east face of the building: A fire escape led to a second-story sash window. Behind the window, a pale yellow light glowed faintly from the depths of a hall. I dragged on my cigarette. Ten minutes later, I lit another. Through the second-story window, a shadow passed along the wall. The shadow disintegrated, and then it was just the pale yellow light.

I pitched my cigarette and stepped out of my car. I crossed the street.

Putting my fingers through the fence, I climbed it, then got over the double row of barbs without a stick. I swung to the other side of the fence, got halfway down its face, and dropped to the pavement in a crouch. My palms were damp; I rubbed them dry on the side of my jeans. Staying in the crouch, I moved across the lot to the bricks of the building.

I touched the wall, put myself flat up against it. My heart pumped against the bricks. I could hear it in my chest, and the sound of my breathing, heavy and strained. Sweat burned my eyes and dripped down my back. I blinked the burn out of my eyes. I waited for everything to slow down.

The air moved in back of me as I stepped away from the wall. I started to turn around, stopped when something cool and metallic pressed against the soft spot behind my ear. Then the click of a hammer and the hammer locking down.

"Don't shoot me," I said.

Coley's voice: "You came back. *Damn,* you know? I was hoping you would."

"You don't have to shoot me," I said.

"You'll live a little longer," he said, "if you keep your mouth shut. You'd like to live a little while longer, wouldn't you?"

"Yes."

Coley pushed the muzzle in on my skin. "You alone?"

I nodded.

"Walk to the door," Coley said.

He kept the gun against my head, put his hand on my shoulder, and pushed me along the wall to the steel door at the wall's end. I looked up, saw the window at the top of the fire escape, saw that it was open—the only way out, if I got the chance. Then we were at the end of the wall.

Coley reached over my shoulder and knocked on the door.

"Listen to this," he said with a chuckle. "My redneck friend Sweet, he's gotten all jumpy and shit since you and your pretty sidekick fucked up his face."

Sweet's voice came from behind the door. "Yeah?"

"It's Coley, man. Lemme in."

"Prove it," Sweet said.

"I'll prove it all over your narrow ass. Open this motherfucker *up*. Right now."

I stood there, staring at the door, unable to raise spit, not wanting the door to open.

"Open it, Sweet," said Coley. "I got someone here you been wantin' to see."

The door opened. Coley pushed between my shoulder blades, and then we were inside. Sweet closed the door, slid a bolt and dropped it, and grinned. He turned the key on the lock and slipped the key in his pocket.

"My, my," he said. The bruised side of his face had gone to purple and one eye drooped where the socket had caved. He wore a sleeveless T-shirt tucked into jeans. The knife-in-skull tattoo contracted on his tightly muscled, drug-thin forearm as he reached behind his back. He pulled his gun and lightly touched the barrel to my cheek. The gun was a .22.

"My, my," he said again.

"Let's take him upstairs," Coley said.

Sweet stroked at the hairs of his billy-goat beard. "Right."

I walked between them down a hall that was empty, then into a large room crowded with garden tools and machinery. In the center of the room was an oak table and some chairs, where several men were seated. I could see a scale on the table, amid many bottles of beer, but I didn't linger on the setup, and I didn't look any of the men in the eye. Coley kept walking, and I stayed behind him. Once in a while, Sweet prodded me on the neck with the muzzle of the .22, and when he did it, a couple of the men at the table laughed. One of them made a joke at Sweet's expense, then all of them laughed at once, and Sweet prodded me harder and with more malice.

Coley cut left at an open set of stairs. I followed, relieved to be going out of the large room. We took the stairs, which were wooden and did not turn, up to the second floor, through an open frame, Sweet's footsteps close behind me. Then we turned into another hall with offices of some kind on either side, the offices windowed in corrugated glass. Through one open door, I saw an old printing press, and I noticed that the outside windows had been bricked up. The hallway of corrugated glass ended and the room widened, shelved floor to ceiling, with paints, thinners, glass jars, brushes, and rags on the shelves. Then there was a bathroom, its outside window bricked up, and then an open door, where Coley turned and stepped inside. I followed, noticing before I did the window leading to the fire escape at the end of the hall. Sweet came into the room behind me and shut the door.

"Keep your gun on him," Sweet said.

"Yes, *sir*," Coley said, amused.

Sweet went to the door, connected a chain from door to frame, and slid the bolt. Coley held his gun, a .38 Special, loosely in his hand and kept it pointed at my middle. He shifted his attention to Sweet, fixing the chain lock in place. Coley's eyes smiled.

The room had no furniture except for a simple wooden chair turned on its side against a wall. An overflowed foil ashtray sat on the scarred hardwood floor, next to the chair. There had been a window once, but now the window was brick.

"Hold this," Sweet said. He handed Coley the .22. Coley took the gun, let that one hang by his side. "Good thing you were outside, Coley."

"Heard that car of his. Some old muscle car with dual exhaust and shit. Makes one hell of a racket. Not the kind of ride you want to be usin' when you're trying to make a quiet entrance. Not too smart."

"Yeah," Sweet said. "Real stupid."

Sweet came and stood in front of me, not more than three feet away. He shifted his shoulders, smiled a little, his vaguely Asian eyes disappearing with the smile. Alcohol smell came off him, and he stunk of day-old perspiration.

"You see what your partner did to my face?" he said.

I didn't answer. I tried to think of something I had that they would want, something that would save my life. But I couldn't think of one thing. The realization that they were going to kill me sucked the blood out of my face.

Sweet said, "Our friend here looks afraid. What you think, Coley? You think he looks afraid?"

"He does look a little pale," Coley said.

"You afraid?" Sweet said, moving one step in. "Huh?"

I didn't see the right hand. It was quick, without form or shape, and Sweet put everything into it. He hit me full on the face, and the blow knocked me off my feet. My back hit the wall and my legs gave out. I slid down the wall to the floor.

"Whew," said Coley.

Sweet walked across the room, bent over, grabbed a handful of my shirt. He pulled me up. The room moved, Sweet's face splitting in two and coming back to one. He hit me in the face with a sharp right. Then he pulled back and hit me again, released his grip on my shirt. I fell to the floor. I swallowed blood, tasted blood in my mouth. Stars exploded in the blackness behind my eyes.

"Fuck!" I heard Sweet say. "I fucked up my fuckin' hand on his face!"

"Go clean it up," Coley said.

"The guy's a pussy," Sweet said. "Won't even fight me back. I think maybe he likes it. What do you think, Coley? You think he likes it?"

"Go clean up your hand," said Coley.

"Lock the door behind me," Sweet said.

"Yeah," Coley said, chuckling. "I'll do that."

Sweet left the room. When the door closed, I opened my eyes and got up on one elbow. Coley did not move to lock the door. I pushed myself over to the wall, sat up with my back against it. I looked at Coley, who stood in the center of the room, looking at me.

"You know," Coley said, "we're just gonna have to go on and kill you."

I wiped blood from my face with a shaky hand. I stared at the floor.

"The reason I'm tellin' you is, I hate to see a man go down without some kind of fight. That little redneck's gonna come back in here, and if you let him, he's gonna bitch-slap your ass all around. I mean, you're dead, anyway. But it's important, and shit, not to go out like some kind of punk. Know what I'm sayin'?"

I flashed on my drunken night by the river, hearing similar words spoken to Calvin Jeter. Spoken, I knew now, by Coley.

"Anyway, you got a little while," Coley said. "I'm gonna ask you a few questions first, partly for business and partly just because I'm curious. Whether you answer or not, either way, I'm gonna have to put a bullet in your head tonight. Just thought you might like to know."

There was a knock on the door.

"It's open," Coley said.

Sweet walked in, looked with disappointment at the chain swinging free on the frame. "I thought I told you to lock it."

"*Damn*," Coley said mockingly. "I damn sure forgot."

Sweet looked at me. "Get up," he said.

I stood slowly, gave myself some distance from the wall. I looked at Sweet's right hand: swollen, the knuckles skinned and raw. He walked toward me, the inbred's grin on his cockeyed face. He balled his right fist, but his right was done; I knew he wouldn't use it, knew he would go with the left. He came in. He faked the right and dropped the left.

I moved to the side, bent my knees, and sprang up, swinging with the momentum. I whipped my open hand into his throat, snapping my wrist sharply at the point of contact, aiming for the back of his neck. My straight-open hand connected at his Adam's apple, knocking him one step back. It felt as if a piece of Styrofoam had snapped.

Sweet grabbed at his throat with both hands. I went in, threw one deep right, followed through with it, dead square where his nose met the purple bruise of his face. Something gave with the punch; blood sprayed onto my shirt and Sweet went down. He fell to his side, moved a little, made choking sounds. Then he did not move at all. His hands dropped away from his throat.

"God*damn,*" Coley said. "You kill 'im?"

"No. You hit the Adam's apple, the muscles around it contract, for protection. Cuts off your breathing for a few seconds. He'll live."

I heard Coley's slow footsteps as he crossed the room. The footsteps swelled, then stopped.

"What'd you call that?" Coley said, close behind me. "That thing you did to his throat?"

"Ridge hand," I said.

"Sweet's gonna want to know," Coley said, "when he wakes up."

I felt a blunt shock to the back of my head and a short, sharp pain. The floor dropped out from beneath my feet, and I was falling, diving toward a pool of cool black water. Then I was in the black water, and there was only the water, and nothing left of me. Nothing left at all.

* * *

I WOKE FROM A dream of water.

"Some water," I said, looking at their feet.

Coley's shoes were between the legs of the chair, where he now sat. Sweet's were near my face.

"Get him some water," Coley said.

"Fuck a lotta water," Sweet said.

Sweet's shoes moved out of my field of vision. Then his knee dropped onto my back. I grunted as the knee dug into my spine. Sweet took my arm at the wrist and twisted it behind my back. I sucked at the air.

"Where's your partner?" he said, his breath hot on my neck. "The one with the shotgun."

"He's gone," I said, my voice high and unsteady.

"He's gone," Sweet said, mimicking my tone. He giggled and pushed my hand up toward my shoulders. He held my other hand flat to the hardwood floor. I tried to dig my nails into the wood.

"Where's he gone *to?*" Coley said.

"He split with his share of the money," I said. "I don't know where he went."

Sweet jerked my arm up. I thought my arm would break if he pushed it farther. Then he pushed it farther. It hit a nerve, and the room flashed white. I tightened my jaw, breathed in and out rapidly through my nose.

"Uh," I said.

"Say what?" Sweet said.

"Where is he?" Coley said.

My eyes teared up. Everything in front of me was slanted and soft.

"I don't know where he is," I said. "Coley, I don't know."

Coley said nothing.

Sweet released my arm. I rested the side of my face on the floor.

Then Sweet grabbed a handful of hair at the back of my

head and yanked my head back up. He slammed my face into the floor. Blood spilled out of my nose and onto the wood. My mouth was wet with it; I breathed it in and coughed. I looked at the grain in the wood and the blood spreading over the grain.

"God*damn*, Sweet," Coley said. "You're just fuckin' this man all *up*."

Sweet twisted my hair, yanked my head up out of the blood. My eyes rolled up toward the ceiling. Purple clouds blinked in front of my eyes and I heard the gurgle of my own voice. I felt Sweet push down on the back of my head. I saw the wood rushing toward my face. The wood was black, like black water. I was in the water, and it was blessedly cool.

I OPENED MY EYES.

I stared at the ceiling. It was a drop ceiling tiled in particleboard, with water damage in some of the tiles. Naked fluorescent fixtures hung from the ceiling. The light bore into my eyes.

I rolled onto my side. A Dixie cup full of water sat on the floor. Beyond the cup, a large roach crawled across the floor. It crawled toward Sweet's boots. Past Sweet's boots, Coley's shoes were centered between the legs of the chair.

I got up, leaned on my forearm, and drank the water. I thought I would puke, but I did not. I dropped the cup on the floor and dragged myself over to the wall. I put my back against the wall, sat there. My nose ached badly and there was a ripping pain behind my eyes. I rubbed my hand on my mouth, flaked off the blood that had dried there. Coley was seated in the chair and Sweet stood with his back against the opposite wall. The .22 dangled in Sweet's hand, pointed at the floor. I looked at Coley. Coley moved his chin up an inch.

"Let's kill him," Sweet said. "You said to wait till he woke up. Well, he's up."

"Not yet. I want to get the word first."

"Fuck the word. Let's kill him now."

"Not yet," said Coley.

It went back and forth like that for a while. I started to feel a little better. Time passed, and I felt better still. The hate was doing it. What they had done to me and the thought of it were making me stronger.

I looked around the room: nothing to use as a weapon. Nothing on me but my car keys and a pack of matches. The keys were something; I could palm one, stab a key into Sweet's eye when he came for me. I could hurt him in an awful way before he killed me. Somehow, I would do that. I would try.

"Go downstairs," Coley said to Sweet. "Go down and call him. See what he wants to do."

"Yeah, okay," Sweet said. "You lock that door behind me, hear?"

"Sure thing."

"I mean it," Sweet said. "I'm gonna listen outside that door, make sure you do it." And then to me: "I'll be back in ten minutes. That's how long you got to live. Ten minutes. You think about that."

Sweet walked from the room. He shut the door, and Coley got up from his chair and went to the door. He jangled the chain around in the bolt, made sure Sweet heard the jangle from the other side of the door. Then he dropped the chain without locking it, chuckling as he walked back to his chair. He sat in the chair. His eyes moved to the door and then to me.

"Don't get any ideas about that door," Coley said. " 'Cause this thirty-eight, at this range? You *know* I won't miss."

"I'm not going anywhere."

"Good. That thing with the door, I just like to rattle that little redneck's cage a little bit, that's all." Coley grinned. "You fucked him up pretty good, too. 'Course, he did you right back. He manage to break that nose of yours?"

"I don't think so."

"But it's been broke before."

"Yeah."

"I can see. Where you get that scar on your cheek, man?"

"Who cut off your ear?"

Coley showed me some teeth. "Some brother, in the showers at the Maryland State Pen. Looked at him the wrong way, I guess. All part of my rehabilitation and shit."

"That where you two are from? Baltimore?"

"Yeah. Roundabout that way. Why?"

"Nothing." I looked Coley in the eyes. "You killed Roland, and the Jeter kid, too. Didn't you?"

"Jeter, huh? That's what that boy's name was? Well, I didn't pull the trigger. I take no pleasure in that, though I'll do it if it's called for. Sweet was the triggerman. He likes it, you know. But I guess you could say I killed those boys, yeah."

"Why?"

"We're runnin' a business here, and we got to protect that. Powder right into the projects, straight up. They turn it to rock and then they kill themselves over that shit. But our end, we keep it clean. Now, my boss, the man who bankrolls all this? He favors boys. Young brothers, that's what he likes. Likes to watch 'em on the videotape. He had this idea, why not get them in here and put 'em on tape, use 'em to run powder on the side. I could have told him that shit wouldn't go. One of them got scared and the other one got greedy. We just had to go on and do 'em both."

"Who's your boss?" I said.

Coley laughed. "Aw, go on. What you think this is, *True Confessions* and shit? Uh-uh, man, you're just gonna have to check out not knowing all that. Now let me ask you somethin'."

"Go ahead."

"Why'd you knock us over? It wasn't for the money, I know that."

"I was just trying to save a kid's life. I was only trying to get Roland out of there. He didn't even know who we were."

"He wasn't with you?"

"No. You killed him for nothing."

Coley shrugged. "He would've made me, anyway. Eventually,

he would've done somethin' to make me kill 'im. He was that way. Just *difficult* and shit."

Coley used the barrel of his gun to scratch his forehead. I eased my keys out of my pocket, palmed them, let the tip of the longest one peek through the fingers of my fist.

"But you know," Coley said, "that don't explain why you came back tonight."

"I wasn't finished," I said. "I needed to know the rest of it."

"Now you know," Coley said. "Kind of a silly thing to die for, isn't it?"

"Yeah," I said. "I guess it is."

Coley exhaled slowly, looked at me sadly. "I seen you pull out those keys and shit. Why don't you just slide them over here, man. I'll make sure what gets done to you gets done to you quick."

I tossed the keys to the center of the floor. Footsteps sounded in the hall, louder with each step. Coley got out of his chair, bent over, and picked up the keys. He slipped them in his pocket.

There was a knock on the door.

Coley smiled. "Come on in, Sweet. It's open."

The door opened.

Jack LaDuke stepped into the room, the Ithaca in his hands.

The smile froze on Coley's face. "Goddamn," he said. "God*damn*."

LaDuke pointed his shotgun at Coley. Coley pointed the .38 at LaDuke.

"LaDuke," I said.

"Nick."

LaDuke kicked the door shut behind him, kept his eyes and the shotgun on Coley. LaDuke was wearing his black suit and the solid black tie. I felt a rush of affection for him then; looking at him, I could have laughed out loud.

"Where you been?" I said.

"Office of Deeds, like you taught me." Without moving anything but his free arm, he reached under the tail of his jacket and drew my Browning. "This is you."

He tossed the gun in my direction. I caught it, ejected the magazine, checked it, slapped the magazine back in the butt. I pointed the Browning at Coley. Coley kept the .38 on LaDuke.

"How'd you get in, LaDuke?"

"Fire escape. The window was open—"

"*Damn,*" said Coley.

"And then I just came down the hall. Heard you guys talkin'."

"Good to see you, LaDuke."

"You all right? You look pretty fucked up."

"I'm okay. Now we gotta figure out how to get outta here."

"Uh-*uh,*" Coley said.

"What's that?" LaDuke said.

"You know I can't let you fellahs do that," Coley said, still smiling, the smile weird and tight. Bullets of sweat had formed on his forehead and sweat had beaded in his mustache.

LaDuke took one step in. The floorboard creaked beneath his weight.

Coley stiffened his gun arm and did not move.

"Let's get out of here, LaDuke."

"Maybe you *ought* to run, Pretty Boy," Coley said.

LaDuke's face reddened.

"And maybe," LaDuke said, "you ought to make a move."

"LaDuke," I said.

His finger tightened on the trigger.

"Know what this thirty-eight'll do to that pretty face?" Coley said.

LaDuke just smiled.

Their eyes locked, and neither of them moved. The sound of our breathing was the only sound in the room.

"Hey, Jack," I said, very quietly.

Coley squeezed the trigger on the .38 and LaDuke squeezed the trigger on the shotgun—both of them, at once.

TWENTY-FOUR

THE ROOM EXPLODED in a sucking roar of sonics and fine red spray. LaDuke's head jerked sharply to the side, as if he had been slapped.

A rag doll slammed against the wall, fell in a heap to the floor, the head dropping sloppily to the chest. The rag doll wore the clothes of Coley. Everything above the hairline was gone, the face unrecognizable; the face was soup.

"I'm shot, Nick," LaDuke said almost giddily. "I'm shot!"

I went to him, pulled him around.

The right side of his jaw was exposed, skinless, with pink rapidly seeping into the pearl of the bone. You're okay, LaDuke, I thought. You turned your head at the last moment and Coley blew off the side of your face. You're going to be badly scarred and a little ugly, but you're going to be okay.

And then I saw the hole in his neck, the exit hole or maybe the entry, rimmed purple and blackened from the powder, the hole the size of a quarter. Blood pumped rhythmically from the hole, spilling slowly over the collar of LaDuke's starched white shirt, meeting the blood that was the blow-back from Coley.

"Nick," LaDuke said, and he nearly laughed. "I'm shot!"

"Yeah, you're shot. Come on, let's get out of here. Let's go."

I went to Coley, kicked his hand away from the front of his pants, where it lay. I reached into his pocket and retrieved my keys. LaDuke stood by the door, facing it, shuffling his feet nervously, one hand on the stock of the Ithaca, the other on its barrel. I crossed the room.

"How many in the shotgun?" I said.

"Huh?"

"How many in that Ithaca?"

LaDuke mouthed the count, struggled to make things clear in his head. "It's a five-shot. Four now, I guess."

"You got more shells?"

He nodded. "And my Cobra. And your extra clip."

"Good. Give it to me." I took the extra magazine, slipped it in my back pocket. "Now listen. There's more of them, and they're gonna be comin' up the stairs. Maybe outside, covering the fire escape, too."

"Okay."

"We gotta go out this door now, see what's what. We gotta go now. We don't want to be trapped in this room."

"Okay."

I jacked a round into the chamber of my nine. LaDuke pumped one into the Ithaca.

"You ready?"

"Yes," LaDuke said, nodding rapidly. "I'm ready."

I opened the door, ran out blindly, LaDuke close behind me. I turned to my left.

A man was coming through the open window at the end of the hall. He was cursing, pulling at his shirt where it had snagged on a nail in the frame. There was a .45 in his free hand.

From the stairway at the other end of the hall, Sweet

emerged from the darkness. Sweet ran toward us, the .22 straight out in front of him.

"You!" he shouted.

I kept my eyes on the man in the window. My back bumped LaDuke's. I heard the pop of the .22, and the round blowing past us, and the ricochet off the metal shelving in the hall.

"Kill Sweet, LaDuke. Kill him."

LaDuke fired the shotgun. Sweet's scream echoed in the hall behind me. Then the .22 was popping and the shotgun roared over the pop of the gun.

The man in the window freed himself, pointed his weapon in my direction. I fell to the side, squeezed the trigger on the nine, squeezed it three times, saw the man was hit, saw him caught in the broken glass. I aimed, squeezed off another round. The man in the window rocked back, then pitched forward, a black hole on his cheek and a hole spitting blood from his chest. The casings from my gun pinged to the floor. I turned around at the sound of the Ithaca's pump.

LaDuke walked between the offices fronted with corrugated glass. He stood over the convulsing body of Sweet, Sweet's heels rattling at the hardwood floor. LaDuke kicked him like an animal. He stepped back, fired the shotgun. Flame came from the barrel and wood splintered off the floor. Sweet's body lifted and rolled.

"Hey, Nick," LaDuke said. Through the smoke, I could see his crazy, crooked smile.

A man in a blue shirt came running out of the stairwell, an automatic in his hand.

I shouted, "LaDuke!"

LaDuke stepped through an open door. Blue Shirt moved his gun arm in my direction.

I dove and tumbled into the bathroom as a vanity mirror exploded above my head. Another round blew through the doorway. The round sparked, ricocheted, took off some tiles. A ceramic triangle ripped at my sleeve. The glass of the shower door spidered and flew apart. Glass rained down and stung at my face.

I looked behind me, saw the bricked-up window. The footsteps of the shooter sounded near the door. I could feel the sweat on my back and the weight of glass in my hair. The Browning felt slick in my hands. I gripped it with both hands. From the hall, LaDuke yelled my name.

Then there were gunshots, and more glass, the corrugated glass of the offices blowing apart. I rolled, screaming, out of the bathroom, looked for anything blue, saw blue and the black of LaDuke's black suit, fired my gun at the blue.

The man in the blue shirt danced backward, shot off his feet, caught between the bullet of my gun and the blast of LaDuke's shotgun. He hit the floor, saliva and blood slopping from his open mouth.

I walked through the smoke toward LaDuke, glass crunching beneath my feet. A steady high note sounded in my ears and blood pumped violently in my chest. LaDuke pulled a fistful of shells from his jacket pocket, thumbed them into the Ithaca. I wrist-jerked the magazine out of my automatic, found the loaded clip in my back pocket. My hand shook wildly as I slapped it in.

"What now?" LaDuke said.

"Out the window," I said. "Come on."

"I say we finish things up downstairs. The rest of them are down those stairs."

"You're bleeding bad, Jack. You gotta get to a hospital, man."

I couldn't tell if he had been shot again. There was an awful lot of blood on his shirt now; blood still pulsed from the hole in his neck.

"You see that turpentine, man, and those jars?"

"Jack."

"Come here, Nick. I gonna show you what we're gonna do now."

He went to the shelved area of the hall, and I followed.

Behind us, from the stairwell, I could hear men shouting at us from the first floor.

LaDuke stopped at the jars and the thinners and the paints. He put his shotgun on the floor. I kept my gun trained on the stairwell. He poured paint thinner into the jars, then ripped some rags apart, doused the rags in thinner, and stuffed the doused rags into the necks of the jars.

I put my hand around his arm, but he jerked his arm away.

"Man," he said, "we are going to light this motherfucker up!"

"Let's go, Jack."

LaDuke smiled, the smile waxy and frightening. The bone of his jaw was jagged and the pink had gone to red. His eyes were hard and bright.

"You're going into shock, Jack."

"You got matches? You always got matches, Nick."

The men continued to shout from below. From the window at the end of the hall, I could hear the faint beginnings of a siren. I found my matches and pressed them into LaDuke's clammy palm.

"Thanks," he said, picking up the jars and cradling them in his arms. "It's all been leading up to this for me. You know that, don't you, Nick?"

"Bullshit. The object is to stay alive. Nothing else. If you got a different idea, then you're an idiot, LaDuke. I'm not going through that door with you, man. I'm not coming with you. You hear me? I'm not."

"See you around, Nick."

He walked down the hall toward the open doorway of the stairwell. I went the opposite way and got to the window. I climbed halfway through the window, then looked back.

LaDuke passed in front of the open doorway. A round fired from below and sparked at his feet. He kept walking calmly with the jars tight to his chest, stopping on the other side of the doorway. He set the jars down on the floor and drew the .357 Cobra from the holster behind his back.

"Jack," I said, almost to myself. Then I screamed his name out with all I had. But he didn't respond. He didn't even move at the sound of his name.

LaDuke struck a match. He touched the match to the three rags, ignited them all. He took one jar and tossed it down the stairs. It blew immediately, sending heat and fire up through the open frame. The men below began to yell. LaDuke threw the second jar, then the third right behind it. Smoke poured up from the stairwell and there was a muffled explosion; the men's voices intensified.

LaDuke pulled the hammer back on the Cobra. He turned the corner and disappeared into the smoke.

There were gunshots then, gunshots and screams. I closed my eyes and stepped out onto the fire escape. It was still night, and two sirens wailed from far away. I went down the fire escape, hung on the end of it, and dropped to the pavement.

LaDuke had driven the Ford right into the fence. There was a hole there now, where the hood protruded into the lot. I walked straight out and crossed the street to my Dodge.

The sirens swelled and there were more gunshots. The spit and crackle of the fire deepened and the screams grew more frenzied. I got in, closed the door and turned the ignition key, and kept the windows rolled up tight. I couldn't hear anything then, except for the engine. I put the car in gear, zigzagged out of the warehouse district with my headlights off. When I hit M, I flipped on my lights and headed west.

I drove across town through empty streets. Fifteen minutes later, I entered Beach Drive and the cool green cover of Rock Creek Park. I touched the dash lighter to a cigarette.

I rolled down my window. The sounds of the guns and the sounds of the fire had gone away. The screams had not.

TWENTY-FIVE

I DROVE TO my apartment and dropped into bed. Maybe I slept. The dreams I had were waking dreams, or maybe they were not. I turned over on my side, stayed there until noon. Slots of dirty gray light leaked through the spaces in the drawn bedroom blinds. I could hear the drone of a lawn mower, and from the kitchen, my cat, pacing, making small hungry sounds. I got out of bed, went to the kitchen, and spooned a can of salmon into her dish.

The *Post*'s final edition was lying out on the stoop beneath a sunless sky, its plastic wrap warm to the touch. I brought the newspaper inside, made a cup of coffee, and had a seat on my living room couch. The burning of the warehouse—the burning and the death—had made the front page. Nothing about violence, though, and no mention of foul play. That would come later in the day, or the next.

I thought of my bullet casings scattered on the second floor of the warehouse. And then there was the matter of my prints. If Boyle and Johnson chose to push it and make the connection, the casings could be traced to my gun. I'd have to get rid of the Browning, and I didn't have much time.

I battered a slice of eggplant, fried it, and put it between two slices of bread, then washed it down with another cup of coffee. Then I took a long, cold shower and reapplied ointment to the cuts in my face, where I had tweezered out the slivers of glass the night before. In the mirror, I looked at my swollen eyes, the area beneath my left eye, black and gorged with blood, and the purple arc across the bridge of my nose. I looked into my own eyes and I thought, That thing in the mirror is not me. But when I moved, the thing in the mirror moved in the exact same way. And I was the only one standing in the room.

I shook some Tylenols out into my hand, ate them, and got dressed. Then I went out to my Dodge and headed downtown.

I PARKED NEAR THE District Building, walked toward the CCNV shelter on D, and cut into the courtyard at the Department of Labor. There was a blind corner there where some men from the shelter gathered to smoke reefer and drink beer and fortified wine during the day. Two men stood with their backs against the gray concrete, passing a bottle of Train in the midday heat. I picked the cleaner of the two, engaged him in a brief introduction, and took him to lunch at a bar called My Brother's Place on 2nd and C. Then I had him clean up in the upstairs bathroom, and when he sat back down at our table, smelling a little less powerfully than he had before, I handed him some written instructions and ripped a twenty in half, promising him the other half upon his successful return. He shambled off in the direction of the Office of Deeds. This man would disappear eventually, become one of the anonymous urban MIA. But looking as I did, even with the benefit of elapsed time, I knew that I would be remembered later on.

I had a slow beer and a shot of bourbon out on the patio and talked to my friend Charles, the bar's dishwasher and unofficial bouncer, an unassuming giant and tireless worker who is one of the few purely principled men left in this city. Then the man from the shelter returned and gave me my information. I sat staring at it, and I laughed, but it was laughter devoid of pleasure, and the man from the shelter asked me what was funny.

"Nothing's funny," I said. "I thought I was pretty smart, but I'm stupid, and I think that's pretty goddamn funny. Don't you?"

He shrugged and took the rest of his twenty. I tore up the written instructions and asked him if there was anything he'd like, and he said he'd like a Crown Royal rocks with a splash of water. I ordered him one and dropped money on the table, then left the coolness of the overhead fan and walked back into the heat.

Back in my apartment, I made a phone call and set the time for the appointment. Then I took a nap and another shower, gathered up the instruments that I thought I might need. On the way out the door, I passed the mirror that hung on the living room wall and saw the thing with the purple nose and the blood-gorged eye—the thing that was not me—walking toward the door.

I PARKED IN THE lighted lot at 22nd and M. It was night, and the heat that had enshrouded the city for days had not receded. Suburban kids locked their Jeeps and Mustang 5.0s and walked toward the New Orleans–style nightspot on the north side of M, the boys clean-shaven and beer-muscle cocky, the girls freshly showered and dressed in the latest cookie-cutter, mall-purchased attire. I lit a cigarette and dangled the cigarette out the open window.

At nine o'clock sharp, Richard Samuels walked across the lot to my car, his fine white hair catching the light. He wore a tie but no jacket, the tie's knot firmly entrapped between the points of his tabbed white collar. He saw my Dodge and then me, and he forced a spring in his step. He opened the passenger door and dropped into the bucket. His face was ridged with lines of sweat.

"Mr. Stefanos."

"Samuels."

"My God, what happened to your face?"

"Your people," I said.

"Yes," he said. "Well."

I dragged on my cigarette, flipped it out, where it arced to the asphalt. "No one knows you're here?"

"No. Of course, you phoned today when my secretary was out. No, no one knows but you and me."

"Good."

Samuels relaxed his shoulders. "I'll tell you, I've had one hell of a day. The police came to me first thing this morning. And the insurance people have been swarming all over me. What with you bringing Vice down on me last week, it's not going to be long before this whole thing blows up in my face, and yours. I'm not waiting around to find out how it plays out. I assume you'll be leaving town, too, after we settle things."

"You're pretty casual about all this, Samuels."

"Just practical." He spread his manicured hands. "I'm a businessman, after all. I've always known when to cut my losses. Surely you would understand. I mean, that's what this is about, isn't it?" I stared ahead. "Now, your partner, the one who you brought along to my office? He didn't understand at all. He let his emotions get in the way of what is, after all, a process of logic. I assume that he died with my men. His emotions were what killed him, isn't that right?"

I gripped the steering wheel, watched the blood leave my knuckles. "How does a man like you get involved in all this, anyway?"

Samuel's wet red lips parted in a weak smile. "Simply put, I saw the demand in the market. In the world I traveled in, in the 1980s, it seemed as if every commercial broker in D.C. was driving around town in his three-twenty-five, a one shot vial of coke lying within easy reach. I thought, Why don't I get some of that action? It wasn't difficult to locate and establish a relationship with a supplier, and soon afterward I was in business. Then cocaine went out of white-collar fashion—for the most part, anyway—and the market went from powder to rock. I simply made an adjustment. My supplier put me in touch with some gentlemen who could deal with the rougher situations, and I moved the powder straight into the inner city. I had the space to run it through—"

"Your real estate holdings. And your profit centers—you make movies; you own the equipment, and the lights. You said yourself, the first time I met you, that you favored control all the way down the line."

"Yes. And I had the manpower to make it work. My own hands never touched the stuff. It was going beautifully, in fact, until you intervened."

"You made a mistake. You had a couple of innocent kids killed."

"Innocent? Mr. Stefanos, don't be naïve. I'm not happy at how it turned out for them, but—"

"Don't. I know all about you, Samuels."

Samuels stared off balefully in a theatrical gesture of remorse. He looked into his lap and spoke softly. "I can't help the way I am, any more than you can change your own proclivities. The decision I made was a business decision, as are all of my decisions. As this is, right now." He straightened his posture. "Which brings us to the real reason we're sitting here."

"Let's get to it, then."

"All right. How much?"

"What?"

"How much do you want? What is it going to take to make you go away?"

"Samuels," I said, reaching beneath my seat, "I think you've misunderstood me."

His eyes widened as I brought up my sap. He tried to raise his hands, but he was too old and way too slow. I swung the sap sharply, connecting at his temple. He slumped forward, his forehead coming to rest against the glove box.

I checked his breathing, then pulled everything else up from beneath the seat. I tied his hands behind his back and covered his mouth with duct tape. A wool army blanket lay folded in the backseat. I arranged Samuels fetally and covered him with the blanket.

I eased out of the lot and headed east.

I PARKED IN THE clearing that faced the river and cut the engine. The lights of the Sousa Bridge shimmered on the river's black water. Through the trees, Christmas lights glowed colorfully, strung along the dock of the marina. Country music and the laughter of a woman lifted off a pontoon boat and drifted in on the river breeze.

I took the blanket off Samuels and sat him up. His silver hair was soaked in sweat, his complexion pale and splotched. I pulled the duct tape away from his mouth, let the tape dangle from his face. His eyes blinked open, then slowly closed. I poured some bottled water on his lips and poured some into his open mouth. He coughed it out, straightened up in his seat, opened his eyes, kept them open as he moved to make himself comfortable. Samuels stared at the river.

"Untie me, please," he said quietly.

"No." I reached over and loosened the knot of his tie. He breathed out, his breath like a long deflation.

"Please," he said.

"No. And don't think of screaming. I'll have to tape your mouth again. All right?"

Samuels nodded blankly. I slipped my cigarette pack from the visor and rustled it in his direction. He shook his head. I lit one for myself. I smoked some of it down.

Samuels said, "*Why?* I don't *understand* this. I can't believe... I can't believe we can't make some sort of deal."

I exhaled smoke and watched it fade.

"I just don't understand," he said.

Some birds glided down from the trees and went to black against the moon. A Whaler passed in the river, the throttle on full, its wake spreading in a swirl of foam and current. I thought of my grandfather and closed my eyes.

Samuels turned in my direction. "Do you ever wonder where dead men go, Mr. Stefanos?"

I didn't reply.

"What I mean is, do you believe in God?"

The woman from the party boat screamed and then there was more laughter, her laughter drunken and mixed with the wolfish shouts of men.

"No," Samuels said. "Of course you don't. Everything is black and white with people like you. People like you can't even see the possibility of a higher power. No, I'm certain that if you were asked, you'd say that there is no God." Samuels's face turned childish, impudent. "*I* believe in God. You're saying to yourself, There's a contradiction here, a man like this believing in God. But you know, I pray for myself every day. And do you think I could have sent those boys to their deaths if I didn't believe that I was sending them to a better place? Do you think that?" He chewed at his lip. "I'm sorry. I'm talking quite a bit, aren't I? I'm nervous, you know."

I stabbed my cigarette out in the ashtray.

"Talk to me," he said, a quiver in his voice. "Why don't you say something to me, please."

I fixed the tape back over his mouth and stepped out of the car. I went around to the other side, opened the door, and pulled him out. He fell to his side, tried to stay down. I yanked him back to his feet. Samuels bugged his eyes, made muffled moaning sounds beneath the tape.

I pushed him along the graveled clearing, his feet dragging, stirring up dust. We got to the bulkhead, where the river lapped at the concrete. Beyond the bulkhead, the Whaler's wake splashed against the pilings and slipped over the rusted window frames of the sunken houseboat.

Samuels's hands squirmed against the rope. I turned his back to the water and kicked him behind the legs. He fell to his knees. I ripped the duct tape off his face.

"Oh, God," he said as I drew the Browning from behind my back.

"There isn't one," I said, and shoved the barrel into his open mouth. "Remember?"

TWENTY-SIX

I BURIED UNCLE Costa in the fall. His grave was next to Toula's, just twenty yards from my grandfather's, in Glenwood Cemetery, off Lincoln Road in Northwest. It was an immigrant's graveyard, unofficially sectioned off, with a special section for Greeks, many of them Spartans, the grounds run down at times, littered with beer bottles and cartons, but clean now and live with the reds and oranges of the maples and poplars on the hills.

A small group attended, old-timers mostly, the very last of a generation, the men who had ruled at the picnics of my childhood, men in white shirts and pleated gray slacks who danced to the wild clarinets and bouzoukis and played cards and drank and laughed, the smell of grilled lamb and fresh phyllo in the air. Lou DiGeordano was there, as frail as I had ever seen him, held at the arm by his son Joey, and a few other men and women, stooped and small, with black marble eyes and hair like the frazz of white rope, men and women I no longer recognized. And

Lyla was there, her red hair long and lifting in the breeze, our hands touching, the touch of two friends.

It hadn't ended suddenly with me and Lyla, as it does not end suddenly between two people who are breaking things off but still in love. We went out a couple of times to our regular restaurants, but the restaurants had lost their shine and the people who served us looked to us as strangers. Lyla had given up drinking and I had not, the change just something else that had dropped between us. We slept together on those nights, the sex needed and good. But the sex, we knew, would not save us. So things continued like that, and one afternoon I realized that I had not spoken with Lyla for a couple of weeks, and I knew then that that part of us was finally over.

The weather did not begin to turn until late September. As the days cooled, I rode my bike more frequently and kept the Dodge parked and covered. Mai went off to Germany to visit her family and Anna returned to school. I took on double shifts at the Spot into October, and in that period there was Costa's funeral and solitary nights and occasionally nights with friends, all of them unmemorable and with the certain sameness that comes with the worn wood and low light of bars and the ritual of drink. My face healed quickly, though when it healed, I noticed that I had aged, the age and a kind of fading in my eyes. My scars had become a part of me now, suggesting neither toughness nor mystery, rarely prompting the interest of acquaintances or the second look from strangers. No one came to me for outside work; I would not have considered it if they had.

In the days that followed the violence in the warehouse, I looked over my shoulder often and listened for the inevitable knock on my front door. The newspaper and television reports stayed on top of the story for a full week and then the next sensational multiple murder took the warehouse story's place. It was always in my mind that Boyle and Detective Johnson knew I was connected in some way. But no one came to interview me and no one came to bring me in. And Boyle continued to come in on a regular basis and sit at his bar stool, his draft beer and shot of Jack in front of him, a Marlboro Red burning in the tray.

Then in late October, on a night when the first biting fall wind had dropped into town, Boyle walked into the Spot at closing time, his bleached-out eyes pink and heavily lidded, drunk as I had seen him in a long while. His shirttail hung down below his tweed sport jacket, and the grip of his Python peeked out of the jacket's vent. He walked carefully to the bar, had a seat on a stool. I stopped the music on the deck and went down to see him.

"Closing time, Boyle."

"Just one round tonight, Nick, before I go home. You got no problem with that, do you?"

"Okay."

I drew him a beer and set it on a damp coaster while he arranged his deck of Marlboros and pack of matches next to an ashtray. Then I free-poured some Jack Daniel's into a beveled shot glass. He drank off some of the beer and lit a cigarette. He knocked back half of the shot.

Darnell's light switched off as he walked from the kitchen. He buttoned his jacket and looked at Boyle. Boyle's head was lowered, his eyes dull and pointed at the bar.

"Hawk's gonna fly tonight, looks like," Darnell said. "You drive down, Nick?"

"Yeah, I got the Dodge out tonight, with the weather and all."

"Mind if I catch a ride uptown with you?"

"Sure, if you can wait."

I nodded toward Boyle and Darnell shook his head. "I don't think so, man. Let me get on out of here. Take it easy, Nick."

"Yeah, you, too."

Darnell touched his hat in a kind of salute. He walked from the bar. I took a few bottles of beer from the cooler and buried them in the ice chest.

"God, I am drunk," Boyle said, pushing his face around with his hand. "Have a drink with me, will ya, Nick?"

"All right."

I opened a bottle of beer and put a shot of Old Grand-Dad next to the bottle. Boyle and I touched glasses and drank. I chased the bourbon with the beer.

"So," Boyle said.

"Yeah," I said.

"Well... I shouldn't be so drunk. But I am. I've been driving around all day, and when I was done driving, I hit a couple bars. You know how that goes."

"Sure. Where'd you go?"

"Out in the country. Frederick County."

I lit a cigarette and shook out the match. I dropped the match in the ashtray.

"Out there in the country," Boyle said, "lookin' for some answers."

"What kind of answers?"

"It's this thing with that partner of yours, Jack LaDuke. How he just disappeared after those deaths in that warehouse. And the Samuels murder—I don't know, it's just been eatin' away at me, you know? I mean, I could have just come to you and all that, but, the way you are, I knew you wouldn't talk."

I put my hand up in protest, but Boyle cut me off.

"Hold on a second, Nick, lemme just go on a little bit."

"Go ahead."

"So I went to talk to Shareen Lewis. Well, she didn't say much of anything. But she did tell me the name of the bondsman—I forget his name right now—who turned her on to LaDuke. So I went to this bondsman, see, and he fills me in on some details on this LaDuke character. I finally found his old man out there in the country, but the old man said he hasn't heard from his son in years. Imagine that, not talkin' to your own kid for years."

"It's something," I said.

"And you?"

"What about me?"

"You haven't heard from him, either."

"No."

"Well," Boyle said, "let me just tell you what I think. What I think happened is—and granted, it's just a theory of mine—I think he checked out in that fire. You remember, fifteen, twenty years back, when all those faggots got caught in that fire down at that movie house, the Cinema Follies? Man, they were just piled up against that locked door. Well, that's the way it looked the morning after that fire in the warehouse. There was a bunch of 'em, piled against the door. 'Course, some of them had been shot up, and there were a few shot-up ones up on the second floor. And we identified a few of them from prison dentals, that sort of thing. The thing is, I think LaDuke was one of the ones in that pile, one of the ones we couldn't identify. What do you think?"

"If he went to that warehouse, he went on his own. I don't know a thing about it."

"Well, anyway, it's just a guess." Boyle walked two fingers over the top of his glass. "Pour me another one, will ya?"

I did it. I dragged on my cigarette and Boyle dragged on his and our smoke turned slowly in the conical light.

Boyle put his glass down, looked into it thoughtfully. "But," he said. "But... if LaDuke died in that fire, it doesn't explain the Samuels murder."

"I don't follow."

"The casings found at the crime scene match the casings found on the second floor of that warehouse. Same gun, Nick. I followed through with ballistics myself. So whoever was in on the warehouse kill also hit Samuels."

I finished my bourbon and put one foot up on the ice chest.

"You know, Nick, we were really close on nailing Samuels, too. I'd say we were one day off. We were working our informants pretty good on the drug angle, man, and we were close. Once we knew he owned both warehouses, after that it was a cinch. But someone just got one step ahead of us. Goddamn, was Johnson pissed off about that. We did find the twenty-two that did Jeter and Lewis, and the man who used it. Guy out of

South Baltimore, just like you said. But we'd still like to clean the rest of this thing up. 'Course, all's we got to do now is find the gun that belongs to those casings."

"There you go, Boyle. Find the gun and you'll have the whole thing wrapped up."

"The gun. The gun was a nine-millimeter, like that Browning you carry." Boyle's jittery eyes settled on mine. "You still carry that Browning, Nick?"

"No. I lost it. The thing is, I was just looking for it the other day, to clean it—"

"Yeah. You probably dropped it in the river or some shit like that, by mistake. Slipped right out of your hands. Funny, you know. If the city could get it together and put up the money to dredge the Anacostia, you wanna know how many cases we could put to bed?"

"Too bad they can't get it together."

"Yeah. Too bad." Boyle closed his eyes and emptied his drink. "Well, I better get home. My kids and all that."

"I'll lock up behind you," I said.

Boyle held on to the bar and got off his stool. I walked with him to the door. When we got there, he put his back against it and wrapped a meaty hand around my arm. He started to speak but had trouble putting the words together, closed his mouth in a frown.

"You're drunk, Boyle. You want me to call a cab?"

"Uh-uh."

"Go home to your kids."

"My kids. Yeah, I got my kids."

"Go on home."

"You know somethin'?" Boyle said. "I feel sorry for you, Nick. I really do. You know...you remember a few years ago, there was this short-eyed motherfucker that was rapin' those little girls in Northeast? Description on him was he was some variety of spic, a Rican maybe, with a bandanna, the whole brown rig. The shit was on the news every night, man—you gotta remember."

"Yeah, I do. They never caught the guy. So what?"

"*I* caught him," Boyle said. "Me and this other cop. We got him in an alley, and he confessed."

"Congratulations. Another good collar for you."

"You didn't read about him being caught 'cause we never took him in. I put a bullet in his head that night, Nick. The other cop, he put one in him, too."

"Go home," I said, pulling my arm away. "That's liquor talk. Save that shit for your buddies at the FOP."

"It's just..." Boyle said. "It's just that I know what's in your head right now. The thing is, I got my kids to go home to. I can go home, I can hold them, and for a little while, anyway, it makes everything all right. I got that, Nick. What do you got?"

I didn't answer. Instead, I opened the door.

"Don't you want to know?" Boyle said.

"Okay," I said. "Why hasn't Johnson pulled me in?"

"Johnson?" Boyle said, a sad smile forming on his face. "Johnson's been there, too, that's why. Johnson was with me when we did that short-eyes. Johnson was the other cop."

Boyle stepped through the open door. I closed it and turned the lock.

I walked back behind the stick and refilled my shot glass. The whiskey was silk; I drank it and smoked a cigarette in the quiet of the bar. The phone rang. I picked it up, the call a misdial. I stared at the receiver in my hand. When I heard the dial tone, I phoned Lyla's apartment. A man's voice greeted me on the other end.

"Is Lyla McCubbin in, please?" I said.

The man put his hand over the phone but did not cover it all the way. He said, "Hey, Lyla, this guy wants to know if he can speak to a Lyla McCubbin. Sounds like a salesman or something. Want me to just get rid of him?"

I heard Lyla laugh, recognized the laughter as forced. I hung the receiver in its cradle before she could reply.

I had another beer, and another after that. By then, it had

gotten pretty late. I thought of my cat, out in the weather, hungry and pacing on the stoop. I dimmed the lights and put on a coat, then locked the place and set the alarm. I went out to the street.

Orange and yellow leaves lifted and tumbled down 8th. I turned my collar up against the wind, walked with my head down, my eyes on the sidewalk.

I passed the riot gate of the shoe store and neared the alley. From the alley, I heard a voice.

"Stevonus."

I turned around.

"LaDuke," I said.

He stood in the mouth of the alley, his face covered in shadow. But the black pant legs and heavy black oxfords were exposed by the light of the streetlamp above; I knew it was him.

I walked to the alley and stood a couple of feet back. The smell coming off him was minty, strongly medicinal.

"Got a cigarette, Nick?"

"You're smoking now, huh?"

"Sure," he said, a slight lisp to his voice. "Why not?"

I reached into my coat and shook one out of the deck. He took it and asked me for a light. I struck a match, cupped the flame. He put his hand around mine and pulled it toward him, leaning forward at the same time. I saw his face then as it moved into the light. He watched me carefully as the flame touched the tobacco.

"Kinda scary, eh, Nick?"

I took in some breath and tried to smile. "It's not so bad."

"Nobody's ever gonna call me 'Pretty Boy' again, I guess."

He was right. No one was going to mistake him for pretty. Whoever had done the work on him had botched the job. His lips were pulled back on one side and stretched open in a ghastly kind of half smile, the gums ruby red and exposed there and glistening with saliva, the saliva dripping over the side of his mouth. Skin had been grafted sloppily along his jawline, unmatched and puckered at the edges, and bluish around the grafted hole in his neck.

"No, Jack," I said. "It's not pretty. But you're alive."

LaDuke took a folded handkerchief from his pocket, the handkerchief damp and gray. He dabbed it on his gums, then shoved it back in his pocket. He dragged on his cigarette.

"How'd you get out of the warehouse that night?" I said.

"When I went down into that mess with my gun, we traded shots. But the fire spread real fast, and then those men knew they weren't going to make it. They ran for the door on the first floor. I guess Sweet had taken the key. Anyway, I kinda woke up, decided that I wanted to live. I booked back up the stairs and ran down that hall. Hell, I was right behind you."

"And then?"

"Shit, man, I don't know. I was going into shock in a big way. The only thing I thought to do was go to my father. So I drove out to Frederick County. I kept my foot to the floor all the way, and I made it. I don't know how I made it, but I did."

"Your father," I said, not really wanting to know.

"Yeah. He did the best he could. Used that horse stitch of his on my face, did some kind of poor man's graft. Wired my jaw together. The main thing was, he stopped the infection, after a couple of days. I don't remember much of it." LaDuke avoided my eyes. "Yeah, my father, he fixed me up."

I felt a chill and pulled the lapels of my coat together to the neck. LaDuke retrieved his handkerchief and blotted the spit from his chin.

"Why'd you come to me tonight?" I said.

"Your cop friend visited my father today. Thought I might warn you."

"Warn me about what?"

LaDuke said, "You took out Samuels, right?"

"Yes."

"How about that gun of yours? You get rid of that Browning?"

"I dumped it over the rail of the Sousa Bridge."

"Good. I just wanted you to know that the law was on it."

"I got a feeling they'll be leaving me alone."

"That's good," LaDuke said. He reached inside his jacket and pulled out an envelope thick with bills. "I came to give you this, as well."

"Where did that come from?"

"Shareen Lewis. My payment for finding her son. Half of it belongs to you."

"You keep it. I don't need it, man. I'm coming into some money, from an inheritance. I'm flush."

"Take it." He pressed the envelope into my hand. "We earned it, you and me."

"All right. I know a kid in San Francisco—he could use the money, I guess."

And then the half of his face that was not gone twisted back into some sort of smile. "We got 'em, Nick. Didn't we?"

"What?"

"We took those guys off the street. I mean, it's something. Isn't it?"

"Yes, Jack. It's something."

He dropped the cigarette under his heavy black shoe, crushed it into the concrete, and began to move away. I touched his arm.

"Where you goin', Jack?"

"I don't know. I gotta go."

"How will I find you?"

"I'll be around," he said.

He turned and walked into the alley. The darkness took him, and he was gone.

I stood there thinking about Jack LaDuke. I looked into the black maw of the alley and blinked my eyes. LaDuke would be deep in that alley now, dabbing at his face with the damp gray handkerchief, in the dark but not afraid of it, because for him there was nothing left to fear. Or maybe he was out on the street, staring straight ahead as he walked down the sidewalk, avoiding his reflection in the glass of the storefronts and bars. Wherever he was, I knew he was alone. Like Lyla was alone, and like me. All of us alone, in our own brand of night.

Leaves blew past my feet and clicked at the bars of the riot gate. I slipped the envelope inside my coat and moved out of the light.

I walked to the corner, crossed the street, and headed for my Dodge. I touched my key to the lock, but did not fit it. I stepped away and walked back to the Spot.

Inside, the room was silent, bathed in blue neon. I went behind the bar. I poured myself a bourbon and pulled a bottle of beer from the ice.

I lit a cigarette. I had my drink.

This one started at the Spot.

BACK BAY · READERS' PICK

Reading Group Guide

DOWN BY THE RIVER WHERE THE DEAD MEN GO

A novel by

GEORGE PELECANOS

George Pelecanos responds to questions from his readers

What do you find to be the hardest and easiest things about writing when you are working on a project?

Well, the hardest thing is starting the book because I don't outline my books beforehand. I have to find the story, and the way I find the story is through the development of my characters. And every time I begin a book, I'm not sure if I'm going to be able to succeed. The easiest part is when you hit that point about a quarter of the way through, where your characters actually begin to write the book for you. And then it's just a matter of sitting down every day and doing the work.

Do you think a mystery writer can read other mysteries and enjoy them, rather than being a critic or reviewer?

Sure. I read less mysteries or crime novels than I used to, but the ones that I really like just make me more stoked to do a better job myself. People like Dennis Lehane, Michael Connelly, James Sallis, Craig Holden, and Jack O'Connell make me think that this is the golden age of crime writing.

Have you ever ventured outside the mystery/crime field in your writing?

I don't really feel like I've written mysteries since finishing the Nick Stefanos books. Increasingly, my books are novels about working-class people in the modern city that have crime elements to them. And I don't think I'll ever leave those crime elements behind because I like conflict in a book. I like storytelling. And in addition to my belief that books should be about something, I think also that within these books things should happen.

What would it take for you to make a big change in the direction your writing has gone so far?

It would just be my desire to do something different. What it would take would be for me to feel like I've already covered all the territory, and that I've exhausted these characters and these stories. And that would probably push me to try something else. But at this point, I'm pretty sure that my life's work is going to be writing about the people of the neighborhoods in Washington, D.C., in the form of the crime novel.

Whom would you envision playing Nick in a film?

Well, I always liked Nick Cage. I think he could do it. It's got to be somebody you can empathize with even as he's going all the way down. Too bad Steve McQueen isn't around, because that would be my guy.

Your novels always have such a colorful cast of characters. Do you draw them from people you really know or once knew?

I take elements of a lot of different people I've known over the years to draw these characters. I worked sales force, selling shoes, electronics, and appliances for many years, and you can imagine all the colorful characters I came across. What I'm trying to do in a lot of ways is put a face on people of a certain working class that many folks simply ignore in their day-to-day lives.

It's been said your settings are superb—language, music, locales. How do you "build" the world that your characters inhabit?

This is going to sound like smoke, but it's really all there in my head. I've created this parallel, fictional world of Washington, D.C., that is alive to me all the time. I've always been a daydreamer. Even when I was a kid delivering food for my dad in downtown D.C., I was making up movies in my head all day long while I walked the streets. And I'm still doing it today.

Do you have any tips for an aspiring author? How hard is it? What do I need to know or do?

Well, I think you've got to get out and live. I think many writers try and start their careers too early, before they've done anything or seen anything. I was fortunate to write my first book when I was thirty-one years old. And at that point I already had a lifetime of material just from the living I had done. It's a long life and you shouldn't rush it as a writer.

Questions and topics for discussion

1. "Hardboiled" crime fiction has been described as fiction that is "tough and violent" and can be said to include the traditions of adventure novels and westerns. Discuss why Pelecanos is so frequently praised for his hardboiled roots. In which ways does he adapt not only the classic qualities of crime fiction, but also those of adventures and westerns?

2. Nick observes: "The thirst for knowledge is like a piece of ass you know you shouldn't chase; in the end, you chase it just the same." Is there anything else that drives Nick in his work as an investigator?

3. Critics have praised Pelecanos for his use of Washington, D.C., as the backdrop for his novels; it's even been described as a character in its own right. Do you agree, and are there examples in this novel you could cite?

4. Nick is not perfect; discuss ways in which his habits and methods set him apart from many thriller protagonists. Do his flaws make him more or less sympathetic to you? Do you think someone can be a good person without also being a "nice" person?

5. Discuss the ways Pelecanos uses details about food and alcohol to help set his scenes and define his characters.

6. "I noticed an old man in a physical-plant uniform sitting atop a small tractor in the cemetery, and for a moment our eyes met. Then he looked away, and we both went back to what we had been doing: trying to find a kernel of spirituality before returning to the cold reality of our day" (pages 47–48). How does this moment affect your impression of Nick?

7. Discuss the aspects of family in the novel. What does family mean to Nick, and would you consider him a "family man" in the traditional sense of the term?

8. In an interview, when asked how he, as a Greek American, feels comfortable writing about black characters, Pelecanos responded, "If you are going to do it, first of all, you should do it right. Show people respect and make sure you get the voices right—if you are even attempting it. It's apparent when you are reading something if the writer hasn't bothered to listen to people or go into the neighborhoods and talk to people, and that sort of thing." Discuss the idea of "respect" as it relates to this novel, and the role of a novelist in exploring identities beyond his or her own.

About the author

George Pelecanos is the author of several highly praised and bestselling novels, including, most recently, *The Way Home* and *The Cut*. He is also an independent-film producer, an essayist, and the recipient of numerous writing awards. He was a producer and Emmy-nominated writer for *The Wire* and currently writes for the acclaimed HBO series *Treme*.

. . . and the next Nick Stefanos novel

Nick Stefanos returns in *Shame the Devil*. Following is a brief excerpt from the novel's opening pages.

ONE

THE CAR WAS a boxy late-model Ford sedan, white over black, innocuous bordering on invisible, and very fast. It had been a sheriff's vehicle originally, bought at auction in Tennessee, and further modified for speed.

The car rolled north on Wisconsin beneath a blazing white sun. The men inside wore long-sleeved shirts, tails out. Their shirtfronts were spotted with sweat and their backs were slick with it. The black vinyl on which they sat was hot to the touch. From the passenger seat, Frank Farrow studied the street. The sidewalks were empty. Foreign-made automobiles moved along quietly, their occupants cool and cocooned. Heat mirage shimmered up off asphalt. The city was narcotized—it was that kind of summer day.

"Quebec," said Richard Farrow, his gloved hands clutching the wheel. He pushed his aviator shades back up over the bridge of his nose, and as they neared the next cross street he said, "Upton."

"You've got Thirty-ninth up ahead," said Frank. "You want to take that shoot-off, just past Van Ness."

"I know it," said Richard. "You don't have to tell me again because I know."

"Take it easy, Richard."

"All right."

In the backseat, Roman Otis softly sang the first verse to "One in a Million You," raising his voice just a little to put the full Larry Graham inflection into the chorus. He had heard the single on WHUR earlier that morning, and the tune would not leave his head.

The Ford passed through the intersection at Upton.

Otis looked down at his lap, where the weight of his shotgun had begun to etch a deep wrinkle in his linen slacks. Well, he should have known it. All you had to do was *look* at linen to make it wrinkle, that was a plain fact. Still, a man needed to have a certain kind of style to him when he left the house for work. Otis placed the sawed-off on the floor, resting its stock across the toes of his lizard-skin monk straps. He glanced at the street-bought Rolex strapped to his left wrist: five minutes past ten A.M.

Richard cut the Ford up 39th.

"There," said Frank. "That Chevy's pulling out."

"I see it," said Richard.

They waited for the Chevy. Then Frank said, "Put it in."

Richard swung the Ford into the space and killed the engine. They were at the back of a low-rise commercial strip that fronted Wisconsin Avenue. The door leading to the kitchen of the pizza parlor, May's, was situated in the center of the block. Frank wiped moisture from his brush mustache and ran a hand through his closely cropped gray hair.

"There's the Caddy," said Otis, noticing the black DeVille parked three spaces ahead.

Frank nodded. "Mr. Carl's making the pickup. He's inside."

"Let's do this thing," said Otis.

"Wait for our boy to open the door," said Frank. He drew two latex examination gloves from a tissue-sized box and slipped them over the pair he already had on his hands. He tossed the box over his shoulder to the backseat. "Here. Double up."

Roman Otis raised his right hand, where a silver ID bracelet bearing the inscription "Back to Oakland" hung on his wrist. He let the bracelet slip down inside the French cuff of his shirt. He put the gloves on carefully, then reflexively touched the butt of the .45 fitted beneath his shirt. He caught a glimpse of his shoulder-length hair, recently treated with relaxer, in the rearview mirror. Shoot, thought Otis, Nick Ashford couldn't claim to have a finer head of hair on him. Otis smiled at his reflection, his one gold tooth catching the light. He gave himself a wink.

"Frank," said Richard.

"We'll be out in a few minutes," said Frank. "Don't turn the engine over until you see us coming back out."

"I won't," said Richard, a catch in his voice.

The back kitchen door to May's opened. A thin black man wearing a full apron stepped out with a bag of trash. He carried the trash to a Dumpster and swung it in, bouncing it off the upraised lid. On his way back to the kitchen he eye-swept the men in the Ford. He stepped back inside, leaving the door ajar behind him.

"That him?" asked Otis.

"Charles Greene," said Frank.

"Good boy."

Frank checked the .22 Woodsman and the .38 Bulldog holstered beneath his oxford shirt. The guns were snug against his guinea-T. He looked across the bench at his kid brother, sweating like a hard-run horse, breathing through his mouth, glassy eyed, scared stupid.

"Remember, Richard. Wait till you see us come out."

Richard Farrow nodded one time.

Roman Otis lifted the shotgun, slipped it barrel down into his open shirt, fitting it in a custom-made leather holster hung over his left side. It would show; there wasn't any way to get around it. But they would be going straight in, and they would move fast.

"Let's go, Roman," said Frank.

Otis said, "Right." He opened the car door and touched his foot to the street.